R.L. PEREZ

SALT & BLOOD

WILLOW
HAVEN
PRESS

SALT & BLOOD

CONTENTS

Ares Jungle
Fulcrum
Realm of Elysium

Portal
Amara
Portal

Acheron
The Undead
Aidoneus's Penthouse
Forest of Thanatos
Sty
Oceanus
Erebos

Cocytus
Portal to Elysium
Tartarus
Pool of Forgetfulness
Lethe
Gate to the Mortal Realm
Realm of the Underworld

Askir Mountains
Faidon
Thanassian Empire
Voiceless Jungle
Sodara
Ruins of Rhea
Realm of Gaia

Emdale
Mountains
Murane
Voula
City
Salwaki
Islands
Krenia
Manos Ocean

For the readers who like a sprinkle of darkness with their romance.

DAUGHTER

PRUE

PRUE STARED AT APOLLO AS HE LOUNGED ON THE throne—*Cyrus's* throne—while her heart flipped in her chest. Cyrus and Gaia stood behind her. The three of them had rushed into the throne room as soon as they had sensed the presence of another god. The chrome walls of the throne room were as immaculate as ever, a stark contrast to the ruins just outside the castle.

Apollo was here.

Her father was here. And he wanted to rule the Underworld.

How was she supposed to stop this man—this *god*? Cyrus was human, and he despised her. She wasn't sure if she could trust him to help her.

She was on her own.

"You have no authority here," Gaia said from beside

Prue, her voice sure and steady. The strength in her tone grounded Prue, reminding her she was not as alone as she thought.

Apollo's dark eyes flashed as he fixed a venomous gaze on Gaia. "Hello, *wife*," he spat. "I didn't expect to see you here."

"I'm sure you didn't," Gaia replied calmly. "But you don't belong here, Apollo. You have made many enemies by isolating the people here. You should leave now. While you can."

Apollo chuckled, sliding off the throne and striding toward Gaia, his movements lithe and graceful. Ever the king.

Prue went rigid, holding perfectly still as her father drew closer. Somehow, she could sense Cyrus behind her, though she didn't dare look over her shoulder at him. The last thing she needed was a reminder of the hateful look in his eyes when he said those terrible things to her.

"I have more authority here than you do, Gaia," Apollo said, his mouth curling into a smirk. "If anyone should stop me from taking the throne, it would certainly not be you."

"The kingdom already has a king and a queen," Prue said, finding her voice at last. "It does not need another."

Apollo's gaze slid to her with a keen interest that made her skin prickle with unease. "Ah. Prudence, is it?

I've waited a long time to meet you." A hungry gleam shone in his eyes, and Prue resisted the urge to step back.

Power, Gaia had told her. *Apollo will do anything for power.*

And he wanted hers.

"And why is that?" Cyrus asked loudly. Prue's breath caught in her throat as her husband drew nearer, standing alongside her, as if the past hour hadn't happened at all.

As if they were still a united front, protecting this realm as husband and wife.

"Why were you so anxious to meet my wife?" Cyrus asked, his voice lethal. In this moment, he might have been powerless, but his tone and his posture oozed authority.

He was bluffing. And Prue prayed to the Goddess that Apollo would fall for it.

Apollo looked over Cyrus with a slight frown. "You look different from when I last saw you."

Cyrus only glared at him, refusing to offer an explanation.

If Apollo suspected anything about Cyrus's loss of power, he didn't mention it. Instead, he said, "Well, don't worry, nephew. I won't harm your witchling. At least, not yet."

Cyrus made a low sound in his throat and bared his teeth at the sun god. "Don't call me that," he bit out.

"What? Nephew?"

Cyrus's nostrils flared as he took a threatening step toward Apollo.

Apollo laughed. "Your father and I were comrades in arms. We grew up together. Fought together. He was my most trusted commander. Even if we were not brothers in the flesh, he was more a brother to me than anyone else."

"I. Don't. Care." Cyrus enunciated each word. "I am not your friend or ally, and I am certainly not your family. Get out of my kingdom."

"Ah, see, I can't do that. Clearly, this realm is not fit to be ruled by the likes of you." He gestured to Prue and Cyrus. "Look what happened under your rule! This entire kingdom is in shambles."

Prue wanted to argue, to claim it wasn't their fault... But *she* had been the one to open Pandora's box.

She had done this. It *was* her fault.

Her response stuck in her throat, filling her mouth with a foul, bitter taste.

"Don't you already have a throne?" Gaia asked. "Why do you need another?"

For a moment, Apollo's expression froze, and a haunted look passed over his eyes. In a flash, his easy smile had returned, and he waved a hand. "Elysium is in good hands. I have left my apprentice in charge. But I've neglected *this* realm for far too long, and I'm here to set things right."

"You cannot simply *claim* the throne," Prue said, and she was relieved to find her voice did not shake. "The magic of the realm must choose you. It has already chosen me. And Cyrus. You are too late, Apollo."

"Well, I think you'll find, Prudence, that once a realm is as broken as this one, the magic that binds a ruler to the throne can be... reclaimed. The magic is reset. A clean slate."

Prue's heart lurched, and she shot a panicked look at Gaia. "Is this true?"

Gaia's mouth grew thin, a telltale sign of her unease. "It is speculation. No one here has experienced the death of a realm before. We do not know what to expect."

"Why do you even *want* the throne?" Cyrus asked. "You despise this place."

"I was wrong to turn my nose up at it," Apollo said with a sigh. "It is time I make amends."

"By taking what doesn't belong to you?" Prue asked incredulously. "By leading a people you know nothing about?" She shook her head. "You are insane, Apollo. It will never work. And if you dare to try, we outnumber you." She lifted her chin, trying to project more confidence than she felt.

Apollo's mouth stretched into a wide smile that Prue

did not like one bit. Her stomach sank with dread as he said slowly, "I think you'll find that no one here can match my power. But go ahead and try. It would be highly entertaining to see you fail."

Prue's breaths came in short spurts, and panic rose in her chest.

Gaia seemed to sense her distress, and she stepped forward. "You know the law, Apollo," she barked. "Either make a formal challenge, or get out."

"I'll issue a challenge," Apollo said, still smiling at Prue. "But not yet. I'd like to take a look around. Get to know my future subjects." His gaze shifted from Prue to Cyrus, and at last to Gaia. Then, he clapped his hands together. "Well, I should be off. Lots to see, isn't there?" He frowned in mock contemplation. "Or rather... I suppose there *isn't*, is there? Not anymore." He grinned, then bowed. "I shall see you all very soon."

With that, he sauntered out the room, the heavy doors slamming with his departure.

Prue held perfectly still, waiting for him to come back, to assault them with his powerful magic. Surely, that was not *all* Apollo intended to do. Couldn't he unleash his sun magic and burn them to ash? What was stopping him from obliterating them all? Gaia might be a match for his power now that her curse had been broken. But Prue wasn't—and Cyrus certainly wasn't either.

"What law?" Prue asked, turning to her mother, heart racing. "What did you mean by a formal challenge?"

"In the realms of the gods, a throne can only be acquired if the monarch dies, or if a formal challenge is issued," Gaia said, her tone solemn.

"That isn't true," Cyrus said, his voice stiff. "I took the throne from Aidoneus without issuing a challenge."

"You fought him, though, didn't you?" Gaia asked. "That counts as a challenge. It might not have been a formal declaration, but the realm obviously recognized it as such. I was waiting for Apollo to strike one of you, to take the crown from you by force. But he didn't." She tapped her chin, her eyes narrowing in suspicion. "What is he waiting for?"

"Apollo likes theatrics," Cyrus said in a bored voice. "He's dragging this out on purpose."

"Perhaps." But Gaia sounded doubtful.

Prue couldn't keep her eyes off Cyrus. She recognized the despair darkening his features. But Goddess, he looked *so different*. Pale blue eyes. No tattoos. No horns. Inky black hair, instead of that otherworldly silver.

He was a stranger to her.

His gaze snapped to hers, locking onto her. Awareness rippled over her spine as she found herself pulled in by the intensity of that look. She wanted to draw closer to him. She wanted to feel his skin on hers, to see if their bodies still fit together like they did before.

All too soon, Cyrus broke the connection and turned away, heading for the door.

"Wait!" Prue blurted out.

Cyrus froze, then glanced over his shoulder, not quite meeting her eyes. "What?" The word was sharp and calloused.

"I—What are we going to do?" Prue sputtered, looking to Gaia for help. "We need a plan."

"I have no part in this," Cyrus said. "When Apollo challenges, I will be unable to stop him. To fight would be useless."

He walked away.

"Cyrus!" Prue called, her voice strained and desperate.

But Cyrus kept walking until he disappeared through the same doors Apollo had gone through. As her husband left, something in Prue's chest shattered, leaving nothing but a hollow ache, an abyss that threatened to drown everything in its wake. When Cyrus left, a piece of her very soul seemed to go with him.

This was her fault. This division between them was *her* doing. If she hadn't been foolish enough to sacrifice her own life... If she had thought of *him* and what he might sacrifice to bring her back...

She should have found another way.

"Come, Prudence," Gaia said, gently grasping her arm. "We must train."

Prue blinked, and it took her mind a long moment to catch up to her mother's words. "Train?"

"Your magic has been reborn. You are not yet powerful enough to face Apollo. But with some training, you can be. You are his daughter, after all. You have the potential to match his power and strength. Let me teach you."

Prue was still staring after Cyrus, willing him to come back. But he didn't. With a sigh, Prue met her mother's gaze and nodded. "Very well."

Gaia smiled, and Prue accepted this small mercy. At least the circumstances would bring her closer to her mother.

She only wished it was enough to heal the gaping hole in her chest from Cyrus's absence.

HOME

MONA

MONA SLAMMED INTO SOMETHING HARD AND unyielding, rock scraping against her skin. Darkness and dust crowded her, fogging her vision. She coughed, waving a hand in front of her face to clear the air. Goddess, the air here was so *thin*. She inhaled several gulps, trying to fill her lungs, but they strained with each breath.

"Evander?" she called out, her voice echoing in some vast space. She squinted but still couldn't make out details. The throbbing cuts and scrapes on her arms led her to believe she was surrounded by some kind of mountainous rock, but when she glanced upward, she couldn't see the stars or moon at all.

Was she in the Realm of Gaia? Or a different realm?

This wasn't the Underworld, and it certainly wasn't Elysium...

The last thing she remembered was jumping through the portal in Elysium as the realm was destroyed by Pandora's magic. Evander had been with her.

Then again, her experience traveling through portals told her how easy it was to be separated from other people. What if Evander had landed in a different realm?

"Evander!" Mona's voice sharpened, piercing the air.

A low groan sounded nearby, and she followed it, stretching blindly toward it. Her feet connected with something solid, and she knelt, hands reaching.

She first felt his leather wings, tattered and sticky with what had to be blood.

"Oh, Goddess," she breathed, running her fingers along the length of one of his wings until she found his shoulder. She squeezed it, then shuffled closer so she could nestle herself behind him, cradling his body. "Evander, it's all right. It's going to be fine."

She had healed him once before. She could do it again. Ordinarily, as an earth witch, she would open her third eye and conjure roses from the ground.

But this was different. She no longer held the blood of a mortal, but the blood of a goddess.

With a deep breath, she conjured her magic, waiting for it to swell inside her.

Nothing happened.

Mona gritted her teeth, pressing her hands into Evander's chest as she tried again. Her magic had come to her so effortlessly before... Why wasn't it working?

After several moments, a faint stirring shifted within her, as if her magic was waking from a deep sleep. Her hands glowed, but it was feeble, and the light faded almost immediately.

She dropped her hands with a growl of frustration as panic welled up inside her. What if he died? What if they couldn't find help in time?

"Mona," whispered another voice.

Mona jolted, her heart slamming into her rib cage as chills worked their way across her body. She glanced around in the suffocating darkness and found the shadow of another figure standing nearby.

"Do you sense it?" the voice asked.

After a long, terrifying moment, Mona finally placed the voice. It was Trivia—or rather, Pandora.

Her sister.

The person behind the destruction of the Underworld and Elysium. The one responsible for Evander's injuries.

And yet... her sister.

Mona had vowed to stand by Pandora, despite her crimes. Because they shared blood.

But that didn't mean she trusted her.

"Mona," Pandora said, more urgently.

Mona blinked and inhaled deeply, trying to awaken her new goddess senses. She still hadn't fully acclimated to them. Closing her eyes, she searched within herself, hoping her magic wasn't permanently blocked.

"I—I can't," she hissed, her head throbbing from her efforts.

"Here." Pandora took her hand and squeezed. As soon as she did, power burst in Mona's chest. Awareness flooded her, heating her blood and quivering over her with violent intensity. She shuddered, and a powerful, stirring presence shifted nearby.

Her eyes flew open, and she was on her feet in an instant. Someone was here. Someone powerful.

"Where are we?" she asked Pandora.

"I don't know. I've never been here before. But this magic feels... odd. Different."

Mona stretched her arms and wiggled her fingers, trying to get a better sense of her surroundings. Pandora was right; the air here was different. The magic had a strange scent to it, like earth and embers. But there was something in that smell that called to Mona's memories, resonating within her.

She dropped her arms. "Witches," she murmured. "There are witches here."

They weren't earth witches, though. Mona knew that magic well. She hadn't often encountered other witch covens. In Krenia, where she'd grown up, the island was isolated, populated only by earth witches and mortals. Occasionally, other covens would visit by boat, but that had been rare.

"So, we are in the mortal realm," Pandora mused.

"Yes," Mona replied. "The other two realms are gone."

She felt, rather than saw, Pandora flinch beside her. There had been no venom or blame in Mona's voice, but she knew the guilt of everything her sister had done sat heavily on her.

The mortal realm. Technically, this was Mona's home. But it felt more foreign to her than ever.

To her, home was a lush forest with a babbling river nearby and a soothing melody swelling around her.

Home was the Underworld with Evander.

Footsteps echoed nearby, and Mona shifted so she stood in front of Evander, blocking him from view. His raspy breathing behind her indicated he still lived, and she clung to that fact. The demon magic within him should have killed him. He wasn't supposed to survive in any other realm.

But he was here. He had survived Elysium. And he was still alive.

Amber light flooded the area, and the lengthened shadow of a woman appeared against the rock wall. As Mona's eyes adjusted, she realized she stood within a large cave. To her left was a metal archway with intricate carvings and designs. It looked similar to the portal in Elysium.

As more light poured into the space, Pandora drew closer to Mona, her shoulders stiff and her chin lifting. The two sisters stood side-by-side as the stranger came into view. She held a ball of fire in her hand that illuminated the thick black hair spilling around her face like a mane. She was tall and lean with brown skin and gold eyes that flared brighter than her flame.

"Who are you?" she demanded, her voice deep and commanding.

Pandora shifted, but Mona elbowed her before she could speak. "We come from Elysium," Mona said carefully. "We seek refuge from the darkness of Pandora's magic."

The woman sniffed deeply, then wrinkled her nose. "*This* one reeks of the darkness." She pointed to Pandora. "I can smell the death and decay."

Pandora stiffened, but Mona said quickly, "We are daughters of Gaia."

The woman straightened, her eyes flaring wide. She cocked her head, looking at Mona with more scrutiny. "Earth witch."

Shock bubbled through Mona's chest. How could this woman tell? Mona had thought her goddess magic had pushed out any signs of her grace, or her witch affinity. But somehow, this woman knew.

"Yes," Mona said. "And you are a fire witch." Mona didn't know much about fire witches, only that they were hunted for their deadly and volatile power. Isolated as her little island was, she had never encountered any before.

"My name is Farah," the woman supplied. "I'm the leader of this coven. We are willing to provide refuge to a fellow witch." She gestured to Pandora again. "But she is not welcome."

"But—"

"We need your help," Pandora interrupted. "There were others who came through before us. Gods and goddesses of Elysium. Have you seen them?"

Farah was silent for a long moment as she appraised Pandora with suspicion in her gaze. "Yes," she said at last. "A few others have come through this portal. Which is why it would be difficult for us to shelter you here. We already have too many people to care for."

"We do not wish to intrude," Mona said hastily. "We just need to locate the other portals, and..." She hesitated, resisting the urge to cast a glance behind her toward Evander. How would Farah react to the presence of someone like him? A death god, possessed by demonic magic.

Gathering her resolve, Mona said, "Do you have a healer? My friend is wounded. I tried to heal him myself, but my magic isn't working properly." She stepped to the side, revealing Evander's crumpled form on the ground behind her.

Farah jerked back, nostrils flared as her gaze settled on the death god. After a moment, her expression smoothed into mild interest. "Ah. A death god. That explains the smell of death and decay." Her eyes roved over his torn and shredded wings. "But this one is different. I have never sensed energy like this before."

"Please," Mona begged. "He is dying. Will you help us? We—I can cook or clean or perform magic for you as payment. Whatever you need."

"You are in a different realm, so your magic must acclimate to your new surroundings," Farah said, still scrutinizing Evander's still form. "And even if your magic was at its full power, I speculate you would still have trouble. The death magic emanating him is... quite potent. Too potent for magic like yours."

Farah's gaze slowly moved to Mona, then shifted to Pandora. "You bring a strange and deadly magic to my coven. To allow you refuge would endanger my people."

Mona's heart sank to her stomach. If this witch wouldn't help her, then what would they do? She didn't seem hostile, so Mona believed—or rather, hoped—the woman wouldn't attack them. Would she let them pass through the cave unharmed?

"But," Farah continued, "I believe there is someone

here who can help you. I will bring you to him. No payment required."

Mona went rigid with apprehension. "Who?"

"If I'm not mistaken, he is his brother." She pointed to Evander.

Hope rose in Mona's chest. "Cyrus?" If Cyrus was here, that meant Prue had to be as well. Had they survived?

Farah's brows knitted together. "No. Romanos."

Mona blinked, momentarily startled by this. Romanos had gone through the portal with her when the Underworld had been destroyed. She had looked for him in Elysium, but Hestia had assured her he was safe in the mortal realm.

Hestia. The thought of the fire goddess, now dead, made Mona's chest ache with grief and despair.

Did Farah know? Did she know the goddess she worshipped was dead? Could she sense it?

"I don't—Is Romanos well?" Mona asked. "Is he safe?"

A smile lit Farah's face, making her features soften. "Yes. He is well. Come. I will take you to him. But I'm afraid you cannot stay here for long."

Mona nodded eagerly. "Of course. We understand."

She hurried to Evander, struggling in vain to lift him under his arms. Pandora was by her side at once, helping her to hoist him up. But he was so heavy.

"Evander," Mona groaned. "You have to move your legs. Please."

Farah—who watched them with interest—gave Mona a puzzled look. "Aren't you a witch? Use your magic."

Mona gaped at her, then shook her head. Of course. She was not only an earth witch, but the daughter of a goddess. She carefully eased Evander back to the ground, where he moaned and trembled. Closing her eyes, she summoned her powers, stretching her arms wide and calling forth her magic from the earth at her feet. The ground quivered, and pebbles and dust rained down from the cavern ceiling. Cracks split beneath her, and thorny vines sprang forth at her beckoning.

Frowning, Mona flicked her wrist, and the thorns were replaced by vines of ivy, achingly reminding her of her sister, Prue. The vines wove together, crisscrossing until they formed a thick net of foliage. With the strength of her magic, she gathered her vines around Evander's body, then lifted him onto the bed of leaves.

Farah nodded her approval and turned toward the tunnel she'd come through. Mona urged her magic onward, and Evander's cocoon of ivy shifted, sliding on the rocky ground with a strange hiss.

Satisfied with this, Mona glanced at Pandora, and the two of them followed Evander's motionless form, making their way through the tunnel after Farah.

TERMS
CYRUS

CYRUS LEFT THE THRONE ROOM, THE SIGHT OF Prue's devastated face imprinted on his brain forever. He stormed to his rooms, letting the doors slam shut behind him. With a roar, he flung a vase across the room until it shattered, leaving broken shards all over the floor.

It subsided his rage but not by much.

He ran his hands through his hair, tugging at the strands until his skull throbbed. He didn't want to destroy his furnishings; he wanted to destroy this weak mortal body. This frail, pathetic vessel was what he loathed the most.

Apollo was here.

Prue was alive.

Cyrus was human.

His pitiful mind couldn't keep up with it all.

Thoughts and questions raced, too quickly for him to take stock of everything.

He collapsed onto the bed, covering his face with a pillow and bellowing into it as loudly as he could, so intensely his throat burned. He screamed, on and on, letting the sound rip through him.

When he was finished and gasping for breath, he dropped the pillow, then glared at the ceiling.

He wasn't sure how long he lay there. All he knew was he had nothing left to do. No purpose. Nothing to fight for.

All he had was this horrible empty void, waiting to devour him. Waiting for his short human life to end.

A knock sounded at the door.

"Go away, Prue!" he barked. The last thing he wanted to see was the pity on her face, the eyes full of despair as she tried to fix what had broken between them.

There was no fixing this. It was irreparable. Nothing could be done.

The tapping sounded again, more timid this time. Then a feeble voice said, "I have a message for you, Your Highness."

Frowning, Cyrus climbed off the bed and opened the door. Before him stood a demon woman with two sets of short horns on her head. Her skin was charcoal and a long, barbed tail flicked behind her. Her eyes darted up to Cyrus's, then dropped, her head bowing in submission. Wordlessly, she extended her hands, revealing a roll of parchment.

Cyrus took it, then waved his hand, dismissing the servant. She seemed glad to depart, her hastened steps echoing down the hall as she vanished.

As Cyrus opened it, dread coiled in his chest. It was from Apollo.

The Sun God requests your presence in the study for friendly negotiations.

Cyrus snorted. What kind of bastard referred to himself in the third person? And *friendly negotiations* sounded anything but. Apollo was here for his throne. There was nothing friendly about that.

He was already moving to toss the parchment out the window when he faltered. If he refused, it would mean he was choosing a side. Choosing *Prue's* side.

It meant he would need to battle Apollo. If the sun god fought *him* during the challenge, Cyrus could not win.

He stroked his chin, contemplating his options. Siding with Apollo seemed like a terrible idea... but perhaps he could work it in his favor.

.   .   .

Half an hour later, Cyrus sat in an armchair in the study, sitting across from Apollo. He sipped the wine from his glass, resisting the urge to wrinkle his nose from the sharp sweetness that assaulted his tongue. These damned human senses wouldn't let him tolerate anything. Then again, he recalled the wine from Elysium to be rather unpleasant.

But ever since he had cast the spell to bring Prue back from the dead, he hadn't felt like himself at all. Not a god. No one powerful. Nothing but this pitiful mere mortal.

He looked over at Apollo, who drank his wine with a contented smile on his face. The mighty sun god and former king of Elysium lounged in a wing-backed chair facing the hearth, within which roared a pleasant fire. If not for the chaos just outside the doors, Cyrus could easily believe this was an ordinary day with the castle staff flitting about and the realm functioning as it should.

The ease on Apollo's face indicated he was not concerned at all that most of the citizens had been destroyed by the darkness of Pandora's box.

Cyrus continued to sip the wine, if only to give his body something to do. Inside him, turmoil raged, his mind racing and his heart seizing. He forced an outward calm as he said in a smooth voice, "You do not seem at all bothered by the situation."

Apollo blinked, his dark eyes flicking to Cyrus with lazy amusement. "The situation?"

Cyrus waved a hand toward the closed doors of the study.

Apollo snorted and took a large gulp of his own wine. "I've seen war before, nephew. This is nothing. It will pass."

Cyrus bristled at the term of endearment. "I've told you not to call me that. There is no shared blood between us."

Apollo arched an eyebrow. "Your father and I shared a special bond. To me, that binds us together far more than *blood*." He spat the word.

Cyrus went perfectly still. Was Apollo speaking of his own parents? His sister? Whoever he was thinking of was someone he loathed, and Cyrus, regrettably, had not properly researched Apollo's ancestral line to know anything about it.

"Even so," Cyrus said slowly, "I held little regard for my father and brothers. So you can imagine I would be far less inclined to call you *family*, especially when you've stolen into my realm and attempted to claim my throne."

Apollo swept another gaze over Cyrus, then chuckled. "Face it, boy. You are in no condition to rule this place. And you know it."

Cyrus decided he loathed being called *boy* much more than *nephew.*

And this proved Apollo knew something was wrong with Cyrus's magic. But perhaps he didn't know the entirety of the situation.

Struggling to rein in his temper, Cyrus said evenly, "Then, why am I here? Why not kill me to make the transition easier?"

"I could," Apollo mused, his dark eyes glittering. "It would be easy. But I think you'll be far more useful to me as an ally."

Cyrus's nostrils flared. "Why would I align myself with someone trying to steal my throne?"

"Why else?" Apollo sat back in his chair and laced his fingers together. "Power. Protection. As I said, I *could* kill you. And I will do just that if you get in my way."

A threat, then. It wasn't surprising. Cyrus knew the kind of man Apollo was. He was just like Aidoneus.

Thinking of his father made Cyrus pause before answering. He needed to pretend it was Aidoneus before him. How would he manipulate this conversation in his favor, if that were the case?

It was nothing more than a game. A show of strength. And, weak as he was, Cyrus was good at projecting confidence.

He needed to play things differently, though. The absence of his power meant the game had changed.

He needed to tell Apollo the truth. Or at least, part of it.

His chin lifted. "That isn't much of a threat. I expected to die two days ago when I cast the spell to bring back my wife. In a weak vessel like this"—he gestured to himself with a sneer—"death would be preferable."

It wasn't a lie. But repeating those words, when he had thrown them in Prue's face earlier, made his chest ache. He still didn't feel fully like himself, and inwardly, he raged at being weak and pathetic. The fury and frustration were still there.

But now they mingled with a remorse so potent it lanced through him like a sharpened blade. The look of hurt and betrayal on Prue's face. The tears in her eyes. The choked words she flung back at him.

He had shattered something between them. And he wasn't sure if he would ever be able to repair it.

"Your life isn't the only one I can take," Apollo said. His tone was low, and the calmness in his expression darkened into something lethal. "I can take that pretty little wife of yours. She's powerful, yes, but she is nothing against me."

It took all of Cyrus's strength to push down the rising roar of his anger at the thought of Apollo with his hands on Prue. *Don't show him your weakness,* he thought. *Just like with Aidoneus.* "You think you can best my wife? When Gaia herself has had her powers restored, and would fight alongside her? I don't think so."

Apollo chuckled without humor. "You are a fool if you don't see the possibilities, Cyrus. You, your witch, and Gaia—all three of you provide an excellent opportunity." He leaned forward, his gaze sharpening with intensity. "*Leverage.*"

Cyrus's heart lurched as he finally understood Apollo's meaning. All the sun god had to do was threaten Gaia, and Prue would comply. If he threatened Prue, Cyrus would comply. And Gaia had already proven she would do anything to save her children.

Apollo was right. He *owned* this realm because he had nothing to lose. No weaknesses to exploit.

But everyone else did.

Thinking fast, Cyrus pursed his lips as if considering this. "You do make an excellent point." He carefully set his glass on the table next to him, scratching his chin with a thoughtful frown on his face. "But you overlook one thing. I don't care for the earth goddesses. Not anymore."

Apollo's brows furrowed. "You can't expect me to believe that."

It was time to stop pretending. Cyrus needed to offer the truth if he wanted to gain Apollo's trust. After all,

Apollo would find out about his human state eventually. That is, assuming he didn't already know.

"As I said, I thought I would die when I cast the spell for Prue," Cyrus said. "I was willing to do that for her. But I was *not* willing to come back in this wretched state. A human." With a disgusted grimace, he gestured to himself once more. He couldn't even bear to look at himself in the mirror. He knew what he would see: a weak human with black hair and blue eyes and no tattoos. No sign of the otherworldly power he'd once held.

"So it's true then?" Apollo asked. "You are mortal? I thought you looked different. And I can sense no power in you."

"Yes, it's true. I can hardly stand the sight of my wife anymore." Cyrus kept his tone idle, as if he were merely discussing the state of his court. "And I told her as much. Whatever existed between us is... gone. You can ask her yourself."

He forced himself to look away, to sigh and gaze at the flames in the hearth, as if this were sad news indeed, but not sad enough for him to do anything about it.

Inside, his emotions raged, thrashing against his mortal form, dragging him downward. He saw the broken agony in Prue's face, the way her gaze had fixed on him in disbelief and confusion. He imagined Apollo speaking with Prue, asking about her marriage, reopening the wound Cyrus had dealt her. Prue would deny it, of course, but she had always been so easy to read. Her expression would turn haunted and full of grief, and in that moment, Apollo would know Cyrus was telling the truth.

"Do what you want with the earth goddesses," Cyrus said, his gaze still fixed on the fire. "Although, I'm a little surprised you don't want to keep them alive."

Apollo shifted in his seat. "What do you mean?"

Cyrus feigned confusion as he looked at Apollo. "To rebuild the realm, of course. You can't rule a broken kingdom. And Gaia and Prudence are the only ones with magic powerful enough to rebuild this place."

Apollo stroked his chin, his eyes calculating. He knew that only earth magic—the magic of new life— could create a realm strong enough for him to rule. Sun magic could only get him so far. "I only need one of them," he said.

"True," Cyrus said. "Gaia is the stronger of the two, and the obvious choice to do the task. But if you kill her daughter, do you really think she'll do what you want? As you said, Prue is her leverage. And without it, you have nothing."

Apollo bit the inside of his cheek and swirled his drink, his eyes narrowing with concentration. Cyrus could practically see the thoughts flickering across his face. He cocked his head and appraised Cyrus with an appreciative gleam in his eye. "All right, then." He set down his drink and clasped his hands together. "Here are my terms. You align yourself with me, help me take the throne, and I will not only offer you protection, but I will give you the highest seat on my council."

Cyrus shook his head. "No. I want my powers back."

Apollo opened and closed his mouth. "But... You... That's not possible."

Cyrus's mouth curved into a serpentine smile. He spread his hands as if in apology. "Then I'm afraid I'll have to reject your terms." He stood and headed for the door.

"Wait." Apollo stood, too, and Cyrus turned to face him, eyebrows raised. Apollo's eyes were wide with panic, his calm demeanor vanishing completely.

That was when Cyrus knew his suspicions had been correct.

Apollo was desperate. He had no allies. No one to trust.

He needed Cyrus. More than Cyrus needed him.

"I—I can find a way," Apollo said quickly. "I *will* find a way to restore your powers. You have my word."

Your word means nothing to me, you bastard, Cyrus thought. But he nodded, offering a satisfied smile. He stuck out his hand, which Apollo shook. "Then, we have a deal."

Let the games begin.

REUNITED
PANDORA

PANDORA'S INSIDES WOULDN'T STOP QUIVERING with fear and dread. At any moment, she expected Mona to abandon her, or perhaps to turn her over to these fire witches. As soon as she said, *This is Pandora*, it would be over.

As Pandora clambered through the narrow tunnel, she paused often to check on the vines carrying Evander's limp form. When they caught on a jagged rock, she was the first to dislodge the vine so it could continue sliding along the ground.

She was determined to be as helpful as she could to Mona as well as Evander. Not only because she wanted them to trust her—or because she owed them, which she did—but because Pandora wanted to be different. She wanted to be helpful instead of destructive. She wanted to change her story.

Inside, she felt the restless darkness churning, hungry for blood, for vengeance. It wouldn't be long before that power consumed her entirely.

She was not strong enough to fight off this curse. Eventually, it would take her.

So she had to make every moment count while she still could.

After what felt like an eternity, the tunnel opened up to a vast cavern with torches lining the walls. In the center, a circle of benches surrounded a fire pit, upon which rested a boiling cauldron. The cavern was filled with witches, some sitting on benches, some trickling ingredients into the cauldron, while others were chatting on the opposite side next to an array of cabinets and shelves.

At Farah's approach, each witch fell silent and bowed their head in reverence to the coven leader. Farah strode toward the crowd of witches, but Mona and Pandora lingered at the tunnel entrance. Pandora noticed the way Mona angled her body protectively in front of Evander to shield him from view.

"If Romanos is truly here," Pandora whispered to her, "he will not let harm come to him." From what she remembered of Romanos, he kept his head down, seeking to stay out of the power struggle between Cyrus and his brothers. But he did still care for them. And he wasn't heartless.

But how would he react to knowing she was behind the destruction of his realm? According to him, she had only been Trivia, the goddess of pathways.

"He might not have a choice," Mona muttered darkly. "This coven is powerful. I can sense it. And they will easily outnumber us, even with Romanos on our side."

Pandora swallowed hard. She couldn't sense the power here like Mona could. Then again, Mona had proven her magic was more powerful than Pandora's when she had shattered the bindings of their bargain. Pandora had tried to keep Mona contained, ordering her to say nothing, to do nothing to stop her from putting her plan in action as Elysium crumbled. And Mona had severed that bond like it was nothing.

Pandora had deserved it. She never should have called in that bargain at all. It was yet another item on her list of reasons why Mona should abandon her and never look back.

Farah was saying something to the witches, who glanced at Mona and Pandora with interest. One witch pointed to a tunnel behind her, and Farah nodded in agreement. The first witch disappeared through the tunnel, while Farah and two other witches made their way to Mona and Pandora.

"Tell them you're Trivia," Mona said quickly.

"I'm not an idiot," Pandora hissed, but she felt a hopeful warmth spread through her as she realized Mona wasn't going to reveal her identity.

But no. Pandora squashed that hope inside her before it bloomed into something dangerous. Something she couldn't trust. Mona would betray her eventually. It was inevitable. She needed to keep her guard up, to anticipate the moment when Mona would exact vengeance for all Pandora had done to her.

Steeling herself, Pandora watched as the three fire witches stood before them. One had curly auburn hair and a prominent chin, while the other had dark wavy hair and skin almost as brown as Farah's. Both had glowing amber eyes that glinted eerily.

"This is Wren." Farah gestured to the first witch. "And this is Dahlia. They will see to your needs while you are here."

"This one has darkness about her," Wren said, her voice blunt as she pointed to Pandora.

Pandora resisted the urge to fidget under the three witches' scrutiny.

"We all have darkness," Dahlia said, her voice softer and more subdued than Wren's.

"My name is Mona." Mona pressed a hand to her chest, then waved a hand toward Pandora. "And this is Trivia. We are daughters of Gaia."

Wren and Dahlia both stiffened. The latter narrowed her eyes at Pandora. "Trivia... as in the goddess of three paths?"

Alarm prickled along Pandora's skin, but she forced herself to respond. "Yes. That is me."

"I did not realize you were also a daughter of Gaia," Dahlia mused. Pandora didn't like the way her keen eyes appraised her.

Farah cleared her throat, giving Dahlia a pointed look.

Dahlia smiled, the motion warming her features. "Apologies. I am a teacher in our coven, so I am well-versed in the histories of our goddesses. I would love to learn more about *your* history, Trivia."

Shit. If Dahlia was a historian, she would easily be able to detect Pandora's lies.

Which meant the sooner they left this place, the better. The moment these witches found out who she really was, they would try to kill her. Pandora was certain of it.

"Did you say Romanos was here?" Mona asked, and Pandora was grateful for the subject change. Mona craned her neck, as if to search for the death god, her eyes full of worry. Pandora knew she feared for Evander and wanted his brother to help him as soon as possible.

"He is coming," Farah said. "While we wait, you can

tell us what happened to your friend." Her gaze slid to Evander, still unconscious on the bed of ivy. "None of the others who came this way looked like that."

Pandora and Mona exchanged uncertain glances. "What did the others tell you?" Mona asked carefully.

"That the magic of Pandora's box obliterated the realm of Elysium," Farah said, her voice eerily calm despite her words.

Pandora felt a lump rise in her throat. *Oh gods, I can't do this.* Between the dark energy roiling within her and her mounting guilt and shame for what she had done, the emotions were enough to overwhelm her. It was a miracle she hadn't fainted from the intensity of the weight bearing down upon her.

Mona was trembling beside her. When Pandora looked at her, she found her sister was paler than usual, her eyes wide with fear. What was wrong?

After a moment, Mona said in a shaky voice, "Hestia... Your fire goddess..." She broke off with a strangled sound.

"We know," Farah said solemnly, her eyes flaring with pain. "Hestia is dead."

The air stilled from the intensity of her words. Chills rippled over Pandora's body as the atmosphere around them seemed to darken. Pandora's eyes closed as echoes of her former life rang through her.

No, she thought. *It was not my life. But hers. The goddess inside me. We are separate beings.*

But it was feeling less and less real. She could not hide behind the former goddess's past. It was no excuse for her actions. Sol had been right; she still had made choices. She was still in control.

Gods, her stomach cinched at the thought of Sol the sun god, at the betrayal in his eyes when he'd found out who she was.

And it was all the more terrible because he and the true Pandora had been lovers. It was a long time ago, but he had never moved past that loss.

Now here I am, reopening that wound and destroying another life for it, Pandora thought bitterly.

"We felt it," Wren said, her eyes haunted, and a wrinkle forming between her brows. "When she died, we all felt that loss in our very bones. Once the gods from Elysium began arriving, they confirmed it for us."

"How many are here?" Pandora asked.

Before anyone could answer, a voice rang out across the cavern. "Mona?"

The witches all turned to find a man striding from the mouth of the tunnel on the opposite end of the cave. He wore fighting leathers and had black hair streaked with silver, cropped close to his scalp. His familiar silver eyes shone in the lantern light.

"Romanos," Pandora breathed, her chest tightening with anxiety as the death god approached them. To her surprise, he swept Mona into a fierce hug. Mona yelped, then clutched him in return, laughing as Romanos set her back on her feet.

"I'm so relieved you're all right!" Mona said, grinning at him.

"Likewise." The warmth in Romanos's demeanor made Pandora's whole body ache with yearning and jealousy. Not that she fancied Romanos. No, she yearned for this bond that he shared with Mona. The two had only known each other for the span of a few days, and already they were comrades. Friends. They cared about each other.

Pandora had never had that. Not once in her life.

Slowly, Romanos's gaze slid to Pandora, and his smile faded. He looked her over, then inhaled deeply. "Trivia, you..." He stilled, his face going pale. "What magic have you brought here?"

Shit. She no longer possessed death magic to disguise the blood of Gaia racing through her veins. That, and the curse of the former goddess still thrumming within her, was a dangerous combination for anyone who could sense her magic.

"I—I—" Pandora didn't know what to say. What *could* she say? She couldn't deny it, nor could she admit who she was.

She was stuck. Trapped.

"What is she doing here?" boomed another male voice.

Pandora went rigid from the sound of that voice. Gods, *that voice.* She never thought she would hear it again. It was both a balm to her soul and a torturous punishment.

Her eyes followed the sound, and her heart stopped within her chest. A shaky breath whooshed from her as she found Sol the sun god standing in front of another tunnel. He must have heard the commotion and come to investigate. His expression was murderous, his dark eyes narrowing and his face twisting in disgust. With forceful steps, he came closer, his fingers curling into tight fists.

Shit, shit, shit...

Pandora found herself edging backward toward the tunnel she'd come through. Could she throw herself into the portal once more? Where would she end up?

It didn't matter. Anywhere was better than here. Even a collapsed realm would be preferable.

When Sol reached them, he gestured toward Pandora. "What is she doing here?" he repeated, his tone icy.

"She came from Elysium, seeking refuge like you," Farah said, her gaze flicking between Sol and Pandora.

"I will leave," Pandora said quickly. "I'll leave at once. I shouldn't be here, I—"

"She is responsible for the destruction of Elysium," Sol said, his eyes blazing. "My mother's death, the loss of my home—it's all her fault. She has the soul of Pandora inside her, and it's because of her that the dark magic has been unleashed."

FRACTURED

PRUE

"Again," Gaia commanded.

Prue wiped sweat from her brow, her arms trembling and her body weak. The two goddesses stood across from each other in the throne room, where they had been practicing conjuring earth magic for hours.

"I want this entire room to become a lush forest, Prudence," Gaia said, her blue eyes sharp and unyielding as she fixed a determined stare on her daughter. "You can do better than this."

Prue let her arms fall on her thighs, gasping for breath. "I'm *trying*."

"You're not trying hard enough. If you ever hope to prevent Apollo from taking your kingdom, then you—"

"I know what's at stake, Gaia," Prue snapped, rubbing her forehead as frustration mounted within her.

Her last attempt with her magic had sprouted trees and roots, with shrubs and flowers spreading over the entire floor. But the chandelier on the ceiling had remained, as had the two silver thrones.

Emotion flared in Gaia's eyes, and Prue knew why. She usually called her *Mama*. But sometimes, Prue couldn't help but be reminded of the divide between them. Gaia had lied to Prue her entire life, keeping her lineage a secret, letting her believe she was nothing more than an ordinary witch.

Prue had forgiven her for this. But it didn't mean they could return to how things were before. Even on Krenia, their relationship as mother and daughter had been strained. Gaia always got along better with Mona.

Mona. Prue's chest constricted in agony. Goddess, she missed her sister. Was Mona safe? Was she well? Prue had to believe she'd gotten out of the Underworld before Pandora's magic had consumed the realm.

"I don't know if I have it in me," Prue said in a low voice. She was so tired, so fragile, so deflated.

Gaia's expression softened just a touch. She drew closer to Prue, her emerald gown swishing on the marble floors. "You do," she said gently. "I know you, and I know your magic. You *can* do this. One last try. Please?"

Prue's gaze flicked to her mother's in surprise. Gaia never said *please*. As a goddess, and, before that, the

Mother of the witch coven, she was accustomed to giving orders and having them followed without question.

So much had changed in Prue's life over a short period of time. She couldn't forget that Gaia had changed, too. Losing her powers and her third child to Apollo, then almost losing her other two daughters as well, had taken its toll on her. As far as Prue knew, Gaia was still prepared to give herself up to Pandora's dark forces. But if Prue could prolong that for as long as she could, perhaps Gaia's mind could be swayed.

"All right," Prue conceded. "One last time."

"Remember, this is not like witch magic," Gaia reminded her. "No grace. No conditions. No third eye. You need to trust your goddess blood."

Prue nodded. With a deep inhale, she spread her arms around herself. Her magic flared to life, making the ground rumble. The lacy blue fabric of her dress rippled from the movement. Her black curls billowed as a powerful wind swept over her.

Still she pulled, drawing out that power and strength, focusing on the new energy churning within her. Ever since Cyrus had brought her back from the dead, her magic had felt different. Foreign. Like it belonged to someone else. Like it wasn't truly *hers* anymore.

Gaia had promised it would take time to adjust. But they did not *have* time. Apollo was already here. Any day now, Prue expected his army to burst into the castle, ready to seize it by force.

He hadn't yet formally challenged her or Cyrus for the throne, which made Prue suspicious. Was he waiting for his forces to arrive? Or was he doing something else? He had announced his intention to rule, but then he'd vanished. Prue could still sense his powerful sun magic and knew he was still in the realm, but she had no idea what nefarious plans he was putting in motion. And she didn't like it.

Focusing her thoughts on her powers, Prue flexed her fingers, coaxing out more and more of her magic. It burst from her, making the wind whistle and the ground quake. Cracks formed in the marble, and vines and roots sprang forth. Sweat dripped from her temples. She resisted the urge to wipe it away, keeping her arms stretched on either side of her.

More, she urged. *More.*

Grass coated the floors, spreading until the entire throne room was covered. Thick oak trees shot up, and the glass of the chandelier tinkled in response. Prue pictured exactly what her mother had asked for: a lush forest. She thought of the beech trees of Krenia, the thick woods where she and Mona had grown up. In her mind, she heard the laughter of children as they padded, bare-footed, through the grove.

The smell of roses tickled her nose, and once again,

she was painfully reminded of Mona. Despair lodged in her throat, making it hard to breathe. But instead of shying away from the emotion, she clung to it, fueling her power with it.

"That's it, Prudence!" Gaia said, her voice full of pride.

Prue's face crumpled, and she felt tears burn in her eyes. But she embraced it, drawing out her agony along with her power. The fractured remains of her heart and soul.

She saw the loathing in Cyrus's eyes when he'd awoken as a human.

She heard Mona's screams as she sacrificed herself to the dark magic that had once claimed her life.

She saw Apollo ripping the infant baby from Gaia's arms, leaving her sobbing on the floor.

Sharp heat burned in Prue's chest, and she groaned, hunching over as the tears spilled freely down her face. Goddess, it was too much. *Too much.*

She threw her head back with a scream, letting it tear at her throat, letting it pull everything from her. Only once had she allowed her magic to take this much of herself—and it had been when the caves of Tartarus were collapsing. It had been the only way to save Cyrus.

That much strain on her body had killed her.

But this time was different. This time, the castle walls trembled, and an explosion of power split the air.

Glass shattered, but Prue's magic swarmed around her, protecting her from the shards. Metal and stone cracked, making a resounding echo that clanged through the room. Dust filled the air, brushing against her skin. Still, she wept. Still, she pushed.

At long last, she fell to her knees, unable to offer any more. Her knees met soft, grassy earth, and the smell of sage and roses and jasmine filled her nose. Slowly, she opened her eyes, blinking away the tears.

It was as if she'd stepped through a portal. A canopy of tree branches had replaced the ceiling, and vines and shrubs coated the windows, cocooning her in darkness. Where the thrones once sat were now two massive oak trees. Rose bushes, beech trees, and vines of ivy lined the walls. Thick grass had completely replaced the floor.

Gaia stood in front of her, a rare smile on her face, her blue eyes gleaming with admiration. She strode toward Prue, and the grass shifted from her movement, bending to her will as the Earth Goddess. She knelt at Prue's side, then grasped her shoulders. Prue leaned into her touch, afraid she would collapse from fatigue.

"Well done, my darling," Gaia murmured, pressing a kiss to her forehead. "Well done."

Prue soaked in the bath for an hour after the ordeal with her magic. Her emotions were still raw and festering inside her, as if a dam had burst, and there was no way to repair it. No way to shove the emotions back into place.

The tears wouldn't stop flowing. Pain and misery clouded her mind, and she couldn't breathe. Even an hour in the soapy water could not cure her of the turmoil racing through her.

She needed Cyrus. She needed her husband.

It had been days since she'd seen him. The day he'd awoken as a human, he had said terrible things to her, and even after they had confronted Apollo together, she'd been too afraid to seek him out. Not only that, but he was making himself as scarce as Apollo these days. She got the sense he was avoiding her.

Well, she had given him time. And right now, she needed her husband. Her king. Her mate.

Swallowing around the lump of grief in her throat, Prue slipped into a red silk gown and gathered her hair into a braid that fell over one shoulder. She brushed her fingers along her collarbone, lamenting the loss of that pomegranate necklace that had bound her and Cyrus together so long ago.

After brushing rouge on her lips and cheeks, she strode from her quarters, chin lifted as she projected a confidence she did not feel. The servants and staff nodded or bowed politely to her as she swept past them. In the corridors, she encountered dozens of demons flitting about, some looking as if they belonged, and others seeming confused and overwhelmed. The realm was in shambles, and her advisor, Lagos, had managed to shelter as many demons as possible before the kingdom had fallen. The castle was warded with powerful magic that had somehow managed to protect its inhabitants from Pandora's darkness. For this, Prue was grateful, but her chest ached at the thought of the people they had not been able to save.

People who had died because of her. Because *she* had opened Pandora's box.

The tightness in her throat only intensified, lodging firmly in her airway until she couldn't breathe. Heat burned in her eyes, and she barely saw where she was going, barely registered her steps moving until she found herself in front of Cyrus's door. Originally, he had resided in the king's suite of the castle, but Lagos had discreetly questioned the staff about the king's whereabouts, and Prue was alarmed to discover he had moved to a guest chamber instead.

Was he not intending to stay? Or did he find himself unworthy to occupy the king's suite?

Or worse—was he abdicating to Apollo? Could he even do that, while Prue still reigned as Queen of the Underworld?

Shoving aside these thoughts and uncertainties, Prue rapped on the door loudly, then frowned. She was his *wife.* She didn't need to knock. Her fingers reached for the door handle.

A low groan sounded from within, halting her.

Cold dread seeped into her, cinching tightly in her stomach. *Oh, Goddess…*

Was he in there with another woman?

Prue didn't think he could hurt her any more than when he'd first discovered he was human. But no, he could. If he decided to bed another woman, then—

Prue gritted her teeth. For the first time, fresh anger swept over her, coursing through her and heating her blood. How dare he?

She flung open the doors, letting them bang against the walls as she strode into the chambers. Her eyes flared wide at the scene before her.

Books, papers, and clothes were strewn all over the room. Pillows had been shredded, leaving feathers every-where. On all fours, gasping for breath, was Cyrus. He was shirtless, his black hair hanging, obscuring his face like a curtain. A sheen of sweat coated his pale skin.

"Cyrus," Prue said, all ire leaving her at once as she hurried to his side.

But at her approach, Cyrus hissed and cringed away from her. "Don't."

She froze at the lethal warning in his voice. He might

not have the same powers he'd possessed before, but he still carried the authority of a god.

"What happened?" Prue asked, trying not to let panic bleed into her words.

To her surprise, Cyrus wheezed a mocking laugh, sitting back on the balls of his feet and shaking the sweaty hair from his face. His blue eyes were like chips of ice as he glared at her. "Nothing, *wife.* Nothing has happened. I am merely winded from the mundane events of the day because of this despicable mortal body. I would be shocked if I lived to see another fortnight at this rate."

Prue blinked at him, unable to process his words. He was wounded... from his mortal blood? Her gaze passed over him quickly, assessing for injuries. Aside from the blue veins standing out starkly on his arms and neck, and the pallor of his skin, he seemed unharmed.

She swallowed hard, uncertain of what to do. It was clear he didn't want her pity or concern. What could she do for him? She wanted to touch him, to hold him to her chest.

But no. He would hate to be coddled. She knew Cyrus better than anyone. And although he had been severely altered from this transformation, she knew his soul. His mind.

He wanted power. Respect. Strength. And he had lost all of that.

Sorrow welled inside her at the sight of her husband like this, and her, powerless to help him.

After a long moment, she said quietly, "Do you wish to leave?"

Cyrus turned to look at her fully, his dark brows furrowing in confusion. "Leave?"

"Leave the Underworld."

His lips parted in surprise, and Prue was alarmed at how refreshing it was to see an emotion other than hatred on his face.

"If you are unhappy here," Prue went on, "I can arrange for you to be taken to the mortal realm."

Cyrus snorted, casting his gaze skyward. "The mortal realm." He said the words with derision.

Prue scoffed and crossed her arms. "You've been there before. It wasn't so bad, was it?"

Cyrus's expression shifted, his eyes flaring with an emotion Prue couldn't place. Something softened in his features for a brief moment, but his apathetic mask slid into place before Prue could scrutinize it. "I suppose not."

"Is that what you want?" Prue asked. "To leave here?" *To leave me,* she wanted to say. But she couldn't bring herself to ask directly.

If he no longer loved her, she would let him go. She would let him live whatever life he wanted to.

Cyrus leaned against the armoire behind him,

draping his arms over his legs as he fiddled with a loose thread on his trousers. "Why?"

"Why what?"

"Why are you offering? To get me out of the way? To be rid of the embarrassment of having a human for a husband?"

Prue's nostrils flared. "You forget that *I* was a human once, too. And you looked down on me, sneering at me at every turn. I will not do the same to you. I lived among humans my entire life. I have nothing but respect for them."

"You were a witch." Cyrus waved his hand, as if her words didn't matter. "You still had magic. That's hardly *human*."

Prue cocked her head at him. "Is magic all that matters?"

Cyrus's lips pressed together in a thin line, but Prue could read the answer in his eyes. *Yes.*

She had to ask. She had to know. "Do you regret it?" Her voice was quiet. "Bringing me back? If you had known... what the spell would do, would that have changed your mind?" She held her breath, unsure if she wanted to know the answer.

Cyrus's gaze sharpened, and he climbed to his feet, bracing one arm against the armoire for support. With a heavy sigh, he ran his fingers through his inky black hair. At long last, he spoke, his voice so soft Prue wasn't sure she heard him properly. "No."

The breath whooshed from her lungs in a sharp exhale. *Thank the Goddess.*

"I still believe you are the best leader for this realm," Cyrus said, his gaze solemn. Something in Prue's chest sank. So, he only brought her back for the good of the kingdom? Not because he loved her?

"That hasn't changed, even with Apollo here," said Cyrus.

Apollo. Prue bristled at the reminder that her throne was in jeopardy. As if she and Cyrus didn't have enough to deal with at the moment.

Cyrus's brows furrowed in confusion, and he said slowly, "He called Gaia *wife...*" His eyes flicked up to meet Prue's, a question in his gaze.

Prue blinked. Did Cyrus not know? Well, it was bound to be exposed soon anyway. "Apollo is my father," she said.

Cyrus's eyebrows lifted, his mouth going slack with surprise. Then, he barked out a harsh laugh, sounding so much like his old self that Prue felt her heart lighten. "Of course he is. Well, it all makes sense now. You broke Gaia's curse, and you are the Queen of the Underworld. He couldn't possibly allow it. He wants revenge."

"He wants to be the most powerful," Prue said. "I

don't believe he would be here if he didn't consider us a threat."

Cyrus's mouth twisted into a bitter smile. "I'm not much of a threat anymore, am I?"

"He doesn't know that."

"Yes, he does." The words were grave and final, and Prue felt her blood run cold.

Shit. Had Cyrus told him he was human?

If so, why was he talking with Apollo at all?

Cyrus stared at her, his throat bobbing as he swallowed hard. "Why are you here, Prue?"

In truth, she had come to Cyrus for selfish reasons—because she needed him. But upon arriving, she realized he had needed her more.

And in that moment, she knew what else he needed: freedom.

Clearing her throat, Prue said in a firm voice, "I came to tell you that I love you. Despite everything we have endured, everything that has happened, and everything you said to me, I am still desperately in love with you. And if, at any point, you wish to be my husband once again, I will be waiting."

Prue paused to take a breath, her pulse racing and her stomach twisting into knots. She took a moment to steady herself before continuing, "But, ages ago, we struck a bargain that bound us together as husband and wife. It was something neither of us asked for, and neither of us were able to be rid of that bond. I'm giving you the chance now. If you wish to part ways from me and seek out your own life in the mortal realm, I will accept this. I will look after the Underworld and do my best to stop Apollo from taking the throne. I swear it."

Cyrus's eyes flashed with pain. A muscle worked in his jaw as he looked at her, his cheeks reddening. He exhaled deeply, dropping his gaze, his nostrils flaring. Prue couldn't tell if it was anger or despair that overcame him.

But she wasn't ready to face it. Whatever it was, she wasn't strong enough yet.

So she said, "You don't have to answer right now. I just wanted you to know where I stood. And what you can expect from me."

Her throat burned as she turned away from him, her eyes stinging with tears. As soon as she left his chambers, not even glancing back at him, she let the tears fall freely as agony consumed her.

JUDGMENT
PANDORA

THE ENTIRE CAVERN WENT STILL AFTER SOL'S bold words. Pandora felt a chill ripple in the air, making the skin on her arms pebble. Her blood ran cold as every pair of eyes fixed on her.

Oh no. *Oh no.*

Farah spoke first, her eyes narrowing into slits as she assessed Pandora with renewed scrutiny. "Do you care to explain this, Trivia?"

Pandora's mouth was dry, and she couldn't form any words. These witches would kill her. If Sol didn't do it first.

"It wasn't her fault," Mona said.

Pandora gaped at her sister. She had *not* expected her to defend Pandora's actions. Not when they had caused her so much pain.

"As Sol stated, she has the soul of Pandora inside her," Mona went on. "And we all know what happened to Pandora."

Pandora blinked as several fire witches murmured to one another, not one of them appearing confused or shocked.

They knew? How did they know what had happened to the goddess? Apollo had taken such care to hide the truth.

"How?" Sol asked, voicing her shock. "How do you know?" His face was pale as he stared at Farah.

"We are witches," Farah said. "Seers and prophetesses. We see things others do not. And our goddesses do not conceal the truth from us."

Pandora's breath caught in her throat. Hestia had told them?

Hestia... who was now dead.

Sol's mother was dead.

Her fault. *Her fault.* This was all Pandora's fault.

"Apollo doesn't care about the mortal realm," Mona said, her voice bitter. "He was more concerned with keeping the secret from Elysium."

Farah's eerie amber gaze fixed on Pandora once more. "Is she controlling you right now?"

"No," Pandora said, finding her voice at last. "What Mona says is not entirely true. Yes, the soul of... the goddess is inside me. I have her memories, and I am fueled by her desire for revenge. But... I am still myself. I possess Gaia's magic. I am capable of making my own choices. Sol—Sol is correct. I am to blame for all this. And I will accept whatever punishment you see fit to inflict." She lifted her chin, trying to appear calm, but her mouth trembled, and heat burned in her eyes.

Perhaps it would be a relief to die this way. The witches would make it swift—they were certainly powerful enough—and Pandora would not fight them. And after it was over, she would finally be free.

Perhaps it was the *only* way to truly be free of her curse.

Farah did not respond at first. She looked at Wren, and the two witches seemed to be silently communicating for a moment. At long last, Farah said, "It will be up to the Gorgon sisters to decide your fate. They are Hestia's chosen vessels, and it is for them to judge what shall be done to exact her vengeance."

Pandora's throat tightened with emotion, but she nodded. She did not know much about the Gorgon sisters. The only texts she had read about them had mentioned they had the power of serpents, and they could turn their enemies to stone.

"Apollo killed Hestia," Mona said loudly. "*He* is to blame for her death."

"He was after *you*," Sol growled. "Perhaps it is *your* fault then."

Mona's eyes darkened for a moment, but she huffed a cold laugh. "Are you so blinded by the love of your mentor that you will not put blame where it belongs?"

Sol bared his teeth and took a step toward Mona. "If you had not challenged Apollo, my mother would still be alive."

Pandora found herself moving before she realized what was happening. She stepped between Sol and Mona, hands outstretched. Her fingers brushed against Sol's tunic, and she hastily withdrew her arms before the feel of him completely undid her.

"This is pointless," Pandora said. "Apollo is not here. I will accept full blame for what happened. We do not need to argue about this."

Sol's eyes narrowed as he fixed his venomous gaze on her. "Since when are you the peacemaker?"

"Since I realized my entire life was stolen from me for no reason," Pandora said coldly. She turned to Farah. "I believed that once Elysium was destroyed this curse would leave me. I thought the soul of the goddess inside me would be freed. But I was wrong. I no longer wish to serve her. I want to be my own person. My own goddess. And I will do whatever it takes to atone for what I've done."

Sol barked a harsh laugh of disbelief, but Farah watched Pandora with calm interest, her eyes sparking with an emotion she couldn't place.

"As I said before," Farah murmured, "we will take you to the Gorgon sisters for judgment."

"You cannot take her anywhere," Sol said, his dark eyes burning with fury. "She will bring the darkness with her. She will betray *all* of you."

"Then what do you suggest?" Farah asked, fixing him with a fearsome look. "We kill her right here? Well, don't let me stop you, little sun god." She spread her arms. "Strike her down. We will not stand in your way."

Pandora went rigid. Was Farah serious?

Sol's brows drew together as he glanced from Farah to Pandora. But he did not move. Anger still brewed in his gaze, but he did not come toward Pandora. His magic could easily end her life. They both knew this.

But he wouldn't kill her.

She had asked him to, when Elysium was burning. He had refused, claiming death would be too merciful for her.

But as she watched him, she saw something haunted fill his gaze. Something she had only seen once before: when she had caught him gazing at the moonlit sea with devastation on his face.

He had been consumed by grief over the loss of the goddess he had loved. The goddess whose soul now occupied Pandora's body.

And in that moment, she knew he was unwilling to

take away that soul once more. He had lost her already. He wasn't ready to do it again.

The thought filled her with despair. It was only the former goddess he cared about. Not *her*. He only saw the lover he'd lost. Nothing more.

She was nothing to him. And that would never change.

"Please," Mona said suddenly, turning to Romanos. "Can you help us? Evander..." She gestured to the figure lying on the bed of ivy.

Pandora had forgotten he was there, and she hated herself for that. The death god looked ghostly pale, his eyes still closed and his expression crumpled in agony.

"Shit," Romanos muttered, drawing forward and crouching in front of his brother. His wide eyes took in Evander's shredded wings and bloodied state. "Gods above, Evander, what the hell happened to you?"

"Can you help him?" Mona asked, her voice strained as she knelt alongside Romanos.

Romanos didn't answer. His mouth was set in determination, his jaw taut as he placed his hands over Evander's body, hovering slightly above the tattered wings.

"Demon magic," he said quietly, his brows knitting together. "I can feel it."

"You can draw it from him," Farah said.

Romanos shook his head. "I haven't practiced enough. Marina should do it."

"You *can* do this, Rom," said Farah.

Pandora frowned. Since when had Romanos and the coven leader become so familiar with one another? What had he been up to here in the mortal realm?

And who was Marina? Another fire witch? Or a goddess Pandora should be wary of?

After a few seconds, Romanos nodded, then closed his eyes. Darkness pooled from his fingertips, surrounding Evander in a black cloud.

Mona yelped, lurching toward Evander with panic in her eyes, but Pandora hurried to stop her, clutching her sister's shoulders to hold her in place. "Wait," she urged. "Just wait."

The shadows swirled, forming a cocoon around Evander's body. Romanos's face was strained, a muscle working in his jaw as he continued to release his power.

Several tense moments passed, and Pandora's heart raged against her chest. What was happening? What if Evander suffocated?

Then, the shadows began receding back into Romanos's hands. Bit by bit, the darkness fell away, leaving Evander's body. But as the magic faded, falling from him like a cloak, Pandora realized his body was different. He no longer had wings. And the bloody gashes on his body had been healed.

Mona inhaled a sharp gasp and brought her hand to her mouth, her eyes wide with shock.

When Romanos had pulled the magic back to his hands, he sank back on his knees, gasping for breath. His hands shook as he stared at them, as if not quite believing what he had done.

Evander groaned, his head turning. His eyes remained closed, but the color had returned to his skin, making him look less sickly.

Mona pressed a hand to her chest, tears filling her eyes. "Evander?" She hesitantly placed her other hand on his cheek.

Evander's eyes flickered open, revealing the silver irises that marked him as a deity. Slowly, his eyes snapped to Mona.

A heartbeat passed. Then another.

Evander lunged for her, drawing his arms around her, sitting up to pull her to his chest. He clutched her so tightly, Pandora was certain it would crush her.

But Mona only laughed, the sound thick with her tears as she buried her face in his chest, muttering something unintelligible.

Pandora withdrew a few steps to give them privacy and found Romanos standing a few paces away. She made her way over to him and asked, "What did you do? And how?"

Romanos offered a smile that didn't reach his eyes. "I called the death magic that festered inside him. And it came to me."

"You—You took his magic?"

Gravely, Romanos nodded, then glanced at Evander, who had tears in his eyes as he pressed kisses along Mona's cheeks and neck, his hand stroking her hair.

Pandora felt her chest tighten. Evander had no magic. He was powerless.

And he didn't know it yet. He was too consumed with the joy of reuniting with his lover.

Unbidden, Pandora's gaze flicked to Sol, only to find he was already watching her. His expression was hard, like a marble statue. Pain burned in his gaze, mixed with longing and desire.

Oh, gods. When he looked at her like that...

She shook her head, breaking eye contact. But she couldn't stop the flood of memories that assaulted her.

His hands on her bare skin. His frantic breaths in her ear. The heat of him as he ravished her body, unraveling her completely.

I had never wanted anyone as much as I wanted you. Not since her.

Those were the words he'd told her on the balcony that night. When he had admitted she had rekindled something lost inside of him.

And now, she'd broken him. Shattered whatever they had shared together.

With a shaky breath, Pandora pushed the thoughts

from her mind and approached Farah. "When do we leave for the Gorgon sisters?"

Before Farah could respond, Sol interjected. "If she is to accept punishment for my mother's death, I insist on being there to witness it."

Pandora stared at the determination in his gaze. Would he be relieved, or devastated if the Gorgon sisters called for her death?

"You have a whole realm of people to look after," Pandora said. "You were Apollo's apprentice. With him gone, they have no one to look to but you."

"Apollo is not gone," Sol said.

Pandora stiffened, and the darkness within her raged in response. "What?"

"He still lives. I can sense his power. He bound my sun magic to his. If he were dead, I would have felt it."

Pandora's eyes flared wide as she looked at Farah, then Mona and Evander, who were watching the exchange with solemn interest.

Apollo still lives.

The darkness did not destroy him.

And deeper within her, a voice hissed, *I will have my revenge.*

Pandora closed her eyes, hunching over from the agony of the fury churning inside her. Darkness. Screams. Blinding white light that seared into her skin...

"Well, where is he?" Mona demanded. "Is he here in the mortal realm?"

"I don't know," Sol admitted, his voice tight.

The conversation pulled Pandora back to the present. She rubbed her chest, trying to catch her breath. Mona was speaking again, and Pandora got the sense her sister was intentionally trying to draw attention to herself instead of Pandora.

Bless you, Mona, Pandora thought. *I do not deserve your kindness.*

"He could have come through another portal," Mona said, then looked at Farah. "There are others, right?"

Farah nodded. "There is one other portal that leads to Elysium. I can take you there."

Pandora frowned. "I thought we were going to see the Gorgon sisters?"

Farah's mouth spread into a smile. "You are in luck, young goddess. The Gorgon sisters and the portal are in the same place: the Voiceless Jungle."

POWERLESS
EVANDER

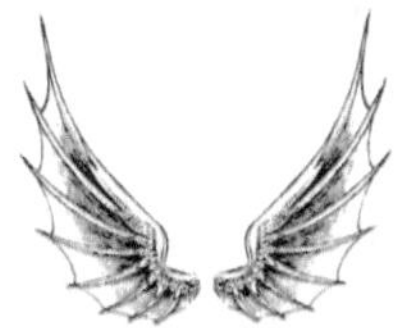

For so long, Evander had been consumed by darkness, despair, and pain. His body was slowly decaying, ripped apart from his connection to Typhon, his demonic alter ego. Typhon was a creature born of the Underworld, and only in the Underworld could he exist.

In Elysium, Typhon had taken over Evander's body, unleashing the beast within, with no restraint or control.

Evander had only managed to survive because of Mona.

And now, with another journey through a portal, Evander feared the strain on his body would be too much. That he would finally give out.

Fog clouded his mind as he waited for death to take him.

What would it be like, for a death god to die? Would his soul traverse the rivers, like all the others? Or was something different in store for him?

Would he go straight to Tartarus, because of his tainted demon blood?

From within the clouds of confusion that obscured his senses, he made out one clear sound, like the pure chime of a bell: Mona's voice. He would know that sound anywhere. He clung to it, to the proof that she was alive and healthy. Her voice was like a melody that called to him, a balm to his soul that soothed the agony that had consumed him for so long...

And then, quite suddenly, a searing, sharp clarity pierced his mind, so intense it burned against his eyes and ears and skin, assaulting his senses. He cried out but had no voice. His back arched as the fog of his mind evaporated, leaving a brilliant and blinding light that illuminated the details around him.

Cavern walls. Burning torches. And people—so many people.

The beast within him stirred, threatened by the presence of so many strangers. Once, Evander might have been able to soothe Typhon, to convince him all was well. But now, he and Typhon no longer knew each other. They were strangers occupying the same body, and Evander was powerless to stop him from taking over.

Before the monster inside him could wrestle control from his weak mind, the clarity exploded, spreading farther and farther into the recesses of his mind, sweeping away darkness from corners he didn't even know existed.

It was a startling shock to be buried in shadows and, mere seconds later, to be shoved into the light. He felt exposed, stark naked before an audience as he tried fruitlessly to return to the safety of those shadows.

The unknown was a terrifying thing. Sometimes it was so terrifying that the pain was preferable—because it was all he knew.

Then he heard her voice again.

"Evander."

The sound washed over him, calming his senses and soothing his body. He felt himself relax as that sound caressed his ears with perfect sharpness. Gods, he had missed how beautiful and perfect his name was on her lips. What had once been muffled was now crisp and undeniable.

Mona. Mona was here, calling for him.

He searched for her, his eyes burning against the sharp details of the room surrounding him... until they landed on her. Her black hair was tangled, her eyes were shadowed, but a fierce determination lit her features. She was so much more than the timid and clever woman he had fallen in love with. She had morphed into a powerful goddess, capable of undeniable strength.

He was so unworthy of her.

When their eyes locked, he lunged for her, clutching her to his chest and breathing in her rose and parchment and saltwater scent. Gods above, everything about her was perfection. His memories of her hadn't done her justice. The softness of her hair. The smoothness of her skin. The way her breath caught in her throat when she was overcome with emotion. The small sigh that escaped her when he touched her.

It was like he was experiencing everything for the first time. He was reborn, though he didn't know how or why. All he knew was that deep within himself a strange silence echoed into a yawning void. Typhon was gone. But more than that, Evander's whole being felt hollow.

Something was missing. Something within him had been severely altered.

But that didn't matter. Right now, he would savor every moment he had with Mona. He pressed himself further into her embrace, stroking her hair and letting his salty tears trace down his cheeks as he clung to her tightly. Gods, he would never let her go again.

An eternity could have passed, and Evander wouldn't have noticed. He could have lost himself in her arms, holding her forever.

But he couldn't deny that something felt different

within him. Now that he was adjusting to these new heightened senses, that strange emptiness in his chest only intensified. Slowly, he withdrew to peer into Mona's eyes. She, too, was crying but she beamed at him, her eyes sparkling with joy and relief. He couldn't resist bringing his mouth to hers in a gentle kiss. He yearned to do more—to ravish her and taste the sensitive parts of her body that would make her moan with desire—but there would be time for that later.

For now, he needed to figure out what had happened, and why he felt so strange and empty.

His eyes reluctantly left Mona to sweep around the vast cavern. A crowd of unfamiliar women with unsettling amber eyes peered curiously at him. He recognized Trivia—or rather, Pandora—and the sun god who had forced her to fuel the portal to let everyone in Elysium through.

Then, his eyes landed on someone he thought had been lost forever. His eyebrows lifted in surprise. "Romanos?"

Romanos offered a tight smile and nodded. Something guarded filled his eyes, making Evander frown. Slowly, he extricated himself from Mona's grasp, taking her hand in his as he made his way to where Romanos stood.

"What are you doing here?" Evander asked, surveying the room once more. "And... *where* is here?"

"You're in the mortal realm," Romanos said. "In the Rhea desert. This is where the fire witch coven lives. They are friends of mine."

Evander's head spun. This was so much information to process. He rolled his shoulders back, and they felt strangely weightless. Then, he froze, realizing why: his wings were gone.

His stomach dipped as he met Romanos's solemn gaze. "What happened to me?"

He was afraid to learn the answer. Had he already died? Was this all a vision from Tartarus, meant to taunt him?

Romanos opened his mouth, then hesitated, his gaze dropping to the floor as he rubbed the back of his neck. "I, ah, siphoned the death magic from your body."

Evander's heart thudded wildly in his chest. "What does that mean?"

"It means, I called the death magic to me, and... it came."

It took several beats before Evander registered what his brother was saying. "You stole my magic from me?"

"He *healed* you," Mona said, squeezing his hand. "Evander, you were dying. It's a miracle you hung on for as long as you did."

Evander's mouth was dry. His death magic—his demonic essence—was all gone. "I—Can you give it back?"

Even before Romanos shook his head, Evander knew the answer. He had to ask, though.

"I cannot. It is irreversible. The death magic within you had become infected, weakening you like a disease. When I siphoned it, it merged with my own magic, changing it and altering it to fit my own powers."

Evander bristled at the notion that Typhon had been a disease. He had simply been another side to his soul.

"Altering it?" Evander repeated slowly.

Romanos's brow furrowed. "Yes."

Evander swallowed, unsure of how to directly ask him if a demonic presence now lived inside him. "I— There was... another being inside me. A powerful manifestation of my death magic. I could sense his presence almost constantly. Do you—Do you feel him?"

A stunned silence rippled over the crowd, and Evander had to fight to keep his gaze from straying from Romanos. He *had* to know.

Romanos's eyes were full of regret when he replied, "I'm sorry. But all the magic I took from you has merged with mine. If there was any presence or being that lived inside of you... it's gone now."

Gone. The word echoed like a haunting melody in Evander's mind.

Typhon was *gone.*

How long had Evander yearned for this, to be rid of

the beast inside him? And now that it had finally happened, he felt emptier than ever.

"It was the only way," Romanos said softly.

"I know," Evander said at once, his throat tight with emotion. "Of course, I understand, Romanos. You did what needed to be done." He didn't sound convincing, even to himself. He knew he should probably be thanking his brother for saving his life, but all he could dwell on was that gaping emptiness inside him.

Romanos had taken a part of himself. And he would never get it back.

"Call me Rom. Everyone here does."

Evander's brows knitted together. It sounded so informal and strange. Then again, he had never been particularly close to Romanos. Not like he had with Cyrus.

Cyrus. Gods, was his younger brother even still alive? The last he'd seen, Cyrus had been about to dive into the pits of Tartarus. Then the Underworld had been destroyed.

Surely he had survived. He had to. He was King of the Underworld.

"Does this mean he's a mortal?" Mona asked cautiously.

"No," Romanos said. "Look at his eyes. They still bear the mark of the gods. His blood is still silver. He only lacks the magic of our kind. But his god strength and lifespan remains."

Mona sighed with relief, but Evander couldn't share the feeling. An entire piece of him was missing. It would take longer than a few moments for him to come to terms with this.

"Why are we here?" Evander changed the subject, looking around once more. The women had stopped staring at him and were now chatting with one another. A few were casting dark looks toward Pandora, who stood on her own, rubbing one arm and refusing to meet anyone's gaze.

She looked... forlorn. Like a lost child. Not at all like the confident goddess who had taunted him, almost killing him by dragging him to Elysium.

"We came through the portal before Elysium was destroyed," Mona explained.

"This one is waiting to be judged by the Gorgon sisters," Romanos added, jerking his thumb toward Pandora. "For her crimes."

Evander's gaze flicked to Pandora. He had once held such venom and hatred for her. Perhaps it was because of his healing, or perhaps it just did not matter now that he was reunited with Mona... But Evander found he felt nothing but pity for the goddess.

"Can't that wait?" Evander asked.

Romanos frowned. "Wait for what?"

"Two realms have been destroyed by Pandora's magic. It's still out there, and the Realm of Gaia is next. We have to do something to stop it. Not to mention, the rivers of the Underworld have stopped flowing. That means there are millions of souls who need to be shepherded to their resting place. It's chaos right now, and I don't think we should be wasting time with punishing criminals when the war isn't even over yet."

Silence rang from his words, and he suddenly realized everyone was watching him once again. The echoing chamber made it easy for his words to be heard, even across the cavern. He felt his cheeks warm from embarrassment. He couldn't remember the last time he'd spoken to a crowd this big. He often kept to himself.

"He's right," Mona said, standing up straighter. "We have to do something."

"We can't *do* anything," snapped the sun god, crossing his arms over his chest. "No one here is powerful enough to stop that darkness. Believe me, I've seen it firsthand."

"I think you'll find the realms are far different now than they were when Pandora's box was first crafted," said a tall, brown-skinned woman with amber eyes. Her graceful form and commanding tone spoke of authority as she speared a sharp gaze at the sun god. "The three Gorgon sisters have harnessed the power of the Triple

Goddess with their united powers. They are a force to be reckoned with."

"This is not their war, Farah," murmured an amber-haired witch beside her.

"With Hestia gone, it needs to be," Farah replied.

"Do you think they can help?" Mona asked eagerly.

"Perhaps. But they aren't the only ones. You yourself possess the magic of Gaia, do you not?"

Mona went rigid, her hand going limp in Evander's. He looked at her and found her face had gone slack, her eyes wide, as if—for one terrifying moment—she had forgotten she was an earth goddess.

After one long, slow blink, Mona's eyes grew unfocused as she concentrated on something Evander couldn't see.

He knew that look well. It meant the clever side of her brain was working.

"You're right," Mona said slowly. "We have two earth goddesses here who can rebuild the realms."

Pandora stiffened, then looked around wildly as if expecting another woman with earth magic to appear. "I'm sorry, *two*?"

"You are a daughter of Gaia," Mona said slowly, as if explaining this to a child.

Pandora crossed her arms. "I wasn't reborn like you, Mona. Your powers are ten times stronger than mine. Besides, I have the soul of a vengeful goddess thrashing inside me. She refuses to let me access the full extent of my powers. Not until her revenge is complete."

The sun god scoffed. "Elysium is gone. Isn't that enough for you?"

"Apollo still lives, Sol," Pandora said darkly. "And so does Gaia."

Mona released Evander's hand and took a step toward Pandora. "What does Gaia have to do with this?" Her tone was sharp and laced with panic.

Pandora grimaced, then rubbed her temples. Her face was a shade paler than before. Evander wondered what shadows she battled inside her. For the first time, he felt he could relate to her. They shared a hidden darkness they could not escape.

Or rather... they *had* shared that. Evander wasn't even sure who he was anymore without Typhon.

"The goddess wants revenge on Gaia, too," Pandora said.

"Why?" Mona asked. "She had nothing to do with what happened to Pandora."

"But she had everything to do with what happened to *me*." Pandora's eyes flashed, and in that moment, she looked like the dangerous goddess who had revealed her true nature to Evander before pulling him through the portal to Elysium.

A tense silence passed between them before Sol said

in slow, measured words, "You said your actions were fueled by *her* quest for revenge. Not yours."

The silence became awkward as Pandora's face grew even paler. She glanced from Sol to Mona and then to the witches who gaped openly at her. "I—I—Oh gods..." She covered her face with her hands. "It's all so muddied. Sometimes, I have trouble discerning what is me, and what is... *her*. I've been angry for so long that it often mingles with *her* anger, and at times, I can't tell the difference between the two."

"You assured us you were of sound mind when you made the choice to betray Elysium," Farah said thoughtfully. "Now you're claiming the opposite."

"No, don't make excuses for her," Sol said, stepping forward angrily. "She is still responsible for her actions."

Farah raised a hand, cutting a sharp glance at the sun god. "You have made your position on this clear. For now, I don't think we should decide anything until we have reached the Voiceless Jungle. We can make our plans from there."

"How far is it?" Mona asked, chewing on her lip in worry. Evander shared her concern. How much time would they waste visiting these Gorgons when the realms needed immediate help?

"A day's walk," said Farah.

Mona nodded, then looked up at Evander with concern in her eyes. "Are you well enough?"

"Yes." He was still wrestling with the gaping emptiness in his chest, but other than that, he was in perfect health.

If the loss of Typhon was what was required to be with Mona, then he wouldn't regret it. He would push through that emptiness and come to terms with it.

It would just take some adjusting. That was all.

Farah lifted her chin, then turned to face the witches behind her. "Sisters, gather your things. We leave within the hour."

VISITORS
CYRUS

Cyrus did not appreciate being summoned.

So when a servant appeared with a letter ordering Cyrus to meet Apollo at the entrance to Tartarus, he swore loudly before ripping the paper to shreds, vowing to ignore Apollo until he had the decency to speak to him like an equal.

After his temper faded, he begrudgingly admitted to himself that to get information from Apollo and earn his trust, Cyrus would need to play along.

And that included responding to his summons.

But that didn't mean he had to be happy about it.

Cyrus took his time. He took the longer route through the palace, and, without realizing it, he found himself standing just outside Prue's bedchamber.

He froze, his heart stilling in his chest as he stared at the door handle. He knew what would happen if he went in.

She would look up, expecting a maid. When she saw him, her entire face would light up with the hope that he had decided to return to her.

His heart wrenched painfully at the thought. Gods, he wouldn't be able to bear seeing that look in her eyes—the look of eager relief—only for it to be smashed later.

He was weak and powerless and about to lose his throne. And even if Apollo weren't here threatening his reign, he had nothing to offer this kingdom. He was a human now, a pathetic mortal who wouldn't even last another fifty years of life.

Prue would outlive him. And the devastation of that loss would almost break her. It was better for her to endure it now, when she was young and healthy and strong, when Gaia was here to help her through it.

You should let her have a say in how she wants to live her life, he thought. She had told him she would be waiting for him, that she would gladly accept him as her husband. But did she truly realize what that meant? She would constantly have to help him, heal him, protect him... It would be as miserable for her as it would be for him.

And Cyrus would resent her for it. Right now, with his hand hovering over the door handle, he yearned to be with his wife more than anything, to wrap her in his arms and feel her skin against his. He wanted to pin her body to the bed and elicit those intoxicating moans from her, to hear her come undone as he thrust inside her.

He wanted it so much that his hands began to shake.

But... he also knew it would not last. Sooner or later, the anger and fury at his new form would overcome him again. He wasn't strong enough to resist the powerful pull of these human emotions. And he would hurt her. Again. And again.

It would keep happening until he broke her completely. One day, there would be no coming back.

A knot of despair filled his throat as he withdrew his hand and forced himself to keep walking down the hall. Every piece of him ached to turn around, to storm into those bedchambers and claim his wife once more.

But he knew this was better. Once he helped Apollo, he would get his powers back. Then, he and Prue could properly challenge the sun god together, as a united front. They would win, and they could rule together.

Everything would be fine after that.

He rehearsed this plan in his mind over and over again until he almost believed it. His steps were automatic as he made his way down the winding staircase, through the castle doors, and toward the crumbled caves that had led to Tartarus.

The air chilled, and a heavy mist surrounded Cyrus, clinging to him with tendrils of smoke and power. He shuddered, rubbing his arms against the cold. It was so unnerving, stepping outside the palace walls and seeing how empty and ghost-like his kingdom was. Only the palace remained intact—everything else had been swallowed by the mist.

He could still make out the broken rocks of the cavern up ahead. When the jagged chunks of debris met his gaze, he faltered, his blood running cold. Within the pile of rocks, he saw the lifeless face of his wife, heard her screams as she shred herself apart to keep the cave walls from crushing them both.

Nausea roiled in Cyrus's gut, and he bent over, hands on his knees as he struggled to inhale properly. His breaths turned into sharp wheezes, and his vision blurred, then darkened.

Gods, he couldn't breathe. Everything was suffocating around him, pressing in on him.

Too much, *too much*.

Prue, dead in his arms. His soul, broken by the loss.

"Prue is alive," he whispered. "She is here. She is alive and healthy and powerful." He repeated the words until his vision cleared and his breathing leveled out.

After what felt like an eternity, he straightened, taking several steadying breaths before he continued onward.

It didn't take long to find the sun god. Bursts of light bled through the mist, guiding Cyrus's way until he stood before Apollo. Streams of celestial golden light glided along his fingertips, gathering together until they formed a massive ball of power. Apollo flung the magic forward, but it crashed against a large boulder, dissolving into the mist.

"Dammit," Apollo grumbled before turning to face Cyrus. His eyebrows lifted. "Ah, there you are. I need your help. How can I access the gates to Tartarus?"

Cyrus frowned, scanning the surroundings. Only then did he realize the giant boulder rested atop what had once been the very pit he and Prue had jumped into together.

This was Tartarus. And it was currently blocked by rocks and debris.

Cyrus swallowed, his throat dry as he tried not to remember the horrifying visions this place had tormented him with. His voice was slightly strained as he demanded, "Why?"

"I need to access it in order for my plan to work," Apollo said, his expression wary. He still didn't trust Cyrus, but that was to be expected.

"Without my magic, there isn't much I can do." Cyrus spread his hands as if in apology.

"Someone else, perhaps?" Apollo asked hopefully.

Cyrus's eyes narrowed. "If I knew *why*, I could be more helpful. For instance, there are several demons who might be able to move the rubble, but if you want the matter kept private, that limits our options."

Apollo considered this, his lips thinning as he gazed absently at the boulder. After a moment, he said, "We will be expecting visitors in this realm very soon. Allies of mine who will ensure I win the crown."

Cyrus's heart lodged itself in his throat. "Visitors... from Tartarus?"

"Yes."

No, no, no, no... "That is *not* a good idea," he growled.

"What could you possibly be afraid of that hasn't already happened?" Apollo spread his arms wide, indicating the broken mess before them. "There is no realm to destroy, no people to slaughter."

"There *are* people," Cyrus argued. "There's a palace and..." *And Prue,* he thought. *Prue could be in danger.*

But he couldn't say that. Instead, he said, "What good would this place be if you didn't have subjects to rule?"

"My allies will take care of that," Apollo said vaguely.

Cyrus's insides twisted with unease. *Allies?* From Tartarus? How could he possibly go along with this?

When Cyrus didn't respond, Apollo turned to face him fully, his eyes flashing with irritation. "I was under the impression you wanted your powers back. Or am I mistaken?"

Still, Cyrus hesitated. He could say he changed his mind. He could turn away and refuse to unleash whatever hellish monstrosity Apollo sought from Tartarus.

But Apollo would find a way. He was powerful and persuasive, and even without Cyrus's help, he would make this happen. And Cyrus would learn nothing of his plans if he refused.

At long last, Cyrus said slowly, "I know the demon overseers who were last in charge of Tartarus. If I fetch them, they should be able to clear this."

Apollo grinned and clapped his hands together. "Excellent. Send for them, if you will."

Cyrus turned, then paused. "Give me your word they will not be harmed after they've completed this task."

Apollo blinked at him in confusion. "You think me so callous?"

"Yes," Cyrus said at once. "It's what I would do." *Or rather, what I would have done before.* He was stunned to find that the idea of losing his subjects tormented him almost as much as the idea of losing Prue. How had that happened? And when had this change occurred?

Apollo sighed. "Yes, yes, I swear it," he said impatiently. "Now, please fetch them. The sooner, the better."

Without waiting for a reply, Apollo turned away from him, shooting more of his sun magic at the boulder in his fruitless attempts to blast it free.

Cyrus watched the sun god for a long moment before turning back toward the palace, wondering if he was making a grave error in helping Apollo.

RUINS
PANDORA

PANDORA KNEW ONE THING FOR CERTAIN: SHE despised the desert.

The caverns opened to reveal a vast expanse of dunes. For miles on every side there was nothing but sand. The relentless sun beat down on her, far more piercing and agonizing than the sun in Elysium. From the moment she stepped out of the cave, the brilliant light assaulted her, bringing her to her knees with flashes of horror and trauma. Apollo's light searing into her, scorching her blood, melting the flesh from her bones...

Only when Mona's warm hand captured hers was she able to ground herself, returning to the present. She shot her sister a grateful look, and, hand-in-hand, they followed Farah across the dunes.

The heat was unbearable. Farah and the other witches used scarves to cover their faces, but Pandora was already sweating so much that the idea of covering more of her body suffocated her. And on the rare occasion when the wind blew, it stung Pandora's eyes with grains of sand, embedding the tiny particles into every crevice of her body until she felt like she was caked in the substance.

Perhaps that's why they cover their faces, she thought bitterly.

Her sandals kept sliding in the sand, slowing down their trek across the dunes. Sol kept shooting her scathing looks every time their party had to wait for her to right herself, but the other witches waited patiently for her.

Even Evander, who, moments ago, had had to be dragged on a bed of ivy, was moving with lithe grace and strength. Pandora tried not to feel irritated by this. After all, it was her fault he had almost died.

"I'm sorry," Pandora muttered.

Mona, who still clasped her hand in hers, looked over in confusion. "What for?"

Pandora snorted. "Do you really need to ask?"

"I need to hear you say it."

Pandora took a steadying breath, but her insides felt shaky. "I never apologized for any of it. And I need to. I'm sorry for what I did to Evander. I'm sorry for what I did to *you*. I'm sorry I didn't look to you as a sister when I needed help. But I was never raised... I never had..." She blinked rapidly, unsure if it was the threat of tears or the stinging dust particles that made her do so. She swallowed hard. "I've never had sisters before. I've never been able to trust *anyone*. It's a new concept for me. The only thing I can do is apologize to you and promise I will do better in the future."

Mona nodded, her face solemn. She did not smile, but she did not have any ire in her expression, either. After a moment, she said, "It's a start. And I appreciate your words. But I'm not the only one you need to apologize to."

Pandora's gaze fell on Evander, who walked a few paces ahead of them. She had no doubt he could hear their conversation, though he was too polite to say so. He seemed deeply curious about their surroundings, his head turning as he gazed in wonder at the dunes. Only then did Pandora remember he didn't have much experience in the mortal realm. All of this was very new for him.

"Yes, Evander," Mona murmured, following Pandora's gaze. "But also Sol. Prue. Cyrus. There are *many* people you've wronged, Pandora."

Pandora flinched at the reminder, but she forced herself to nod. "I do. There is much to atone for. And I'll do the best I can." Her eyes found Sol, and she stared hard at the place between his shoulder blades, trying not to admire his figure as he walked firmly though the sand.

"I've tried apologizing to him," she said, her voice barely above a whisper. "He doesn't want to hear it."

"Can you blame him?" Mona asked. "His mother just died. And he blames you. Apologies are necessary, but so is *time*. I'm not saying he will forgive you—he may not. But it's not something that will happen overnight."

Pandora wasn't even sure why she cared. She still despised Sol. Or at least, she told herself she did. Even on his better days, he was loathsome and arrogant and...

And it was all a mask to keep people at a distance. He preferred the freedom of solitude, of no expectations or responsibilities. Pandora knew that now, because she had seen *behind* the mask. She had seen him come undone. For her.

"You're right," Pandora said in a tight voice. "I don't think he will ever forgive me." Because if their roles were reversed, she certainly wouldn't have forgiven him.

When the crowd of witches and gods crested the tallest dune, Pandora, covered in sweat, took a moment to brace her hands on her legs and catch her breath. But when Mona jolted and gasped beside her, she found herself drawn to the scene below.

It had once been a town, but now, it was nothing more than ruins. Buildings had been reduced to hunks of concrete. Ash lined the streets. Stains of charcoal and blood coated the ground and the walls.

"What—What happened?" Mona asked, her hand pressed to her heart.

"Harpies," Farah said gravely. "Ever since Pandora's box was opened, the dark creatures have been roaming our realm, destroying everything in their path."

Pandora's head whipped to Farah. "The creatures are *here*? But how? I've seen the darkness. I brought it to Elysium. It shouldn't be here yet."

"Do you think darkness has boundaries?" Farah's eyes flashed as she pinned Pandora with a fierce stare. "Opening that box created cracks between the realms. These creatures slipped through those cracks. The openings will grow wider until there is no separation between our world and theirs."

"Their world?" Mona asked. "What is their world?"

Pandora spoke at the same time as Romanos. "Tartarus."

A chilled silence passed between them. Even Sol looked worried, his thick brows furrowing together. His eyes darted to Pandora and then flicked away just as quickly.

"With the Underworld destroyed, all the creatures bound by the wards of Tartarus were unleashed,"

Romanos said, staring at the desolation before them. The wind tossed strands of his black and silver hair across his forehead, and a wrinkle formed along his brow. "And the longer this goes unchecked, the more creatures will continue to invade the Realm of Gaia. Not just from the Underworld, but from Elysium as well."

"Elysium?" Evander said sharply. "What creatures could possibly have lived in Elysium?"

"You think Apollo didn't have enemies?" Sol said with a derisive snort. "The Underworld isn't the only place capable of monsters."

"Kelpies were creations of Tethys and Neptune," Farah said. "For all we know, there were other Elysium gods who created such abominations."

Pandora stiffened, then glanced at Farah. "Tethys and Neptune?" She hadn't heard those names in ages. In addition, if there were *other* gods that had dabbled in the same dangerous magic as the original Pandora, then perhaps they could help stave off the darkness unleashed from that box.

"Neptune is dead," Romanos said, and his voice was filled with a savage pleasure that made the voices whisper louder in Pandora's mind. She knew that thirst for blood quite well. "Courtesy of the Gorgon sisters."

"And Tethys has fled," Farah said. "We don't know where she is, but she has no allies left."

Pandora's throat went dry. The Gorgon sisters were

powerful enough to *kill* Neptune? Neptune had arguably been as powerful as Jupiter—whom Apollo had been too afraid to challenge head-on. He'd had to steal the throne through trickery and betrayal.

"Can the Gorgon sisters coerce Tethys into helping us?" Pandora asked.

Farah frowned. "Helping us do what?"

"Well, stopping *this*!" Pandora waved a hand at the ruins below them. "If we do nothing, the darkness will spread, and this realm will be destroyed like the others."

"And how can Tethys help with that?"

"She's familiar with the magic of the Titans," Pandora said.

Sol sucked in a sharp breath, his eyes flaring wide. Evander went perfectly still, and Mona chewed on her lower lip, glancing in worry between Farah and Pandora.

Farah lifted her chin, her eyes narrowing. "You know of the Titans?"

"I'm Pandora," Pandora said impatiently. "Of course I know."

"Then you know that Titan magic isn't to be trifled with."

"So you're just going to stand by and *let* this happen?" Pandora argued. "You'll do nothing?"

"I will not risk my coven and my people by dabbling with the exact magic that started all this!" Farah said sharply, her eyes burning with fire. For a brief moment, her pupils turned into narrow slits.

"You're risking them already by doing nothing!" Pandora cried, unfazed by this woman's strength and authority. "If this Titan magic is so uncontrollable and unstoppable, then perhaps we need that same kind of magic to end it."

"You are a *fool*," Sol hissed, baring his teeth at her. "You carry the soul of the woman who was torn apart for daring to do exactly what you suggest."

Pandora turned to face him, prepared to argue her point. But when she saw the anguished devastation in his eyes, she stopped short, the words dying in her throat.

She couldn't.

She couldn't fight him on this, not when it was her fault this fresh agony was haunting him so violently.

Mona gave her hand a squeeze and shook her head slightly. Pandora knew it was a doomed cause.

No one would trust her on this. And even if they did, she couldn't be sure this idea would work at all.

So, she clamped her mouth shut and ducked her head in submission, letting the subject drop.

The party continued their descent down the dune. As the sand gave way to cracked concrete, Pandora couldn't help but cling to this idea of the Titans' magic. Apollo and Aidoneus had used the essence of Pandora to close the box, only because she had dabbled in the power of the Titans.

This meant the only force strong enough to cage these dark powers... was the same magic that brought them to being.

The Titans' magic was quite possibly the only power in all the realms that could stop this.

TRAITOR
PRUE

FOR DAYS, PRUE WORKED TIRELESSLY ALONGSIDE Gaia to strengthen her magic. After she had successfully turned the entire throne room into foliage, Prue had been so drained she had slept for seventeen hours straight. Once she'd awoken, Gaia instructed her to withdraw all the foliage and return the throne room to what it was before. Conjuring and diminishing were both important skills to develop.

She also worked Prue harder than ever. Each day, Prue summoned her earth magic, twisted it, shaped it, and worked on specific details according to Gaia's instructions. Once she had succeeded, Gaia ordered her to siphon it all back, to erase what she had created, to recycle that energy to re-fuel her magic.

"In training, many gods and goddesses overlook the

usefulness of building endurance," Gaia told her. "You were exhausted after transforming the throne room. But after training with me, I can make you so strong that you could transform the throne room three times in one day with no fatigue whatsoever."

The idea had been so appealing that Prue's determination had bolstered her onward. But it hadn't lasted long. She'd forgotten how ruthless her mother could be. Growing up on Krenia, Gaia had always been harder on Prue—because Prue was reckless and rebellious. Mona, however, had always been a star pupil, eager to learn and dive into her studies.

But Prue had wanted more. Adventure. Romance. Excitement.

Well, she had certainly gotten her wish…

The thought was bitter as she created vines of roses and draped them along the walls of the throne room. Her hair was matted and tangled, sticking to the sweat on her face. She hadn't bathed in days. She didn't even know *what* day it was.

Her thoughts were constantly on Cyrus. She hadn't seen him since she'd offered him freedom.

Freedom from the Underworld.

From their marriage.

From anything to do with her.

She was a coward, but she didn't care. She couldn't bring herself to face him, not if his answer would be,

Yes, I would be happy to leave and part ways from you forever.

"Excellent," Gaia said, jolting Prue from the misery of her thoughts. "Now, transform those rose vines into jasmine."

Prue said nothing, her hand automatically moving, fingertips fluttering over rose petals as she effortlessly changed each flower. The deep red velvety flower shrank to the tiny white sprouts of jasmine, the scent filling the room and tickling her nostrils.

"The grass at your feet," Gaia said. "Change it to soil."

Prue wordlessly obeyed. More sweat trickled down her face and neck, but she ignored it as she worked, immersing herself in her training, letting her thoughts dissolve into nothingness.

She wasn't sure how much time had passed before Gaia stood before her with a frown on her face. Prue's hands remained outstretched, waiting for the next command.

"Prudence," Gaia said. The impatience in her tone told Prue it wasn't the first time she'd said her name.

Blinking slowly, Prue met her mother's gaze. "What?"

"When was the last time you slept?"

"I sleep constantly. When I'm not training with you, I'm sleeping."

Gaia's frown only deepened. "You are wasting away, my darling. Tell me how I can help."

"Bring my husband back." The words left Prue's mouth before she could stop herself. Her lips clamped shut, and her eyes closed briefly. "I'm sorry, I just…" She sighed. "I miss him. And I can't force him to be who he was before. It will just take some adjusting, that's all."

Gaia was silent for a long moment. "Has he decided to leave you?" Her voice was quiet, almost gentle, which was rare for her.

"I don't know," Prue whispered. "I don't think he's decided yet." Her eyes burned, and she dropped her gaze, instead focusing on the rich brown earth at her feet. Emotion welled up in her throat until she couldn't breathe. "Goddess, I miss Mona." Her voice was strained. At times like these, she always longed for her sister. They had shared everything together.

"She is alive," Gaia said. "Don't fear for her."

Prue's eyes flicked to Gaia. "How do you know?"

"A part of my soul is tethered to her, as it is to you. I know she is alive and unharmed, but that is all."

Prue considered this. "What did you feel when she died? When she sacrificed herself to close that grimoire?"

A chilled silence fell between them. Prue tried not to think about the day Mona had given up her life to stop the dark magic from devouring their tiny island. It was why she had sought out Cyrus in the first place, why she had struck the bargain with him and bound them together—to bring Mona back.

"My powers were muted back then," Gaia said. "But... I remember feeling a gaping emptiness. A hole that could not be filled. I thought for certain she could not return; that the sacrifice she had made would be permanent. I thought the powers binding that grimoire together would take her soul. But I was wrong."

Prue nodded, remembering how adamant Gaia had been about keeping Mona's soul where it was, lest her sacrifice be undone. Vasileios, Cyrus's brother, had somehow managed to swap Mona's soul with another to fulfill that sacrifice, stealing Mona for himself.

Goddess, that had been ages ago. So much had changed... Prue hadn't even been to the Underworld yet when Mona had been resurrected.

"As an earth witch, I managed to bring her back," Prue said in a hollow voice. "But as a goddess, I can't bring *him* back." A tear streaked a path down her sweat-coated cheek.

Gaia drew closer to her and clasped both her hands in hers. Her eyes blazed as she looked upon her daughter. "You are fierce, my child. A force to be reckoned with. You feel weak now, but this will pass. Remember who you are. You are a *goddess*. And you have an eternity of possibilities before you. For now, your misery seems endless, but I swear to you, *it will pass.*"

Prue met her mother's gaze as if seeing her for the first time. Tears sparkled in Gaia's blue eyes, and Prue realized she was referring to Pandora. And after all this time, Gaia had *still* not been reunited with the daughter she had lost.

The knot in Prue's throat only tightened, and she swallowed hard, the motion painful. "You need to go to her, Mama."

Gaia blinked. "What?"

"Go to Pandora. You must see her. You've waited long enough."

"Prudence, you need me *here.*"

"We've trained for days. I'm as ready as I'll ever be. This magic"—she gestured at the foliage around them—"is effortless to me."

"But we've only just begun. Apollo—"

"Apollo is *my fight.* Not yours. You have your own battle to face." Prue's voice only strengthened as she spoke, a certainty burning within her that this was the right thing. "I brought Mona back without your help. I can do this, too."

Gaia's mouth twisted with uncertainty, and more tears brimmed in her eyes. "Prudence, I—I—"

Prue stepped forward and embraced her mother

tightly. "I love you, Mama. I will always love you. No matter what happens."

Gaia squeezed her tightly. For a long moment, the two held each other, both reluctant to let go. But at long last, Gaia released her and stepped back, her face shining with tears.

"I am so proud of you, my darling," Gaia whispered, touching Prue's cheek.

Prue could only offer a watery smile. Gaia pressed a hand to her heart before turning and leaving the throne room. Prue watched her exit, and a shuddering breath escaped her. Gaia would no doubt make her way to the portal. She likely had enough magic to fuel it on her own.

And then she would be gone, leaving Prue to fight this war on her own. No Cyrus. No Mona. Only herself.

"That was very brave of you," said a voice.

Prue whirled to find Apollo leaning casually against the wall, inspecting the jasmine that surrounded it. "Or perhaps very foolish. It depends on how you look at it." With one finger, he lifted the tiny petal of the white flower. "Very creative, what you've done here. I like it."

Prue crossed her arms. She did not have the energy for this. "What do you want, Apollo?"

"I wanted to introduce you to a guest of mine, and the first official member of my court here in the Underworld." Apollo stretched his hand toward the open doors as a figure appeared.

A foul and familiar scent assaulted Prue's nostrils, and she recoiled, eyes flaring wide. She *knew* that scent. It reminded her of the day Pandora's box had been opened. In her mind, she saw a tall, smirking figure, urging her not to open the box.

Kronos.

Her blood chilled as she backed up until she hit the wall. Terror and panic seized her, forming a vise around her heart.

But the figure who appeared was not Kronos; it was a man with dark skin, a shaved head, and piercing black eyes that seemed to peer into Prue's very soul. He was tall and so muscular, she felt he could wrap two fingers around her throat and strangle her in one swift movement.

Prue wet her lips and shot an uncertain look at Apollo.

Apollo smiled widely, the expression almost catlike. "Prudence, please meet Hyperion. He was an apprentice of mine long ago."

Prue's chest constricted even further until she couldn't breathe.

No. No, no, no.

"Hyperion," she repeated, staring at the stranger. "You're—You're—"

"A Titan," Apollo supplied, his grin widening.

Prue looked at Apollo in alarm. He couldn't be serious. "How? It's impossible for a Titan to be here. They are currently bound in Tartarus."

But Prue wasn't completely certain of this. After Pandora's darkness had destroyed the realm, were the restraints of Tartarus still active? Or were the prisoners of Tartarus now freed?

Before Apollo could respond, more footsteps echoed, and another figure appeared. This one elicited a strangled whimper from Prue as she felt something inside her crack, then shatter.

It was Cyrus, and he wore a look of boredom and apathy on his face. "Yes," he said idly. "It *would* be impossible—without my help. You see, dear wife, *I* brought him here."

CIVILITY

PANDORA

WITH THE CITY OF SODARA IN RUINS, THERE WAS
no place to stop for the night. Farah told Pandora of an
inn she often frequented before the city had been
destroyed, and Pandora had to admit, the idea of resting
on a soft mattress and having a hot meal in her belly
seemed like a dream come true.

But with each step she took through the destroyed
city, the ache in her stomach only tightened, coiling
tighter and tighter until she felt like she might burst.

My fault. This is my fault.

When they finally reached the edge of the city, her
insides were squirming so much that the idea of eating
anything made her want to retch.

"That's the Voiceless Jungle," said a low voice
beside her.

Pandora turned to find Wren, the witch with curly ginger hair, standing next to her. She pointed to something barely visible in the distance. The sun had already set, but the sky was just light enough to make out a line of trees along the horizon.

They stood at least a mile away. Pandora glanced at the sky and then back to the forest. "Will we make it before it's completely dark?"

Wren smirked. "You forget you are among fire witches. We can light the way."

Pandora nodded, unable to manage even a small smile.

Wren's expression sobered. "Are you afraid?"

Pandora glanced at her. The witch's golden eyes burned in the darkness. "No," Pandora said. "At least, not for myself. Whatever my fate is, it's nothing less than I deserve." She sighed and glanced toward the forest again. "But I *am* afraid of how much worse it's going to get. I'm afraid of seeing the consequences of my actions and how many people I've hurt. I—I don't know if I'll survive it."

Wren was silent for a long moment, her lips pressing together thoughtfully. "Perhaps *that* is your fate, then. Whatever the Gorgon sisters decide for you, perhaps you can consider this"—she gestured to the ash and debris around them—"a part of your penance."

A knot formed in Pandora's throat, and she nodded.

"I know that doesn't help," Wren said quietly. "But I don't think any of us would ever change if we hid ourselves from the darkness around us. The destruction is necessary for our growth. It teaches us to change, and it makes way for new life."

"I don't know if I'm capable of change," Pandora said. "Not with this vengeful soul inside me." She shook her head. "At any rate, I cannot be convinced that the loss of an entire city—full of innocent people; children, even—would be considered a good thing. I don't care how much I would grow from it; I would much prefer for these people to be alive."

Wren's gaze turned soft. "That is an admirable sentiment."

Pandora snorted. "I don't feel admirable at all. I feel like shit. But you're right. It is part of my penance, and I will continue to bear it."

Wren offered a wry chuckle. "I like you, Pandora. You're a dark soul, but you own it. And you still have a heart, in spite of what you've endured."

Pandora could only manage a half smile. Here she was, making friends, all because of the deceit and betrayal she'd worked throughout her life. It didn't seem right. Everyone should despise her.

She thought of Mona, who was next to Evander, drinking from a waterskin and smiling at something he said to her. Mona, who had every right to despise her, and yet, she had stood by Pandora.

Another kindness she did not deserve.

Pandora watched her sister for a moment when something in her peripheral vision caught her eye. Next to Mona, standing only a few paces behind Pandora and Wren, was Sol, his solemn gaze fixed on Pandora.

She felt her breath catch at the intensity of his gaze. The usual hatred wasn't there, but a hardness lined his features, making him look fierce and formidable. She had no doubt he'd heard every word of her conversation with Wren. She wasn't sure what to make of that.

Her mouth turned dry, and she looked away, unable to endure his scrutiny any longer.

After resting and hydrating, the group set off across the small plain between Sodara and the Voiceless Jungle. The closer they got to the forest, the wilder it became. From a distance, the treeline looked unassuming. But with each step, the branches became more jagged, the leaves more tangled, and the woods themselves seemed to tremble with an otherworldly awareness.

Having never been in the Realm of Gaia before, Pandora did not know what to expect with this place. But she wasn't afraid. Whatever awaited her in this jungle, it couldn't be worse than witnessing the destruction of her past choices. Choices she could never take back.

"Did you mean what you said?" asked a soft voice beside her.

Pandora simultaneously felt a bolt of heat and a chill of foreboding spread through her at the sound of that voice. She took a steadying breath, refusing to look at Sol as she answered, "When I said what?"

"That we should seek power from the Titans."

Pandora frowned. That was *not* what she had expected him to ask her about. "Yes. I meant it."

"Explain."

In another lifetime, Pandora would have bristled at the command in his tone, or perhaps replied with something snarky and sarcastic. But right now, she was far too tired for it. She sighed and said, "What's there to explain? The forces we're fighting are too powerful for us to match on our own. We need something else to give us an edge. Something to even things out between us. Because right now, we don't stand a chance."

"And who's to say the magic of the Titans won't rebel against us and join with the dark powers of the box?"

Pandora shrugged. "There's no guarantee. But we're going to die from this either way. There is no escape."

"That's a bleak outlook."

She gave him a grim look. "My outlook was never going to be sunshine and rainbows, Sol. You know this."

He scoffed. "Did you expect any less, Pandora? With the choices you've made and the lives you've destroyed, you shouldn't be at all surprised that this is your fate."

Shock and indignation rippled over her. For one brief second, she'd believed they were sharing a civil conversation where he was actually trying to understand her perspective.

But no. He still hated her. And he wanted to remind her of it. Again.

Agony shattered through her, and she dropped her gaze before he could see the tears in her eyes. Within herself, she rebuilt those walls she had constructed to keep herself from caring. The walls that allowed her to do what needed to be done. "You can hate me all you want, Sol. I know I deserve it. But it's not *my* outlook I'm trying to change. It's everyone else's. There are people I care about, people I can still save if I—if I can find a solution to the problem I started."

"And you think repeating *her* mistakes is a solution?" Sol huffed a laugh, running a hand through his hair and shaking his head in derision.

"What's *your* solution, Sol?" Pandora bit out, unable to stop herself. "Lie down and just accept your own destruction? Roll over for the demons sweeping over the realm, like you rolled over for Apollo your whole life?"

Sol's whole expression darkened with fury, and he closed the distance between them, looming over her with loathing in his eyes. For one moment, she thought he would strike her. She welcomed it. All this restless energy and guilt worming its way through her was unbearable. Perhaps if he attacked her, she would finally feel something different. Something other than the pain of her emotions.

"My solution," he said in a low voice, "is to let the Gorgon sisters sentence you to death. Once you're gone, the magic you unleashed will go with you."

She snorted. "Killing me won't close the box that's been opened."

"But killing you will end her curse. And, hopefully, her magic will go with you to the grave."

Pandora crossed her arms, glaring at Sol. She refused to let him see how much his words affected her. How much it hurt to hear him speak of her death with such optimism. "That's a gamble. What will you do if it doesn't work?"

He shrugged, as if watching her die would be a mere inconvenience and nothing more. "Then, I will think of a new plan."

Pandora laughed without amusement. She was finished with this conversation. "Then, end it now. Why wait for the Gorgon sisters?" She spread her arms. "What the hell are you waiting for, Sol?"

His brows lowered, his eyes burning with fury. But he didn't move.

She smirked. "Because you can't, can you?"

A muscle worked in his jaw, and his nostrils flared.

Pandora leaned closer to him until their noses almost touched. "I know you hate me. You have good reason to. But if you aren't going to *do* something with all that anger, then just leave me the hell alone."

"You don't have the right to order me around," he growled.

"No, I don't. But if you insist on tormenting me, then I'll do the same to you."

He chuckled. "You can't hurt me, Pandora."

She offered a cruel smile. "You know what I think? I think it's your guilt that's fueling you. Guilt for letting this happen to her. For not even *realizing* what your beloved mentor was doing, right under your very nose. *That's* why you can't kill me. You're angry with yourself for standing by while Apollo lied to and deceived everyone."

She turned away, ready to put distance between them. He grabbed her arm, his grip bruising, and whirled her to face him once more. "Don't you *dare* pretend to know me just because you have her soul inside you," he hissed. "You are not her."

"I know that," Pandora whispered. "But do you?" She stared at him for a long moment until he released her, his expression going slack. She took advantage of his confusion and slipped away from him, weaving through witches until she stood beside Mona. Her sister looked her over with a slight frown but said nothing, resuming her conversation with Evander.

Pandora rubbed her arms, but a chill seemed to seep into her very bones, icing her blood. She didn't want to hurt Sol. But he was in agony, and he was lashing out at her for the wrong reasons. Yes, she deserved it, but he was broken, and until he realized that, he would never heal.

Pandora walked silently with Mona and Evander until they reached the edge of the jungle. Farah took the first step. She entered the Voiceless Jungle without hesitation, her form vanishing between the shadows. When the rest of them followed, setting foot on the sacred soil of the jungle, the darkness swallowed up every sound, leaving nothing in its wake.

Leaving Pandora to the torment of her thoughts and memories.

SILENCE

MONA

Mona had been warned the Voiceless Jungle was ominously silent, but nothing could have prepared her for the jarring absence of sound. Even her footsteps made no noise. It felt like she had stepped into a yawning void of nothingness, a stasis between worlds that trapped her forever.

She had been between worlds before. She had been in a state of helplessness, disconnected from her soul and unable to fix it. Unable to move or do anything.

This felt a lot like that.

Mona swallowed hard, her heartbeat thundering louder than anything around her. From beside her, Evander's warm hand captured her own and squeezed. If anyone understood how this would feel for her, it would be him. He had been her anchor during that time in the Underworld. Her guardian. Her savior.

Mona squeezed his hand in return and clung to the warmth of his body next to hers. Alive. Whole. Healthy.

It didn't matter to her that he was altered. But she knew it bothered him. It would take some adjusting. He had lost a central part of himself that would never come back. And she was prepared to stand by him for as long as it took for him to come to terms with it.

On her left, she felt Pandora trembling beside her. She'd seen her sister conversing with Sol, and judging by their venomous expressions, the conversation had not gone well. Sol was full of a hatred that couldn't be quenched, and Pandora was masochistic enough to let him torture her. Because she was in love with him.

But Mona knew it wasn't her place to interfere. Both had to work out their own issues in their own time. Besides, the last person Sol would want to hear from was the woman who had gotten his mother killed. The reminder of Hestia's sacrifice still ate at her, and being surrounded by the fire goddess's acolytes only worsened Mona's guilt.

If she hadn't taken a stand before Apollo, Hestia would still be alive.

If Sol should blame anyone—besides Apollo himself —it should be Mona.

Mona's steps were slow and careful as she followed

the shadowed forms of the witches in front of her. Darkness surrounded her, but Farah's palms were lit with the smallest of flames, providing a dark orange glow that guided their way. The coven leader seemed to know the right path to take, although there was no trail that Mona could see. Nothing but wild foliage and overhanging trees blocked the moonlight.

No twigs snapped. No leaves crunched. Not a single insect chirped.

There were no noises at all. The jungle might as well have been a graveyard.

A chill skittered across Mona's skin, and she drew closer to Evander until his arm was pressed against hers. The warmth of him warded off the ice in her bones, and she inhaled his scent, clinging to that strong presence beside her.

Farah had warned them not to speak, that it would disturb the spirits that lived here. But all Mona wanted to do was talk to Evander. How did he feel? Was he all right? After they reached the Gorgon sisters, what did he want to do? Try to return to the Underworld? Stay here in the Realm of Gaia? Mona wanted to remain with Pandora, to support her sister. But if the Gorgon sisters determined she should be executed or imprisoned, Mona wasn't certain what she could do.

Her heart twisted at the thought, even though, logically, she knew Pandora's crimes were great. Many had perished because of her choices. If the Gorgons sentenced her to death, it would be warranted.

But that didn't stop Mona from feeling guilt and anguish at the thought of losing her sister.

Pandora was cruel and vicious and conniving. But she was Mona's blood. And, despite everything she had done, Pandora still had a heart. She was trying to make things right. She was trying to change her ways. People like Sol were making that difficult, but Mona could acknowledge the effort her sister was putting in.

It meant there was still some good in her, and Mona hoped this meant Pandora was strong enough to conquer her curse and the vengeful soul inside of her.

Farah suddenly lifted a hand, the glow of her flame burning in the darkness. The crowd of witches stopped, and Mona's heart lurched in her throat with apprehension at what was coming.

"You are not welcome here," said a low, threatening voice.

Mona went rigid, scanning the dark forest for the source of the voice, but she saw nothing. No one.

"We have come to see the Gorgons," Farah said, her voice solemn and strong.

"You bring darkness and death with you," hissed the voice. "And your flame threatens our sacred flora."

Mona straightened, her breaths coming sharp and fast. *Sacred flora.* Was this stranger an earth witch?

"The flame is contained," Farah promised. "It is only to guide our way. The Gorgons are part of our coven. We have a right to see them."

"The Gorgon sisters are visitors on our land, protected only by the god blood that flows in their veins," said the voice. "You have no such protection."

"But I do," Mona said, surprising herself by how firm and determined her voice was.

A few people gasped, and the witches parted, forming an aisle through which Mona walked to reach Farah. Her hand was still clasped in Evander's. He followed, his body taut, as if he expected a fight.

Only when Mona reached the front of the crowd did she make out a figure of shadows standing before Farah. It was shaped like a tall, slender woman, but Mona could not make out any details; only darkness, as if the woman was born of the shadows themselves.

"The blood of Gaia flows in my veins," Mona said. "And I am one of you, earth sister."

The shadowed figure withdrew slightly, as if in surprise. Mona's skin tingled as she had the distinct impression this witch was looking her over, scrutinizing her carefully.

"I smell earth on you," she said. "Earth and life. Yes, you are one of us. And you are welcome."

Hope rose in Mona's chest. "These people are with me."

But the shadow shook her head. "No. We cannot allow so many intruders. Our soil is too sacred."

Uncertain, Mona glanced at the witches behind her. Her eyes met Farah's, and the coven leader shook her head.

"We have never come here with this many before," Farah murmured. "In the past, they have always let us through."

A knot formed in Mona's throat as she looked at the dark specter. "How many? How many will you allow?"

A moment passed. Then, the woman said, "Five."

A protest formed on Mona's lips, but before she could utter it, Farah grasped her arm. "This is acceptable, so long as the earth witches allow us to await the Gorgon sisters out here. We will use no flame." When Mona looked at her in confusion, Farah offered a grim smile. "Your matter is urgent, and you need the sisters more than we do. Council with them. See what they can do for you. And we will be waiting when you finish."

Mona licked her lips, feeling uncertain about the idea of following this dark stranger and leaving the safety of Farah and her coven. But there was no other choice, and the earth magic rippling from the shadowed woman was strong. It smelled of sage and forests and *home.*

It smelled like Gaia.

A pang of longing filled Mona's chest at the thought

of her mother. Gaia had made many poor choices, but that didn't mean Mona didn't miss her.

"Evander, you're with me," Mona said. Then she turned and called into the crowd of witches. "Sol. Romanos. Pandora. Come with us. We will need you."

The three figures emerged from their party and stepped forward. Sol shot a nasty look at Pandora, who calmly ignored him and stood next to Mona. Romanos seemed utterly unfazed by the entire situation, as if this happened to him every day.

The shadowed figure inclined her head. "Very well. Follow me. I will take you to the king."

Mona stiffened. "King?"

"Yes. The Gorgon sisters are conversing with King Midas now. I will take you to him."

Shock coursed through Mona as if a bucket of ice water had been dumped on her. *King Midas*? The man who had been cursed to transform everything he touched to gold? Mona had read about this man in books, but all the stories she'd read said Midas had died long ago.

She was still trembling with apprehension and disbelief when Evander gently guided her toward the shadowed witch. Shoving her emotions aside, Mona took a deep breath and followed after the witch, descending further into the darkened jungle.

CONVINCING

CYRUS

PRUE'S EXPRESSION OF BETRAYAL AND heartbreak flashed across Cyrus's mind as he sat in his chambers, sipping the despicable Elysium wine Apollo had given him.

He couldn't shake that sight from his thoughts. It was the ultimate treachery, to turn against his wife and side with her enemy—her wretched father who had caused her family so much suffering.

He closed his eyes, allowing the sickeningly sweet nectar to slide down his throat with another gulp. His skull throbbed from the strain of having to play his role for Apollo so perfectly.

He needed to convince Apollo to trust him. The only way to do that had been to allow Hyperion to enter his palace.

Hyperion had been the least dangerous of the Titans, though he was still lethal in his own way. It was just much more subtle. He seemed the best option out of all the Titans to bring back.

But first, Cyrus had needed to convince Lagos to break open Tartarus for him to retrieve Hyperion. Only an overseer of Tartarus had access, and Cyrus, in his human form, no longer had the power to do it himself.

"You wish for me to bring a Titan here?" Lagos had asked, his voice strangely calm. "Why?"

"Apollo will find a way," Cyrus had said, sitting forward in his chair and rubbing his temples with his fingers. "With or without our help, he'll do it somehow. You know he will."

"That's not a good enough reason."

Cyrus sighed, looking up at Lagos, who stood in front of him, arms folded over his chest, his animal eyes betraying no emotion.

"I need Apollo to trust me," Cyrus whispered. "And this is the only way."

"You need to tell Prue."

"I can't," Cyrus said through gritted teeth. "Apollo loves to gloat. And he will lord this over her once she finds out. Prue's emotions are so easy to read. If she *knows* where my true allegiance lies, Apollo will be able to read it on her face. Her surprise, her shock, will not be convincing enough for him."

Lagos was silent, his face stoic as ever. He was the complete opposite of Prue. He had a bull's head, which made him impossible to read. He simply blinked once at Cyrus.

"I serve Prue," Lagos said slowly. "If I do this, I will be betraying her trust."

"You are the only overseer left," Cyrus said, his voice on the verge of pleading. "You are the only one who can do this. And I would much prefer *you* do it than some Elysium lackey of Apollo's."

Lagos released a low huff of disapproval, and Cyrus knew the demon was envisioning some fool from Elysium tampering with the magic of the Underworld and causing even more problems with their ignorance.

"What is your plan?" Lagos asked quietly. "How do you intend to betray Apollo?"

"Apollo has promised me a way to get my magic back."

Lagos snorted. "And you believe him?"

"No," Cyrus said at once, although that wasn't entirely true. "But if there *is* a way, only someone like Apollo would be able to find it."

"So, that's your plan? Trust this god, who lies to everyone, that he will grant you your powers back, making you strong enough to defeat him?" Doubt filled Lagos's voice.

Cyrus resisted the urge to cringe. Gods, when he put

it like that, it did seem like a stupid plan. "It's not the only reason I'm doing this."

"Oh, good. Because for a moment there, I was worried you were trying to convince me to betray Prue all so you could get your magic back."

Cyrus winced. He was a horrible, terrible person. He knew this. But there were sound reasons for his plan. He needed Lagos to see that. "If Apollo trusts me, he will tell me more of his plan. For instance, I know he intends to eventually release *all* of the Titans."

Lagos grew very still. "Are you serious?"

"Yes. He thinks it's the only way to stop Pandora's magic."

Lagos shook his head. "That is an awful idea."

"I agree. But if we unleash just *one* Titan, and Apollo trusts me, then perhaps he will tell me how he intends to release the others. If I refuse to help him, he'll never tell me anything."

"Why does he need you to release one Titan if he has a plan to release them all?"

"I don't think he can release them all on his own. He needs a stronger magic. A more powerful magic. I have to figure out what that is and how he is accessing it. I have a feeling it involves Titan magic. Perhaps with one Titan free, Apollo will use that Titan's magic to craft a spell that will grant him the ability to unleash them all."

Lagos nodded slowly. "And if Apollo can do that with Titan magic, then perhaps you and Prue can utilize such magic as well."

"Exactly. With that amount of power, we could stop Apollo. We could banish him from the realm."

Lagos sighed. "Very well. I will help you."

Relief surged in Cyrus's chest. "Thank you, Lagos."

"On one condition."

Cyrus froze, dread coiling in his gut. "What?"

"As soon as Apollo has finished *gloating*, you tell Prue everything."

Cyrus's heart sank into his stomach. Oh, gods. That was the last thing he wanted. Prue would be so angry and hurt, and to confront her after betraying her... Would she even believe him?

When Lagos blinked expectantly, Cyrus swallowed hard, then nodded. "All right. I agree."

So here Cyrus sat, drinking the disgusting wine and struggling to gather the courage to seek out Prue and explain everything. She deserved the truth. And he could alleviate her suffering by telling her of his plan. Perhaps it would lessen the blow of his treachery.

And Gaia had left... Cyrus hadn't been expecting that. Now, Prue was truly alone. She needed him more than ever.

With a groan, Cyrus climbed to his feet, his head

buzzing from the alcohol in his system. Gods, his pathetic human form was so weak. He used to be able to drink several glasses of wine before feeling its effects. Now, after only two, he was already muddled.

He rubbed a hand down his face and strode to the door. Before he could open it, a heavy pounding echoed from the other side.

Cyrus straightened, his heart hammering painfully in his chest. With a deep breath, he opened the door and found his wife on the other side, eyes blazing. Her face was red and puffy from crying, but pure hatred burned in her lavender eyes.

"We need to talk," she bit out.

Shit. Cyrus was too late. There would be no convincing her now.

Wordlessly, he stood to the side to let her in. She stormed past him, and Cyrus closed and locked the door before turning to face her. Her fists were clenched at her sides, her hair even wilder than normal. Her eyes were so wide and feral that Cyrus expected her to lunge at him at any moment, like a deranged animal.

Prue took several shaky breaths before she spoke, her voice low and menacing. "How dare you."

"Prue, just let me explain," Cyrus began, palms out as he tried to appease her.

Her nostrils flared. "I gave you an out! If you wanted to be rid of me, you could have left this realm.

You didn't have to run off to *Apollo* to stab me in the back!"

"Prue—"

"Are you—Are you *punishing me*?" she cried, spreading her arms. "Is that what this is? You still blame me for that spell that turned you human?"

"Gods, Prue, no! I was—"

"Well, congratulations." Prue's voice cracked, and tears brimmed in her eyes. The sight nearly undid Cyrus completely. "You've officially broken me. I'm not strong enough to face you *and* Apollo. Even with my mother here, I didn't think I could do it. But now? I—"

Cyrus surged toward her, unable to help himself. She was so shattered, so devastated, that he couldn't take it anymore. He brought his hands to her face, cradling her cheeks, and drew her mouth to his.

She stiffened, uttering a small gasp of surprise as their lips met. The kiss was soft and pleading at first, as if Cyrus were asking a question. His lips moved gently over hers, capturing her mouth over and over with deliberate slowness.

He dragged his fingertips down her cheeks, his touches tender and delicate. Her form wilted, and she made a sound that was a cross between a sigh and a sob.

Cyrus pulled away to look at her, and she was weeping freely. "What—What was that?" she asked in a strained voice.

"That was my answer." Cyrus's voice was low. "I choose you, Prue."

She shook her head, still crying softly. "I don't understand. You chose *Apollo*."

"It's a game, Prue. I'm playing the game the only way I know how. I'm weak and powerless, so I needed an edge. Without it, Apollo would have killed me easily. But now, I can get close to him and figure out his plan. I can feed you all the information I learn from him. I'm *on your side*, Prue."

She shook her head, biting her lip. "How am I supposed to believe you? Just days ago, you were yelling in my face about how much you despised me."

Cyrus's chest constricted at her words, because she was right. He had made awful choices lately. He was weak and angry and utterly foolish. He blinked rapidly as heat burned behind his eyes. "I'm so sorry, Prue." He couldn't stop his voice from breaking. "I'm so terribly sorry. As soon as I said those things, I wanted to take them back. I just—I couldn't rein in my emotions. They are so overwhelming, and my need for power is so strong, that... Gods above, Prue. You don't know how much I wish I could change it. How much I wish I could erase all the pain I've caused you. I was weak. And I will spend every day of the rest of my pitiful existence proving to you how much you mean to me."

Prue's brows knitted together as if she were still

confused by his words. She still believed he hated her. She believed *this* was the act. Not what she had seen with Apollo.

She truly thought he was despicable enough to betray her.

And that broke him more than anything else.

At a loss for words, Cyrus gripped her waist and kissed her again, this time with more force. His mouth claimed hers with bruising intensity, his tongue gliding between her lips and colliding with hers. She moaned in his mouth, her hands gripping his shoulders to bring him closer. He tasted her thoroughly, again and again, willing her to believe him, if not with words, then with actions.

He walked her backward until she was pinned to the wall, his hips aligned with hers. She gasped, arching against him, her head thrown back as he ran his tongue along the column of her throat. Gods above, she tasted divine. Her scent, her skin, was so much sweeter than he remembered. He thought he could resist her. He thought that, for the good of his kingdom, he could refuse her touch. But this right here was like a starving man given a feast. He was dying of thirst, and this was a bottomless well for him to drink from.

He groaned in part agony part satisfaction as her hips ground against him, rubbing directly along his hardened length. His skin burned from her touch, his blood boiling with an intensity he'd never known before. Ever since he'd awoken as a human, he had loathed himself for how weak and pitiful he was. But this... He could feel everything so acutely. Each sensation rippled over him with more force and fervor than he could ever imagine.

He couldn't help himself from whispering her name, dragging his hand through her soft curls. He wanted to worship her body, to show her just how devoted he was. Each touch, each movement sent fire coursing through him, and gods, it was the most delicious and exhilarating feeling.

Prue was panting, her hips moving, her lips parted as she stared at him with a dark and heated look that he knew too well.

"I am yours," Cyrus rasped. His body was so consumed by her that he almost couldn't find his voice at all. But he needed her to know. He needed her to understand. "I am *yours*, Prue."

Her cheeks flushed, her eyelashes fluttering as her hands came around his neck to pull him to her again. She kissed him violently, teeth and tongue scraping, devouring him completely.

He growled in her mouth, hoisting her up until her skirts came up and her legs wrapped around him. He was weak—much weaker than before—but he could still carry her. His hands gripped her thighs, holding her against him as he brought her to the bed and lay her before him.

He wanted her naked, but the growing need pulsing through him demanded he take her like this. There wasn't time to remove all the layers of clothing. He needed her *now*.

Her dress was already bunched up well past her thighs, revealing the tanned skin of her legs. His fingers danced up and down those legs, and her back arched as she sighed with contentment. He worked the fabric up higher until his thumb skirted over her slick center, and she cried out.

Gods, she was pure perfection. How had he denied her before? How had he not seen how perfect this goddess was?

In this moment, power didn't matter at all. As he removed his trousers, watching as Prue's eyes dipped to his firm arousal, he realized there had *never* been power between them when their bodies tangled together. He hovered over her, his black hair forming a curtain over them as he brought his mouth to hers in a long and slow kiss, running his tongue along the seam of her lips. Her tongue met his, coaxing him forward until he plunged deeper into her throat, tasting as much of her as she could.

Her hand gripped his arousal firmly, and he jerked wildly with a strangled gasp.

"You are mine," she whispered. "Only mine."

"Only yours," he echoed in a strained voice.

She guided him closer, and he felt the heat of her surround him when he entered her slowly. He slid in, deeper and deeper, letting her fit around him so perfectly, so fully, that he couldn't see straight. Pure pleasure rocketed through him like a violent tidal wave, and he let it overtake him, let it drown him completely.

"Oh, gods, *Prue*," he groaned when he was completely inside her. She rocked her hips, and he met her movement with a thrust of his own.

Here and now, power and magic did not matter. He lost himself in her and the feel of her body. Human or not, god or not, he was still hers, and she was his. When he was with her like this, everything else fell away. Politics, power struggles, court responsibilities, looming threats... There was nothing but Prue and Cyrus.

He gripped her thighs, shifting his angle so he could drive even deeper inside her. She cried out, her arms around him, fingernails dragging along his back. Sweat trickled down Cyrus's face and neck as he pushed into her again and again. Her legs wrapped tightly around him, her heels digging into him. His movements became more wild, more unhinged as feral sounds escaped him. She met his thrusts with her own, hips bucking, making the bed frame rattle.

"Cyrus," she gasped. "*Cyrus.*"

He leaned in and captured her plea with his lips, drinking in her frantic breaths. He caught her lower lip between his teeth and tugged. A soft whimper escaped her. Her hands trembled as she ran them through his hair.

Tension built and coiled inside him, driving him closer and closer to that edge. He moved faster, harder, pounding with furious intensity, eliciting all manner of desperate sounds from her. His tongue met her throat, tasting the sweat on her. His teeth clamped down on the small space where her neck met her shoulder, and he bit down hard.

Her body quivered as release exploded within her. He felt her spasm around him, and it sent him over the edge with her. He gave one more powerful thrust as he spilled inside her. He ground out her name again as he came undone inside her, letting himself fill her, savoring the way their bodies fit perfectly together as she met his need with her own.

"My wife," he whispered, his body spent and his breaths still hard and fast. "My queen."

Her hands came around the back of his neck as she gazed up at him, her eyes still wild but full of bliss. She was satisfied. *He* had satisfied her completely.

Even as a human. A mortal. Someone weaker than she was. He had elicited those sounds, that pleasure from her.

"I am yours," she murmured, tracing her hand down his cheek. "No matter who you are. Or *what* you are. I am yours, Cyrus. Always."

He kissed her again, and she met his mouth eagerly as if they were making up for lost time, kissing and touching for all those moments when they had been apart.

Prue pushed against him and rolled until she was on top of him. Cyrus leaned his head back, still gasping for breath, and managed a weary chuckle.

"I—I can't," he groaned. "You've exhausted me."

Prue only smiled, tugging at the sleeves of her dress. When she lifted the fabric over her head, leaving her in nothing but her thin shift, Cyrus felt his mouth go dry.

"Prue—" he began, but she cut him off with another kiss.

"Let me do the work this time," she breathed before kissing him again. "I just want to be naked with my husband. Is that all right?"

He found himself nodding as she undid the strings of her shift before pulling it off and tossing it to the floor.

She was bare before him, and he let his gaze rove slowly over her tanned shoulders, her perfect breasts, her smooth stomach. She was utter perfection.

"Gods, you are a masterpiece," he said softly.

Her cheeks flushed again. "As are you, husband."

She kissed her way down his throat, then worked on

unbuttoning his tunic. He resisted the urge to recoil, to hide himself and his pale expanse of unmarked skin. She had always liked his tattoos. Would seeing him now without them only remind her of how different he was?

But Prue didn't react when she opened his shirt and tugged it free before discarding it on the floor. She withdrew from him, lifting her hips so their bodies were no longer connected, and he immediately mourned that loss. But then she resumed her mouth's exploration of his body, dragging her lips down his chest and abdomen. He jerked when she hovered just above his arousal, which was still coated in his seed.

Her tongue met his length, tasting him thoroughly, and he gasped, hips jerking. He wasn't hard again, but he could still *feel* her lips and tongue, the minute sensation quivering over him until he shuddered.

"Gods, Prue," he groaned.

Prue smiled before taking him completely in her mouth.

And he let her. For hours, he let her touch him, kiss him, lick him anywhere she pleased. Because he belonged only to her. Even when his body could do no more, she continued to worship him as he had her. And when his goddess was finally spent, they lay tangled up in the sheets, legs twisting together as they held one another, rekindling what had been lost between them.

And not once did he think of his lost magic or his

god blood. Not once did he regret being alive. Because nothing could compare to the bliss of holding Prue in his arms, of binding their bodies together.

She was his. And he was hers.

And that magic was more powerful than anything else in all the realms.

MIDAS
PANDORA

PANDORA WAS ACUTELY AWARE OF SOL STANDING so close, even with Evander between them. She secretly wished Mona had ordered Sol to stay with the witches. But deep down, she knew it was pertinent for him to meet the king with them.

Pandora had heard of Midas. He had once been an alchemist who worked for Apollo. When Midas discovered a magic that could turn light into gold, Apollo stole the power from him and cursed Midas. Pandora never learned what became of the alchemist after that; she was only well-versed in Apollo's history to better serve her plot for revenge.

Now that she thought about it, Sol was likely old enough to have known Midas before he was cursed. But she wasn't sure if this was a good thing. It was possible

Midas would see Sol as an ally of Apollo's and turn them away.

Then again, Pandora herself came from the Underworld. So did Evander and Romanos. That didn't exactly put their party in a positive light either.

The mysterious shadow witch led them through a curtain of ivy, holding it open for the group to pass through. Mona and Evander continued without hesitation. Sol paused uncertainly before stepping through.

Pandora lingered for a moment, trying to steady her breaths. Beside her, Romanos nudged her shoulder with his.

"The witches won't hurt you," he whispered.

"It's not the witches I'm afraid of," Pandora said darkly. With a deep breath, she passed through the curtain of ivy. The air immediately chilled around her, and she rubbed her arms, glancing around in amazement.

Tiny bobbing lights floated from underneath a massive willow tree whose leaves formed a dome-shaped canopy around them. As soon as the ivy curtain fell closed once more, the shadowed witch stepped into the light. The darkness surrounding her fell away, revealing a tall woman with a wild mane of curly red hair. She had fair skin and pale green eyes that seemed to glow as brightly as the lights from above.

"My name is Saffron," the witch said, her voice

solemn. "In allowing you passage into these sacred lands, you are swearing a vow to protect the secrets of my coven. Should you forsake this vow, you risk incurring the wrath of the Triple Goddess herself."

Pandora might have laughed were it not for the ringing authority of the woman's words, and the way the air seemed to quiver around them ominously. She swallowed hard as Saffron took the lead, guiding them toward the trunk of the mighty willow tree.

Pandora fell into step beside Mona and whispered, "Have you ever encountered earth witches like this?"

Mona shook her head. "We were very isolated on Krenia, so there was no need for such secrecy."

"But... the way she speaks of the Triple Goddess... the *authority* in her voice, it's—" Pandora couldn't find the words.

Mona looked at her with a frown. "You haven't encountered witches before, have you?"

"I haven't encountered *any* mortals before," Pandora pointed out. "Before you, that is."

Mona smiled. "I'm not exactly a mortal, though, am I?"

"I suppose not."

The notion sobered Pandora as she recalled what Mona had told her when Elysium had fallen. *The three of us were bound by a powerful enchantment that kept us locked in our mortal bodies. Only upon death can our true powers be freed.*

Mona had died and come back again, resurrected by her sister, Prue. But Pandora would never be able to access these goddess powers. Because if she died, no one would care enough to bring her back. No one loved her. No one even liked her, except perhaps Mona. But to resurrect the dead was a dangerous deed. Mona would never sacrifice what she had with Evander just to bring back a sister who had betrayed her. If there was even a chance the spell would go awry and Evander would be harmed, Pandora knew her sister wouldn't risk it.

So, Pandora was doomed to be a mortal forever. Or die without any hope of returning.

Her thoughts turned to Prue, whom she had assumed had perished with the Underworld. But now, she wasn't so sure. If she *had* died, perhaps someone had brought her back. Cyrus loved her enough to do it. Gaia did, too, and she was capable of creating life from anything.

The thought soured Pandora's stomach and made her face twist into a disgusted grimace. Gaia, Mona, Prue, Cyrus, Evander... They all possessed a love stronger than any other force in the world. A love Pandora could never be a part of because more powerful gods and goddesses had decided she wasn't worth it.

"This way," said Saffron, urging the group forward.

Pandora realized she had fallen behind and hastened to catch up to Mona. Sol was watching her, and she hadn't realized how long his gaze had been fixed on her. Only when she looked at him did he finally turn away from her to follow Saffron.

Saffron led them directly to the center of the willow tree where a massive trunk stood, thicker than five men standing side-by-side.

To Pandora's surprise, Saffron didn't stop when she reached the trunk. She walked right into the center of it, her form dropping suddenly into some space below that Pandora couldn't see. Her heart lurched in her throat. Was there a hole at the base of the tree?

It wasn't until she got closer that she realized a gap in the ground led to a narrow set of moss-covered steps that wound underground.

Awe and unease mingled in Pandora's chest as she followed the group down the steps. The smell of earth and moss swelled around her, filling her with an acute awareness of her own magic. It surged to the surface of her being, floating higher and higher, blotting out any sign of the trapped soul within her. For the first time in her life, her entire body seemed to quiet with the resonance of that potent earth magic. A calmness, a relaxing sense of peace, filled her to her core, warming her bones and soothing her agitated soul.

Miraculously, the memories and the goddess who

owned her were silenced. The earth magic here was stronger than she was.

Pandora felt a slow smile creep across her face as she descended farther and farther below ground.

The winding steps ended at the mouth of a wide tunnel lined by the same floating lights from under the willow tree. Earth and roots surrounded them, and the air seemed warmer down here.

Saffron said nothing as she led them through the tunnel. It wasn't quite wide enough for Pandora to walk shoulder-to-shoulder with her sister, so she lingered behind, her eyes catching on the way Mona's fingers coiled tightly within Evander's. The two were always linked. Never to be separated.

And Pandora's heart ached with the notion that she would never have that because of the choices she had made.

"Midas isn't so bad," Romanos muttered from behind Pandora.

She glanced over her shoulder at him. "He isn't?"

"Just don't mention his curse. Or Apollo."

Pandora huffed a laugh. "That will be a bit hard, since Apollo wronged everyone here and is directly responsible for my own curse as well as Midas's." She paused before asking, "Why do they call him *king*?"

"He was once king of the Thanassian Empire. His ability to turn anything into gold made him wealthier than any other king or noble, and for a while, he brought prosperity to the continent. But, once his enemies discovered the power of his touch and tricked him into turning his own daughter into gold, he disappeared, going underground so no one could exploit him again."

Sorrow twisted in Pandora's gut from the tragedy of such a tale. "And what do the Gorgon sisters have to do with him?"

Romanos paused before answering. "Midas's knowledge of alchemy is incredibly valuable, especially to the witch community."

Pandora frowned and glanced at him. Romanos had a closed expression on his face. There was clearly something he wasn't telling her.

But that was fine. She was used to other people's mistrust. He had no reason to share information with her to begin with.

"Do you think they will be merciful?" Pandora asked. "The Gorgon sisters?"

Romanos took another moment to consider this. "It's hard to say. I wronged one of them many ages ago, and it took quite a lot to earn her forgiveness. But once I did, we were connected, our souls bonded for eternity. Now, she's my wife."

Pandora stumbled over a root, and Romanos gripped her arm to keep her from falling on her face. "Your *wife*?" Pandora choked, eyes wide.

Romanos smirked. It was clear he had intentionally hidden this information. "Yes. Marina and I exchanged vows just last month."

Marina. Pandora had heard the other witches use that name.

So Marina was a Gorgon. Pandora wasn't sure what to do with this information.

The group halted at the end of the tunnel, which was shrouded by another curtain of ivy. Saffron turned to face them, her expression as somber as ever.

"When we reach the king, you will bow to show your respects," she said. "Address him only as *Your Highness*. Nothing else. And if he orders you to leave, you must do so. We follow his command."

Pandora's brow furrowed. Since when did witches obey the command of a man? It didn't make sense. The confusion on Mona's face indicated she, too, was baffled by this. But they said nothing as Saffron led them through the ivy.

Brilliant gold light shone through the curtain, nearly blinding Pandora as she stepped through. Her breath stuck in her throat as she took in a magnificent throne room covered in layers of golden leaves. A massive chandelier hung from the earthen ceiling, but it wasn't lit by candles. The same strange witch lights from before gleamed, bathing the room in an amber glow. A single throne rested on a mound of flattened earth, also covered in golden leaves. On that throne sat a man with auburn hair and blazing red eyes. He wore a golden tunic and trousers, a golden belt, and a golden sword. A matching gold crown rested atop his head, and a thick tan beard lined his face. Even his leather gloves gleamed with the same golden sheen as everything else about him.

But Pandora's gaze snagged on the crimson fire of his eyes, her heart stilling in her chest. Beside her, Mona went rigid, noticing the same thing.

His eyes were the same as Hestia's.

Sol drew forward, approaching the king first. He took a knee, pressing his fist to his chest and bowing his head. "Your Highness, it is a great honor to finally see you again."

Midas smiled, rising from his throne and spreading his arms. "No need for that, nephew. But you are right. It has indeed been too long."

Pandora's blood chilled as realization hit her.

Midas was Hestia's brother... and Sol's uncle.

DEMONS

EVANDER

THE MAGIC IN THE ATMOSPHERE WAS overwhelming. Even without the presence of Typhon, Evander could still sense the energies in the air. They smelled and tasted just like Mona's magic, but amplified so intensely it felt as if the power was swelling around him like a tidal wave.

He was momentarily jolted from his awe of the earth witch haven when both Mona and Pandora stiffened beside him, their wide eyes fixed on the king. Sol was bowing before him, but Midas rose and brought his gloved hands to Sol's shoulders, his face splitting into a wide smile.

And he called him *nephew.*

Evander hadn't known Hestia well, so her death hadn't affected him nearly as much as Mona. But he did have a certain reverence for the fire goddess. She had stepped in the path of Apollo's fury when Evander could not. Ultimately, she had made the sacrifice Evander intended to make himself.

He had been too weak to absorb the blow. And for that, he felt he owed Hestia—and her bloodline—his life.

He felt the sudden urge to lay himself at Midas's feet, to beg his forgiveness, to offer his sincerest apologies that his sister was dead.

Did Midas even know? If Apollo had cursed him, Evander presumed this meant the god was unable to return to Elysium. Did he realize his sister had died? Had he somehow sensed it?

Midas and Sol were speaking in undertones, both of them grinning. The sun god looked unrecognizable. Evander had grown so accustomed to his scowl that to see his dark eyes light up and crinkle with delight was strange.

"And who have you brought with you?" Midas asked, approaching the rest of their party. Pandora inched behind Mona, the movement almost imperceptible. She looked as if she wished to melt away from the room entirely.

Evander couldn't blame her. Sol clearly despised her. And if Midas was Sol's uncle, then Pandora was right to fear him. Would the king seek retribution by punishing

Pandora? Saffron had mentioned Midas's word was final, which made it seem like *he* held the authority, not the Gorgon sisters.

When Midas stood before them, Mona curtsied low, and Evander followed suit with a bow. Pandora lowered herself as well, head bowed and hands trembling as she held her skirts.

"Greetings, Your Highness," Mona said, her head still inclined politely toward the king. "We thank you for allowing us entry. We come with grave tidings from Elysium and have come to seek your aid."

This wasn't entirely true; technically, they were there to see the Gorgon sisters. But if Midas harbored ill will toward Apollo, it likely meant he could be their ally.

Evander found himself smiling at Mona's wit. Instead of speaking of Hestia's death, shifting the focus on the loss of Elysium and Apollo's disappearance would hopefully inspire Midas to work alongside them.

Midas's expression sobered. His brows lowered, and he nodded gravely. "Yes. I know all about what's happened in Elysium." His eyes shifted to Pandora and they seemed to darken with fury.

Evander straightened. "How?" he asked. "Your Highness," he added quickly.

"I have a reflection bowl, courtesy of that damned sun god when he cursed me." Midas's voice lowered to a growl. "I think he enjoyed gloating, knowing I was watching him live the life of a beloved king while I wasted away here in the mortal realm."

Something prickled in the back of Evander's mind. If he recalled correctly, there were two reflection bowls in existence. One was in the Underworld, likely in Cyrus's palace somewhere. The waters in the bowl allowed a person to observe any place in any realm whenever they wished.

"So, you saw what happened?" Sol asked. His gaze also flicked to Pandora, but there was no anger there. Evander could have sworn he saw concern in that expression, but it vanished almost immediately.

"I did," Midas said. "I witnessed my sister's death and the attack of that horrible darkness. Not only that, but I know where that asshole father of yours ended up." He gestured to Mona, who went rigid.

"I—I beg your pardon?" Mona asked, her voice rising to a squeak.

The entire room seemed to grow still with awareness. Pandora's eyes were round as saucers. Sol's face had drained of color, and Evander felt his own blood chill.

Midas snorted, unaffected by the horrified reactions to his declaration. "You did not know? Well, my condolences. I would not wish that kind of father on anyone."

Mona shook her head and raised a hand, stepping toward the king with a panicked expression on her face.

"Forgive me, Your Highness, but... who are you referring to?"

"Apollo, of course," Midas said, his face twisting into a sneer. "Such a coward, hiding in the Underworld. As if that place is worth anything anymore."

Evander's heart slammed wildly in his ribcage as his mind struggled to keep up with Midas's words. "The Underworld?"

"No, hold on." Pandora drew closer to the king, her eyes wild and full of terror. "You—You said *Apollo*? He's —He's her father?" She pointed to Mona with a shaking finger.

"Are you daft?" Midas snapped. "Yes, that's what I said."

Pandora inhaled a ragged breath and pressed a hand to her chest. Her eyes rolled back, and she sank to her knees, her breaths turning into sharp wheezes.

Mona rushed toward her, clutching her shoulders before she collapsed on the ground. "Trivia? *Trivia*! Look at me."

Pandora's head lolled backward, but Evander could tell this was no ordinary fainting spell. After a moment, her body began to twitch and thrash, her head jerking away from Mona.

"No," Pandora moaned, the sound strangled and anguished. "No, Apollo, *please*." Her voice was deeper than normal, and Evander's skin tingled with awareness.

She was seeing something that wasn't there. Was this a memory from her past life?

"Trivia, you need to wake up!" Mona shouted, shaking Pandora's shoulders. The urgency and desperation in Mona's voice made something within Evander rise to the surface. He joined Mona and gently grasped her arm, grounding her. She, too, was trembling.

"Breathe, Mona," he whispered. "You know what to do."

Mona turned to him, her green eyes wide. He held her gaze, his expression calm, willing her to expand her mind. Mona had a tendency to get swept up in her fear, but when she was able to cast it aside, her mind proved to be a powerful weapon.

Gradually, awareness crossed her features, and her breathing slowed. She nodded, holding Pandora with one arm while she plunged her free hand into the golden leaves at her feet. Evander knew she was seeking the earth beneath her. If there was anywhere for Mona to use her magic, it was here in an earth coven.

Mona closed her eyes, muttering something in a low voice that Evander couldn't make out.

"What is she doing?" Midas whispered.

Sol shook his head, his brows furrowed. His eyes were tight with worry, his gaze fixed on Pandora with a startling amount of concern.

Perhaps the sun god did not harbor as much hatred toward Pandora as Evander believed.

"*Sano,*" Mona murmured, her voice firm and brimming with power.

The earth rumbled, and the leaves shifted with an eerie hissing sound. Cracks split the earth, and brambles and thorns sprang forth, coiling around Pandora.

"Stop!" Midas ordered, surging forward, but Sol extended an arm to stop him.

Mona's eyes closed, her brows knitting together in concentration. She pressed her hands to Pandora's chest, and the thorns continued to circle around them. Evander drew closer to Mona, huddling toward her as the brambles formed a cocoon around them. Pandora's body began to glow, the white light intensifying until it burned against Evander's eyes. He shut them tightly as Mona continued muttering in another language.

Pandora threw her head back and cried out, the sound strangled and full of anguish. From the gaps in the thorns, Evander saw Sol draw closer, hand outstretched, as if he could reach for Pandora.

But the next moment, Pandora's eyes were open and clear as they fixed on Mona. Both women were gasping for breath, and a sheen of sweat coated Mona's forehead. Gradually, the thorny vines receded, slithering back into the cracks of the ground. The light had vanished, and the air went still once more.

Midas gaped at Mona, his face pale. "That—That was Gaia's magic."

Evander's eyes narrowed. "I thought you said you knew everything that happened in Elysium."

"I—Well—I don't—" Midas blustered.

"The reflection bowl doesn't work that way," Romanos said, speaking for the first time. He had lingered in the back, arms crossed as he watched the events unfold. Evander wondered if he was entertained by the show. He certainly seemed unperturbed by Pandora's condition or the revelation of who her father was. He also seemed less than impressed by Mona's magic, which made Evander wonder exactly what kind of magic Romanos *was* accustomed to. "The bowl only shows you what you wish to see. Nothing more. It is not omniscient, and it cannot show you more than one scene at a time."

Evander frowned as he stared at Romanos. His brother seemed to be speaking from experience. Had he used this bowl before? Or had he used the one in the Underworld?

"What happened to her?" Midas waved a gloved hand toward Pandora, who was climbing to her feet with Mona's assistance.

"What happened was you just informed her that her father is the same bastard she's been plotting against for the last two decades," Pandora said, her voice raspy as she rubbed her temples. "And the memories of the soul trapped inside her completely took over, triggered by the thought of Apollo and what he's done to us both."

Midas's mouth opened and closed as he no doubt struggled to process everything Pandora had said. After a long moment, he stammered, "N-No. I said he was *her* father." He pointed to Mona.

"Yes, Your Highness," Pandora said in a tired voice. "She's my sister."

From the way Midas's face paled even further, it was clear the king was not the only one delivering earth-shattering revelations. He opened his mouth to speak when a high-pitched shrieking sound filled the chamber, making the walls rattle. Dust and dirt rained from the ceiling.

Evander instinctively drew closer to Mona. She took his hand in hers, her eyes raised toward the ceiling. The chandelier quivered, and the lights flickered.

A chill of awareness skittered down Evander's spine as the air filled with a familiar scent. The smell awakened something primal and feral within Evander, an echo of when Typhon had occupied his body.

He knew that smell. He knew that presence.

It was demonic, and it reeked of death magic.

"What is that?" Mona asked.

"Dammit," Midas murmured. He moved toward a servant who stood against the wall and whispered something. The servant nodded and darted down a tunnel behind the throne. With a fierce expression, Midas turned to face Mona and removed his gloves. His hands were the same brown color as his skin, but a strange golden glow surrounded them like a transparent glove.

"You best summon your earth magic again, little goddess," Midas said. "We've got demons approaching."

DRAINED

PRUE

CYRUS WAS FAST ASLEEP WHEN PRUE CREPT OUT of his chambers. But she had allowed herself a moment to gaze upon him without interruption. Since his transformation, every time she had looked at him for too long, she had feared he would lash out at her or think she was staring only because she was horrified by who he was now.

But it wasn't true. He was still utterly and devastatingly beautiful. From his thick black lashes fanned out on his cheek to his fit and sculpted body. His inky black hair, mussed from sleep, had fallen around his face, partially obscuring one eye. His skin was smooth and pale, and although there were no tattoos, Prue couldn't help but admire the muscles lining his arms and chest. The way her hands and tongue had explored those muscles...

She shook her head before the heat pulsing between her thighs became unbearable. She had exhausted them both last night. With his human form, Cyrus's stamina wasn't the same, but he had still managed to completely satisfy her. Afterwards, she had wanted to do the same for him. She wanted to show *him* how much she adored this new body of his. And she hoped that when he woke, he would remember that.

After pulling her dress back on, Prue slipped out of the room, checking to ensure the hallway was clear before she tiptoed back to her own chambers. She heaved a sigh and pulled on a fresh dress, this one a brassy gold, then tugged her impossible hair into a messy knot at the top of her head. She couldn't send for a maid for fear word would get to Apollo that Prue hadn't spent the night in her own chambers. This secret needed to stay strictly between Prue and Cyrus.

After ensuring she looked at least somewhat decent, Prue emerged from her chambers and made her way downstairs. With the Underworld in its broken state, she didn't know what time it was. Ordinarily, an enchantment had the sun rising and setting every day, and, although it was only an illusion, it had always brought Prue a sense of comfort, reminding her of home.

Home. Goddess, what *was* home for her anymore? For a long time, it had been Krenia. But even there, Prue had felt a sense of restlessness, a desperation for a thrill or an adventure.

She supposed the Underworld was her home now, although it wasn't the same as when she had first come here. Still, it felt empty and lonely without Gaia or Mona to support her. Cyrus was on her side, or so he claimed. She couldn't help but harbor doubts about his allegiance, especially given his past behavior. Back and forth, they seemed to dance. And she wasn't sure what was real and what wasn't.

Even if he *was* on her side, they could only be together in secret. Apollo had to believe Cyrus was loyal to him, so, outside of their chambers, Prue was completely alone.

"My queen," said a voice, startling Prue from her thoughts.

She jumped and turned to find Lagos bowing before her. They stood at the bottom of the staircase, and Prue's hand was absently resting on the bannister. She wasn't sure how long she'd been standing like that, lost in her confusing thoughts.

Prue found herself smiling, realizing she wasn't as alone as she thought. She still had Lagos, who had proven his loyalty to her on more than one occasion. "Lagos, it's so good to see you. Are you ready to get to work?"

"There's no need, my queen. I have found what you were looking for."

Prue's pulse quickened, and she pressed a hand to her chest. She and Lagos had been searching for days for answers to the question of the realm's magic. She wanted to know if what Apollo said was true, or if there was a way to reconnect her magic to the Underworld once more.

"Show me," Prue said breathlessly.

Lagos nodded and turned to stride down the hall. Prue hurried to match his pace, her heart thundering in her chest. But as Lagos led her down another set of stairs, her chest tightened for an entirely new reason. He was leading her to the lower vaults of the palace—the same room where Cyrus had brought her back to life, then awakened and spat those hateful things at her. This was the place where Prue had broken her mother's curse, but it was also the place where her husband had shattered her heart.

His anger and venom toward her had been so potent, so raw, so *powerful*... She had believed nothing could bring him back from that.

She had truly believed he was lost to her.

Swallowing around the knot of emotions in her throat, Prue took a steadying breath and followed Lagos down the stairs.

He is on your side, Prue, she reminded herself. *He said as much last night.*

But he also said other things, another part of her whispered. *How are you to know what's real?*

Shaking her head, Prue followed Lagos across the room, past boxes and crates and furniture covered in white sheets. Prue's fingertips drifted over a dusty set of shelves upon which rested various jars and vials of potion ingredients. The smell of sage and earth magic whispered in the air, strangely reminding her of her home back in Krenia.

"Here." Lagos crouched low to the ground before hoisting a hefty book from the bottom shelf and setting it onto a dusty end table. Prue coughed as dust particles floated in the air before her. Then, she squinted at the book Lagos had found. Power thrummed through it, and as she scrutinized the book, she had the strange feeling it was watching her in return. And there was something familiar about that leather cover...

With a yelp, she jerked backward, her blood chilling as panic and alarm raced through her. She stumbled, barely catching herself before falling. "L-Lagos, where did you find that?"

Lagos straightened, glancing from the book to Prue and back again. "It was here, my queen. It must have been here for ages."

Prue shook her head, hands trembling as she covered her mouth. "No. No, it was *not* here. This book was once in Krenia with me when I used it to summon Cyrus. After that, it showed up in Faidon when I resurrected Mona. That—That's the *Book of Eyes.*"

A dozen memories assaulted her at once. Her and Mona opening the book. Darkness seeping out of it, devouring their village. Mona, stepping into that darkness, sacrificing herself to save everyone else.

Pomegranate seeds and candles surrounding the book as Cyrus appeared in the sarcophagus. And then, in Faidon, when Vasileios had stabbed her and she'd been bleeding out, Prue had used the book to reunite Mona's body and soul.

Blinking rapidly, Prue rubbed her chest, struggling to calm her racing heart. Goddess, it was too much. This book had been involved in so many dark and dangerous spells. And now it was here again.

"How did it end up here?" Lagos asked, as if reading Prue's mind.

Prue shut her eyes against the storm of her thoughts and emotions, trying to think logically like Mona. What would bring the book here?

In a flash, awareness hit her, and her eyes snapped open. "Cyrus. His powers are gone. His magic was linked to this book. It must have returned when he lost it."

Lagos grunted in surprise, turning to look at the book once more. Prue kept her distance. Even from across the room, she could still feel the book reverberating with power. She felt like it was watching her, eager to devour her magic. Now that she had the power of a goddess, she feared the book would be even more drawn to her, hoping to suck everything out of her.

"Do you think his magic returned to the book?" Lagos asked thoughtfully, clearly unaffected by the book's power. Perhaps it wasn't a threat to him, since he was a demon.

Prue inhaled deeply and straightened, staring hard at the book that had caused her so much pain and suffering.

But... it had also brought her to Cyrus. Without it, they never would have met.

Light bled through the uncertainty fogging her mind, and she chewed on her lower lip as she considered this. "Perhaps. This book is how he got his powers in the first place." Her eyes flared wide as she looked at Lagos. "Do you think... Is it possible he could get his powers *back* from this book?"

Lagos turned to her, the movement quick. His dark animal eyes narrowed, but she couldn't tell if it was in concentration or warning. "Even if he could, would his body be able to handle it? He is still a mortal."

Prue's heart sank. This was true. What if the intensity of that power ended up killing him? She nibbled on her fingernail, struggling to come up with an idea, something she could bring to Cyrus. He would be thrilled to know there was a way to get his magic back. And perhaps that would mean he wouldn't have to put on a show for Apollo anymore.

"Prue," Lagos said sharply.

She frowned at him. He rarely used her given name. But the alarm in his voice set her on edge. His head was turned toward the staircase. Prue whirled, her heart lurching in her throat when she found Hyperion standing at the top of the stairs, watching them.

Oh, shit. How long had he been there? Had he heard everything?

"What are you doing here?" Prue demanded.

Hyperion said nothing as he slowly descended until he stood before them, his dark eyes sweeping over the contents of the dusty room. "Fascinating," he murmured, his voice strangely accented.

Prue didn't like having a Titan here in this vault, where all manner of powerful and enchanted objects lived. She drew closer to the man, then faltered when his body seemed to ripple with a foreign energy. Her own earth magic rose to meet it, forming a transparent shield between them both.

Hyperion chuckled, the sound low in his throat. "Clever goddess. Gaia has taught you well. But... she is not here, is she?"

Prue went rigid but refused to back down as he drew closer. She reinforced her shield of magic, holding it in place for whatever attack was coming.

Metal clanged loudly, and then Lagos stood between them, a dirty blade in his hand. He must have grabbed it from the shelf.

"You will not harm my queen," Lagos growled, baring his teeth. A low growl rumbled from within him. He had the face of a bull, but this sound made him seem more like a feral tiger than anything. Prue had never seen him like this.

Hyperion did not even glance at Lagos. His dark gaze was still fixed intently on Prue. Lagos raised his blade. Prue cried out, reaching for her friend, but she was too late. With one lazy sweep of his hand, Hyperion sent Lagos flying backward until the demon collided with the shelves. Jars and glass shattered, and he fell to a crumpled heap on the floor.

"No!" Prue shrieked, surging toward Lagos.

Hyperion was in her face, his movements startlingly quick, like a blur of motion. His arm lashed out, and he caught her throat, his fingers wrapping tightly around her. In her haste to help Lagos, she had neglected her shield.

Now, Hyperion was choking the life out of her.

Pain split through her, her neck burning and her lungs straining for air. She couldn't breathe. Spots danced in her vision. She choked and gagged, fingers clawing at Hyperion's hand, but he was too strong. His hand was thick and meaty and her thin fingers could do nothing against his strength.

You are a goddess, she reminded herself. *Not a mortal. You can stop this!*

Fighting past the pain, Prue summoned her roots. The earth cracked, and several vines wrapped around Hyperion's feet. They tugged, and he cried out before sinking to his knees.

Prue gasped, inhaling a shuddering breath as she massaged her throat and stepped away from the Titan. "You... will pay for this," she rasped, stretching her arms and summoning more power. Grass sprang from the ground, followed by bushes and shrubs. More brambles emerged, latching onto Hyperion's arms and ankles until he was properly restrained.

But the Titan didn't even struggle. Instead, he grinned, the flash of teeth making Prue's blood run cold.

"You *are* powerful, little goddess," he said.

Prue gasped as Hyperion tugged at the vines surrounding him. Black shadows poured from his fingers, engulfing the vines completely until they turned to ash. The particles floated in the air, and then Hyperion *inhaled* them.

Prue staggered back in horror as he did the same to the other vines that were wrapped around him. One by one, he destroyed her earth magic and drank it in, absorbing it inside him.

He shoved his arms toward her, palms out, and a blast of her own earth magic exploded from him.

Prue threw up a shield, but she wasn't quick enough. A burst of power slammed into her chest, and she flew backward, head cracking against the stone wall.

Darkness clouded her mind. She willed herself to wake up, to *get up now* before Hyperion killed her. But she couldn't move. Her body was limp, her mind foggy as pain coursed through her.

A moan sounded nearby, and Prue blinked rapidly, trying to see through the haze.

"Prue," Lagos groaned. Glass tinkled as he tried to move. "Prue, you have to get up!"

Heavy footsteps drew nearer. Gradually, her vision cleared and she made out Hyperion standing above her, a sinister smile on his face. With one hand, he grabbed the front of her dress and lifted her until she was at his eye level. Her arms hung limply, and she was too wounded to stop him. Warm blood trickled from her head.

He was going to kill her.

No... he was going to *drain* her.

"Your magic belongs to me now," he whispered. The fabric he'd gathered in his hand was blackening, slowly turning to ash.

Soon, *she* would be nothing but ash.

A kernel of energy burned within Prue's chest. She clung to it, reminding herself she was a goddess, and she was powerful. She had the strength of Gaia in her veins.

She could overcome this bastard.

She closed her eyes, letting her body relax in Hyperion's grip as if surrendering to him completely. But inside, she focused on her magic. Branches stretched along the floor, working their way toward the Titan.

Hyperion chuckled, then leaned in, his face close to hers.

In a flash, a sharpened branch buried itself into Hyperion's chest, spearing completely through him. Black blood spurted, coating Prue's face.

With a roar, Hyperion dropped her, and she crumpled to the floor. Lagos was by her side, his head and arm bleeding, but he still wielded the dagger from before. With a swift movement, the demon dragged the blade across Hyperion's throat.

Prue scrambled backward as the mighty Titan fell to the ground, choking on his own blood.

She grabbed Lagos's hand. "Come on!" She tugged him forward, and he stumbled, one leg dragging. Prue glanced down to find his left trouser torn and bleeding. His ankle jutted out at an odd angle.

"I'm fine," he panted, squeezing her hand. "Let's go."

He managed to hobble forward, and Prue helped him up the stairs, one arm wrapped around him as they fled the vault before Hyperion could siphon more of her magic.

ECHOES

MONA

Mona's blood turned to ice from Midas's words. *Demons were coming.* For a moment, she stood there, frozen in place, terror numbing her completely.

Why? Why were they here? What were they after?

Most demonic creatures are drawn to power, she thought, remembering what she had studied. She lifted her hands, which were caked in dirt, and stared at them in horror.

Her power must have drawn the creatures here.

This was her fault.

She barely registered Romanos surging forward and asking the king, "Where is Marina?" His voice was full of furious desperation.

"The Gorgon sisters were called away," Midas said as

he slid several daggers into his belt. "Harpies were spotted in the southern edge of the jungle."

Romanos swore and ran a hand through his hair.

They were alone. The Gorgon sisters weren't here.

Somehow, the notion cleared Mona's thoughts, chasing away her fear. No one was coming to save them.

They had to save themselves.

"Salt," Mona said, turning to King Midas. Urgency pulsed in her veins, driving her to action. "I need salt. Do you have any?"

Midas shot her a bewildered expression before his eyes grew wide with awareness. "Ah, yes! Salt wards off demons."

Mona's head reared back. How did Midas know that?

To her astonishment, the king put his gloves back on and withdrew a small pouch from his belt. He tossed it to a nearby soldier. "Sprinkle this on the floor as fast as you can."

"No, it's too late for that," Mona said quickly. "They're coming for us. For *me*. But we need to contain them here where we can kill them."

Midas spread his arms, gesturing to the large, earthen throne room. "This is an underground palace. To draw demons here could destroy these tunnels."

Mona shot him a fierce look. "Better to destroy the tunnels than the entire community of witches here." She looked at the soldier. "Sprinkle the salt on the outskirts of the throne room. Keep the demons from reaching any of the other tunnels."

The soldier blinked, uncertain, as he glanced between Midas and Mona.

"You heard her," Midas snapped, waving a hand in irritation. After a moment, the soldier darted away with the pouch of salt in his hand.

"You keep a pouch of salt on your person?" Mona asked, still confused by this.

"I do." Midas looked over Mona with more scrutiny, as if he hadn't noticed her properly before. After a moment, he handed her a dagger, hilt out.

Mona's stomach twisted, and she shook her head, backing away from the blade. "I'm no warrior, Your Highness."

Midas laughed and slid the blade in his belt with the others. He slid off his gloves once more. "Your demonstration from earlier would suggest otherwise. But perhaps you're right. Your magic alone can do enough damage."

"And what about *your* magic, Your Highness?" Mona's eyes dipped to his gloveless hands, which still glowed gold.

Midas's eyes darkened, all humor vanishing from his face. "It is a blessing and a curse. Mostly a curse. But in this case, I can do some damage as well."

Curiosity nibbled at the corners of Mona's mind, but

she stifled it, knowing there were more important matters at hand than scrutinizing Midas's magic. Her gaze swept over the room, which was in a frenzy. Guards were arming themselves, just like Midas. Romanos accepted a blade from someone, then tossed another to Evander, who caught it by the hilt. Mona's heart seized in her chest at the uncertainty in Evander's eyes as he lifted the blade, as if weighing it in his hand. It was clear he knew how to use the sword, but he was uncomfortable with it. He, too, was accustomed to relying on his magic.

But in this case, he couldn't.

Mona stared at her own hands, remembering the ease with which she'd healed Pandora. She looked at her sister, who was standing in the middle of the room, arms folded across her chest and face pale with fear.

Mona strode to her sister and touched her shoulder. Pandora jerked, as if startled from her thoughts.

"Are you all right?" Mona asked.

Pandora rubbed her arms, then shook her head. "I'm not—I can't—" She broke off, her eyes fluttering closed. "I can't believe it's *him*. I can't believe he's our father."

Mona flinched at the reminder. The horror that had spread through her—knowing that vile god was her own flesh and blood—made her want to retch. She cast a thoughtful look on Pandora. "How did you not know?" Her words were gentle and not accusatory.

"How *could* I have known?" Pandora asked, voice rising. "I've lived in the Underworld my whole life."

"Yes, but... you studied Apollo. You knew him well because you wanted to take your revenge on him. I would think..."

Pandora's expression crumpled into a pained grimace. "Gods, you're right. You're right. I should have known. I just—" She heaved a sigh and ran a hand through her dark red hair. "I didn't want to know. I liked to think my father was Jupiter or Hermes or some other god who had passed long ago. The idea that my father was out there somewhere and didn't want me was... too painful to consider. It was already too much for me to think of my mother abandoning me."

"She didn't abandon you," Mona said at once.

Pandora shot her an incredulous look. "You don't know that."

"I know *her*. And she didn't abandon you. Apollo was the one to place the curse inside you. I know Gaia would have done everything in her power to try and stop him."

Pandora's eyebrows lowered. "You may think that. But I don't. From my experience, the gods wear many different faces. I believe Gaia wore the face of a doting and loving mother while she raised you. But it was only a mask and nothing more. None of us can know her true nature."

Mona wanted to argue this, but the protest died in

her throat. Because hadn't Gaia lied to her for years, making her believe she was nothing more than an ordinary earth witch? Gaia *had* worn different masks. The mask Mona was accustomed to was the mask of the Mother of their coven in Krenia. And she was still coming to terms with the fact that that was *not* her mother. At least, not entirely.

The ground trembled, the walls shook, and more dust and dirt rained down from the ceiling.

"Sentries!" Midas bellowed. Several soldiers hurried toward the tunnel where Mona and the others had come from. "I need to know what we're dealing with and how close they are."

"It's a hydra," Evander said. His voice was so quiet that for a moment, Mona wasn't certain he'd spoken at all. But his eyes were distant and unfocused, his expression hard.

Mona's skin tingled with awareness as she gaped at Evander. How did he know that, if he had no magic?

Midas faltered, glancing warily at Evander. "Come again?"

Evander's eyes cleared, and he stepped closer to Midas. "It's a hydra. It must have escaped from Tartarus when the Underworld fell."

Mona's heart dropped like a stone. "*A hydra?*" she repeated.

Another deafening boom shook the ground, this one

so violent that Mona toppled over, barely stopping herself from falling on her face. Palms out, she landed on the soft earth, then scrambled to her feet, trying to quell the quivering fear that wracked her body. Her mind flitted through every book she'd read about hydras. Multiple heads. Two heads would grow back if one was cut off. Serpent-like body. Often frequented marshes before it was captured and thrown in Tartarus.

Marshes. Mona shook her head in confusion. If it preferred the water, why was it here in a coven of earth witches?

Right, she thought, her stomach sinking with dread. *Because of me.*

A soldier rushed into the room, stopping to bow quickly to King Midas. "It's a hydra. My men caught sight of it less than a mile from here. Our blades do nothing to its flesh, and we were careful not to remove any of its heads."

Midas nodded, expression grave. He was gazing at his own hands in contemplation.

"Your Highness, if you get too close to it..." The soldier trailed off.

Mona knew what he'd been about to say. *If you get too close to it, it could tear you apart.* A hydra was known for its sharp teeth, which were strong enough to tear through flesh.

Mona was grabbing Pandora's hand before she knew

what was happening. Pandora yelped in surprise but allowed Mona to tug her forward until the two sisters stood before the king.

Mona lifted her chin, trying to project more confidence than she felt. "We can provide a distraction so you can get close enough to touch the hydra."

Pandora shot a bewildered look toward Mona.

Midas glanced between them, eyes narrowing. "You just told me you were no warrior. Do you really expect me to believe you can get close to this beast without faltering?"

"We don't need to get close to it," Mona said. "All I need is enough power to trap it with my vines."

Midas frowned, considering this.

"Your men can flank it on the opposite side," Mona said. "Attack it on both fronts, while you slip into its blind spot, undetected."

Midas's dark eyes took on a hungry gleam. "You know, for a woman who doesn't know battle, you certainly strategize like a captain."

"If this thing has multiple heads, then it won't have a blind spot," Pandora pointed out.

"Under the belly," Mona and Midas said together.

Pandora looked at Mona as if *she* had grown two heads. "Who are you? How do you know all this?"

"I read a lot," Mona said with an embarrassed chuckle.

An earth-shattering *crash* echoed through the room as something large shoved through the ceiling. Rocks and dirt fell around them. Mona lifted her arms over her head, and a magical dome of protection surrounded her and Pandora. Squinting through the particles in the air, she looked up, and her stomach roiled.

A gray, clawed foot protruded from the ceiling. It was half the size of Mona's entire body. Her pulse quickened, and she suddenly felt like she might be ill.

"It'll bring the whole cavern down!" someone shouted.

Mona's eyes widened. Without another thought, she stretched her arms toward the creature's foot and *pulled*.

Soil and rocks fell, but Mona's magic absorbed it all, catching each piece before it fell to the ground. The hole around the monster widened, and the chandelier shattered. Mona widened her shield so the shards bounced off it. Sweat beaded along her brow, and then a hand was gripping her arm.

Pandora. She offered Mona a sure nod before stretching her other arm toward the ceiling, pulling the creature down.

"What the hell are you doing?" Midas roared.

Mona couldn't see him through the dust around her, but she shouted back, "If I can control its descent, I can ensure the rest of the cavern remains intact! Once it's dead, we'll rebuild it! This way is safer."

She interpreted Midas's silence as assent, so she continued drawing the earth downward. Her magic swept up each piece of dirt and dust that fell, but the strain of controlling so much falling debris made her arms tremble.

"A little further," Pandora assured her.

Mona's vision darkened, but she nodded, gasping for breath. She struggled to focus, to home in on that beast's gray, scaly flesh as it sank lower and lower. An almighty screech filled the air, making the walls tremble again.

At long last, the hole was big enough, and the hydra fell to the earth before them. Mona tugged Pandora backward before they were crushed by it. Goddess above, it was *massive*. Bigger than Mona's home back in Krenia, the beast had five heads, each one resembling a large snake. The scaled body stretched behind it on four legs, with a long, barbed tail swishing on its end.

"Seal it in!" Mona cried.

She and Pandora sent their magic toward the gaping hole in the ceiling, filling the gap with the powers of the earth. The energy shifted around them as the hydra whipped its heads toward them, drawn in by their magic. Crimson eyes flared wide with interest, locking onto the two sisters. Mona pushed and pushed, even as the beast drew closer with another screech.

Then Evander was there, sword slicing into the creature's side. Black blood oozed from the wound, and the hydra staggered backward, its heads now craning toward Evander.

"No!" Mona screamed as the beast drew nearer.

Evander dropped his sword and stretched his arms wide. Something silver and transparent flared behind him, and Mona's breath caught in her throat. Even the hydra staggered backward in alarm.

Behind Evander, spreading outward from his shoulder blades, was a gleaming echo of the dark wings he used to have—like a translucent replica of his demonic form. Mona's eyes widened as she recognized the small horns atop his head, also silver, like a ghost.

He looked just like when he and Typhon had merged, only this time, his wings and horns and claws were sheer like glass.

Evander's wings beat, and he rose into the air, hovering until he was at eye level with the beast.

"Is that—" Pandora whispered, following Mona's gaze.

"It's Typhon," Mona breathed, jaw slackening in shock. "But... a ghost."

INSTINCTS

PANDORA

Having grown up in the Underworld, Pandora had seen all manner of demons. She'd encountered ones with horns, tails, fangs, claws, scales, and skin of varying shades of color.

But the hydra was something else entirely.

It was the biggest creature she had ever seen. And while the demons of the Underworld were intelligent, sentient creatures, this monster was all animal. No awareness in those all-black eyes; only bloodlust.

The ground shook as the creature tried to rise. Beside Pandora, Mona was frantically working to knit the ceiling back together with her earth magic. Hand still clutched in hers, Pandora returned to the task at hand, summoning as much of her own magic as she could. As soon as they closed up the hole in the ceiling with their magic, they would be able to trap the creature here. It would not be able to escape.

Then they could kill it.

But with the presence of this dark being, her memories rose up, threatening to drown her. From inside her, the soul of the goddess thrashed and raged, desperate to be unleashed, to join in the powerful fury of the monster. She could *sense* its energy, its kinship to the Titan magic used to create the box and all the creatures inside.

No, Pandora thought, gritting her teeth. *You will stay put. You are not in control.*

A deep, resonant part of her laughed in response, and a chill swept over her body. Cold awareness seeped into her, clouding her mind and weakening her resolve.

She was a slave to the memories, to the past life harbored inside her. And she would never be free.

Pandora's magic flickered, and her arms went slack. Her stomach sank, and she had the urge to drop to her knees and cry out in despair.

I can't win this battle. She will always control me. I will never be rid of her.

The darkness continued to rage inside her, slamming against the walls of her mind, desperate to be free.

Pandora wanted to give in. She was just so damn tired of fighting...

A shout rang out nearby, and Pandora's ears prickled

with recognition. Her head snapped up, and she locked eyes with Sol across the room.

The hydra had cornered him, drawn in by the brilliant sun magic flowing from his fingertips. He provided a diversion while Mona finished repairing the ceiling, but the distraction was *too* effective. The hydra was fixated on him. Saliva dripped from its fangs, and its maws opened wide, prepared to devour the sun god.

Something snapped within Pandora. All darkness, all uncertainty and confusion fled her body, and she lunged without thinking. A bolt of clarity speared through her, silencing the fury mounting inside her.

Save Sol. I have to save him.

The goddess's presence within her vanished. The memories faded. Pandora could see nothing but Sol before her, fear creeping into his features. He glanced behind him, suddenly realizing he'd been backed into a corner as the monster closed in on him. Blinding white light burned from his fingertips, luring the beast closer. When Sol realized he had nowhere to turn, he dropped his hands, dousing the light.

But the hydra had already decided on its target, and it would not be deterred.

Sol darted left, but one of the hydra's five heads intercepted, gnashing its teeth. Sol ducked to avoid the full strike, but the creature's fang caught on his elbow, drawing blood.

Pandora roared in anger, sprinting at full speed toward the hydra. Its back was to her, so it didn't notice when she summoned her roots right next to its tail. Thick oak trees sprang forth, and Pandora caught a branch in her hands before thrusting it into the monster's side.

The hydra screamed, the sound shrill and deafening, making Pandora's ears throb. But she didn't stop there. She shoved and twisted until the sharp branch had fully impaled the monster. Her roots kept moving, surrounding the creature, climbing over its legs and claws. One of the hydra's heads turned to leer at her, eyes blazing and fangs bared, but Pandora glared right back at it, undeterred. Half its focus was still on Sol—the benefit of having multiple heads.

But it also meant its attention was divided. And Pandora could take advantage of that.

The underbelly is its blind spot, she reminded herself. She didn't know where Midas was or what he was waiting for—the beast was plenty distracted, and this was the perfect opportunity. So, if he wouldn't take it, she certainly would.

If it meant saving Sol's life, she would do this.

More branches snapped as she gathered one in each hand, wielding their sharpened points at the hydra. Another head turned in her direction, and the creature tried stepping backward to draw closer to her.

Her roots tightened over the beast's feet, restricting its movements. It stumbled, falling over as it struggled to right itself.

Taking advantage of its disorientation, Pandora dived forward, sliding underneath its torso and thrusting the branches into its scaly flesh.

The creature shifted, managing to free one foot and slide out of the way. One branch missed, but the other sank into its chest, drawing black blood that spattered on Pandora's face. She choked and coughed, spitting it out of her mouth and struggling not to retch.

The hydra fell, and Pandora wasn't quick enough. Before she could roll out of the way, its torso pinned her legs, trapping her underneath its massive weight.

Shit. This was bad. So very bad.

The monster sensed her writhing underneath it. It stretched its long, scaly necks, craning to inspect her with part curiosity, part hunger. Keen red eyes fixed on her, narrowing with intense fury.

Someone cried out, and the hydra's head turned. Hovering in air, suspended by his strange, ghostly wings, Evander drove his sword into the monster's eye. The beast reared back with a shriek, its body shifting just enough for Pandora to wriggle free. Gasping for air, her left thigh screaming in pain, Pandora hobbled away from the creature as quickly as she could manage, slamming into something hard.

Arms wrapped around her, stilling her. Pandora froze and looked up into Sol's face. He seemed as startled as she was. She hadn't realized she'd run straight into his arms. He looked over her with alarm and concern, taking in the inky blood staining her face and clothes.

"Are you—Are you hurt?" he asked. The desperation in his voice tugged at something within her.

Pandora shook her head, even though her leg throbbed in pain. She gazed up at Sol, running her hand along a deep gash above his eyebrow. He winced but did not flinch away from her touch. Warmth radiated from his chest as it lined up with hers. They hadn't stood this close to one another since that night on the balcony. The night he had fully ravished her.

"Evander, *no!*" Mona screamed.

Panic burst in Pandora's chest, jolting her from the hazy stupor of being so close to Sol. She whirled in time to see Evander's sword slice through the neck of the hydra.

"Oh, shit," she whispered.

The severed head fell with a resounding *thud* on the earthy floor. Brief silence filled the space as black blood gushed from the open wound. Pandora gaped in horror as the flesh stretched and flexed, slowing the flow of blood. The skin split and elongated, forming two long necks. In an instant, two more heads appeared, red eyes gleaming with triumph.

Pandora hadn't seen the blow, but now she wondered if the creature had intentionally placed itself in the path of Evander's sword. He had blinded it; perhaps the hydra had decided it was worth the pain to grow back two fresh heads.

This creature was smart. *Too* smart.

Evander's face was ashen and stricken with horror. His translucent wings flapped harder as he withdrew, putting more space between himself and the hydra.

Mona was there, arms outstretched as vines and thorns sprang from the earth. A quick glance upward told Pandora the ceiling had been repaired. The monster was trapped.

But so were they.

The monster reared back as Mona's vines encircled it, tying down its feet just like Pandora's roots had. Screeches filled the air as the beast pulled at the vines, snapping them easily. It stomped backward, away from Mona—and toward Pandora and Sol.

Sol shoved Pandora behind him, her hands meeting the rocky wall as he shielded her from the beast. A serpentine head lunged for him, and his anguished shout made Pandora's heart seize in her chest. Silver blood spurted—Sol's blood.

A scream tore at her throat. She spread her hands, summoning every drop of power she possessed. The ground quaked and split, and this time, more than roots emerged. Vines and bushes, flowers and shrubs—all manner of foliage burst forth from the ground, seeping across the floor like oozing blood. Alarmed, the hydra drew back from Sol, who crumpled, cradling his right arm. It was so covered in blood that Pandora couldn't even see the wound. Massive shrubs grew in size, trapping the creature in like a hedge maze.

"Midas!" Mona screamed. "Midas, *now!*"

Another jolt of energy filled the room, and Mona's vines latched onto each of the creature's necks, tying it down. It wouldn't hold for long. But then Midas was there, sliding under the beast's belly, eyes hard with determination and fire. He thrust his hands upward, fingers grasping the hydra's chest. Gold light flowed from his fingertips, encasing the creature's scales. The light shimmered and spread, bleeding across the hydra one scale at a time. The beast shrieked, heads thrashing, but part of its torso was already frozen, and it couldn't move. Mona's vines snapped, but she conjured more. Pandora added more of her magic to keep the beast at bay. Its chest might be turning to gold, but its long necks could still lash out at the others.

Pandora didn't let herself glance down at Sol, though she felt him near her feet. He wasn't moving.

He's alive, she told herself. *He has to be. He's alive.*

She pushed and pushed until she had nothing left, pouring all her magic into the earthy cage she had crafted. Midas's hands moved to the beast's legs, spreading more gold as the hydra slowly transformed into a gold statue. Each spot where the king touched brought more brilliant gold light that glistened and shimmered. Slowly, the hydra's movements halted. Now, its torso and legs were transformed into gold. The light moved upward, creeping forward until the monster's necks were contained.

One last desperate screech echoed in the air as the hydra struggled in vain to avoid its fate. And then, it fell completely silent as the gold encased it completely.

Gasping for breath and struggling to see through the dizzying fog of her mind, Pandora stared up at the frozen hydra, waiting for it to break free and attack once more.

But it didn't. It was now nothing more than a gold statue, forever preserved in that one moment of fear and desperation.

When Pandora was certain the beast was dead, she dropped to her knees, her hands on Sol as she tried to rouse him.

"Sol!" she cried. "Gods above, Sol, please… *Please.*"

His eyes were closed and his face was ghostly pale. She gingerly touched his arm and choked back a sob.

Three of his fingers were missing. That damned monster had chewed off half his hand. Silver blood gushed from the stumps where his fingers had been.

He was bleeding too much. Even a god could bleed out.

"Mona!" Pandora screamed. "Mona, I need you!" She wasn't strong enough to heal him, but Mona was. Her sister could fix this.

He just had to hold on another minute. He had to make it.

But Mona didn't come. Pandora glanced up, anger and terror warring within her as she searched for her sister. She couldn't see a damned thing past the massive gold statue filling the room.

"*Mona!*"

A figure appeared, and Pandora almost exhaled in relief before she realized it wasn't her sister. This woman had long black hair and vibrant green eyes. In a flash, her eyes had shifted to a brilliant amber—identical to the eyes of the fire witches.

Pandora stilled, her pulse racing as the woman drew nearer. Every ounce of her resonated with power and authority. She stood in an emerald dress that fell over one shoulder, looking regal and commanding as she glanced over Pandora and Sol.

Then, she knelt before them, placing her hands on Sol's injured arm.

"What are you—" Pandora demanded, but the woman shushed her, eyes closing.

Orange light burned from her hands, and for one

horrifying moment, Pandora feared she was like Midas and was turning Sol into gold. But heat filled the air, and Pandora realized it was *fire* emanating from her hands.

"You're burning him!" Pandora shouted, prepared to shove the woman away.

"Be silent," the woman hissed, and when she glared at Pandora, her pupils had turned into long slits, like a snake's.

Only then did Pandora realize who this was. She was a Gorgon sister. She had to be.

The glow of the woman's magic intensified, burning against Pandora's eyes. She squinted, eyes watering, but she was determined to keep them open to see what would happen to Sol.

At long last, the light faded, and the woman withdrew her hands before fixing a solemn look on Pandora. "He is healed."

Pandora lunged for Sol, dragging him half onto her lap as she cradled his face. "Are—Are you sure? There's so much blood."

"I am certain. The fingers will not grow back, I'm afraid. But the wound is closed. He will live."

Tears burned in Pandora's eyes as she stroked the bloodied hair out of Sol's face. He was still unconscious, but the color in his cheeks had returned, and his breathing was steady.

Pandora turned to the woman in gratitude and

amazement. Tears flowed freely down her face as she said in a strained voice, "Thank you. Thank you so much."

The woman nodded, half her mouth tugging upward in a smile. "I saw what you did. Your power is incredible. What is your name?"

Pandora faltered. Her true name didn't really feel like it belonged to her. It had always belonged to someone else, to a life that wasn't hers. So instead, she said, "Trivia. My name is Trivia."

"A pleasure to meet you, Trivia. My name is Marina."

ABSORBED
CYRUS

Cyrus had only just awoken when Prue burst into his chambers, panting as if she'd sprinted through the entire palace. She slammed the door shut and bolted it behind her, then pressed a hand to her forehead.

Cyrus froze in the middle of pulling on his shirt, one arm through the sleeve as he looked at his wife in alarm and panic. "What is it? What's happened?"

Prue wiped sweat from her brow and leaned her head against the door. Only then, with her neck arched, did Cyrus notice the faint bruising around her throat.

Rage coursed through him, hot and merciless, blinding him and consuming him entirely. A low growl escaped him, and he stifled the urge to smash the furniture in the room, knowing his wife needed him in this moment. He drew closer to her, teeth bared, and said in a low voice, "Prue. Who did this? Who touched you?"

Prue's eyes fluttered open and fixed on Cyrus. Slowly, she shook her head. "Cyrus, don't. He'll kill you."

"Who. Did. This."

Prue's face crumpled, and Cyrus watched as her resolve weakened. He stepped toward her, closing the distance between them. Cupping her face in his hands, he forced her to meet his gaze. Terror and despair burned in her eyes. Never before had he seen her so helpless. So afraid. It filled him with a mixture of devastation and fury.

Someone had broken her. And Cyrus would ensure they paid for it.

"Tell me what happened." His voice was gentle because he knew she needed that side of him right now. Not the monstrous, vengeful side, but the side that showed compassion and understanding toward her.

A tear streaked down her face, and Cyrus brushed it away with his thumb. Her lower lip wobbled, and, after a moment, she relented.

"Hyperion," she whispered. "He—He was *draining* my power. Cyrus, it was like he was... eating it." She shuddered, her face twisting into a disgusted grimace. "My earth magic could do nothing against him. It only fueled him."

Cyrus stared hard at the mahogany door behind her,

his gaze unfocused as he tried to recall what he knew about the Titans. He had assumed allowing Hyperion entry into the Underworld had been safe. Nothing he'd read indicated the Titan had any siphoning powers. Was it possible he picked it up in Tartarus? Would the wards even allow a power like that to develop?

"Cyrus," Prue said, her voice gaining strength. "If he has weakened me, I don't think I can face Apollo when he challenges me. I won't be strong enough. I—I think that's Apollo's plan. To drain me completely so I can't fight."

Cyrus's jaw flexed as his mind worked furiously to put the pieces together. After a moment, he shook his head slowly. "No. He wants to *steal* your power. With Gaia gone, you can no longer be used as leverage. You have no reason to help him rebuild the realm. But if Hyperion can steal your power, he can use it to rebuild in your place. Which means Apollo will be free to kill you."

Prue's face paled. It was clear she hadn't considered this. "Oh, Goddess. What can we do?"

The anger rising in Cyrus's chest reached boiling point. He took a shaky breath before stroking his fingers gently along Prue's cheeks, traveling lower until he brushed the bruising of her neck. Red crept into his vision, and he wanted to roar with rage, to drive his fist into the wall.

"I'm going to see Apollo," he bit out, unable to keep his voice from quivering with rage.

Prue's eyes flared wide. "Cyrus, you can't! You have to keep up the ruse. He has to believe you're on his side."

"He knows I'm not on his side," Cyrus sneered. "Otherwise he wouldn't have done this. Part of our agreement was that he wouldn't hurt you. And he's broken that."

Cyrus reached for the door handle but Prue stilled his hand, her eyes full of worry. "Cyrus, he could kill you," she breathed.

"He won't. He still needs me." But Cyrus wasn't sure how much he believed this anymore. He had shown Apollo that Lagos had the power to unlock Tartarus. All Apollo had to do was coerce the demon, and he could unleash the rest of the Titans.

"I cannot do *nothing*, Prue," he said. "He has made a threat against you, and I have to do something. If anything, I have to know what he is planning next. Let me confront him. Perhaps I can... convince him to leave you alone."

Prue arched an eyebrow, her expression full of doubt. Cyrus almost smiled, but the fury brewing inside him was too potent for amusement right now.

"There's something else," Prue said, her face sobering. "I found the Book of Eyes."

Cyrus's blood ran cold, and his pulse quickened. *The*

Book of Eyes. The grimoire that had bound him to the mortal realm. The very book that had granted him enough power to overthrow Aidoneus and take the throne. His throat went dry, and he wasn't certain if he should feel excitement or dread.

"Lagos and I think it returned because your powers are gone," Prue went on. "Do you think it's possible the book can give you your magic back?"

Cyrus shook his head. "I don't want it to."

Prue's head reared back, her mouth falling open. "You—You don't?"

"No. Not like that. The way that book tethered me... It was too restrictive. It held too much power over me. I would rather have no powers at all than to be controlled by it." The conviction with which he spoke surprised even himself. He didn't realize how true his words were until he uttered them. Yes, the book had granted him power. But it had also pulled him to the mortal realm against his will, forcing him to leave the Underworld when it was in danger. He had no choice in the matter.

And what if Apollo got his hands on the book? If Cyrus's magic was linked to it, would that mean the sun god would be able to control *him*? He couldn't risk that.

"Leave the Book of Eyes," Cyrus murmured, resting his thumb underneath her chin. "Let Apollo toy with it. If the book steals his magic or wrestles control from him, then all the better. But I don't want anything to do with that grimoire. Not anymore."

Prue leaned in and kissed him, her mouth salty with tears, but smooth and warm and soft. He captured her lips again and again. His movements were fervent and desperate until he was pinning her against the door, his chest aligned with hers. Her arms wound around him, tangling in his black hair, dragging him ever closer. His tongue twined with hers, and he angled his head to ravish her fully. She uttered a soft sigh in his mouth, and he swallowed it hungrily. An aching, urgent part of him wanted to hike up her skirts and thrust into her this very moment, just to prove to himself that she was alive, she was safe, and she was well. The panic coursing through him was so volatile, so frantic that he needed to do something to quell it. He needed to prove to himself that Prue wasn't in danger. He wasn't going to lose her again.

He caught her lower lip between his teeth, and her hips rolled against him in response, grinding directly into his arousal. He groaned, the sound low in his throat, and pulled away before this woman completely undid him.

"You don't have to see Apollo right now," she said breathlessly, her mouth pink from their passionate kisses. "There is time."

He leaned in, brushing his nose against hers. "I know," he whispered. "Believe me, there is nothing I want more than to take you to that bed, rip off your clothes, and thrust so deeply into you that you forget your own name."

She shuddered, her eyes closing and her lips parting. "Then do it," she challenged.

Cyrus bit back a growl and kissed her again, forceful and bruising, his tongue plunging between her lips to taste her thoroughly. She gripped his shoulders tightly, her body writhing against his in silent demand.

When he broke away, he pressed his forehead to hers, struggling to catch his breath. "I need to do this, Prue. In my former life, I stood by while others threatened my kingdom. I did nothing for my people. I have to be different, even if I am weaker. At the very least, I must tell him our deal is off. I will not help him anymore."

Prue searched his eyes. What she was looking for, Cyrus didn't know. But after a moment, she nodded, and Cyrus stood back to free her from the door he'd pinned her against. She stepped aside, and Cyrus opened the door.

"Be careful," Prue said.

"Don't leave this room," he warned her. "Lock the door when I leave." A lock wouldn't do much good against Apollo's magic, but hopefully, Cyrus's guest chambers would be the last place he'd look for her.

He strode into the hallway, the energy flowing within him reaching an unbearable intensity. He found himself running, breaking into a sprint, desperate to work off this feeling of frustration and helplessness.

His wife had been threatened. Choked. Almost killed. He wouldn't stand by and do *nothing*.

He bolted down the hall and flew down the stairs, knowing Apollo would be in the throne room. That bastard wouldn't be able to resist the opportunity to gloat. He had to be expecting Cyrus. Apollo was too smart not to.

Cyrus burst into the throne room, and, sure enough, Apollo was lounging casually in the throne, sipping that damned Elysium wine. There was only one throne in the room now; at some point, Apollo must have had the other one removed.

Cyrus bared his teeth, his hands forming fists at his sides. With lethal calm, he moved toward Apollo, who watched him with a lazy smile.

"Nephew," Apollo said, lifting his chin. "So good to see you."

"Spare me your bullshit," Cyrus spat. "You swore you wouldn't harm Prue."

"Ah." Apollo sat forward, setting his glass down on the floor before bracing his arms on his knees. "So you *do* care. That was a test, nephew. A test you failed."

"This wasn't part of our agreement," Cyrus snarled. "I'm sending Hyperion back."

Apollo's eyes glinted with amusement. "I'd like to see

you try to overpower that beast of a Titan. He is stronger than he looks. A fact I'm sure your wife is well acquainted with by now."

Cyrus unleashed a roar of rage and lunged, his fingers closing around Apollo's throat. With strength he didn't know he had, he lifted the sun god in the air and slammed him against the wall behind the throne. Apollo gagged and struggled against his grip, his eyes bulging and his face turning red. He clawed at Cyrus's hand, but Cyrus held firm, his grip unrelenting. Heat and power coursed through his blood, making him feel powerful for the first time since he'd woken up human.

"You will not touch her," Cyrus hissed. "Hyperion will not touch her. If either of you so much as *looks* at her again, I will tear off your balls and shove them down your throats."

Apollo's legs flailed as he continued to struggle, his face now turning purple. Vaguely, Cyrus wondered why the sun god didn't blast him with his magic, but he didn't care. The anger flowing through him was so potent, so uncontrollable, that he felt he could take on anything and anyone. He could even take on this sorry excuse for a god.

But then Cyrus's hands began to glow. Warmth pressed into his palm, burning hotter and hotter until smoke wafted from Apollo's neck, filling the air with the putrid smell of scorched flesh.

Cyrus's eyes widened, and he immediately dropped Apollo, letting him crumple to the floor. The sun god fell on all fours, choking and wheezing.

Cyrus raised his hands, which were shaking, his mouth falling open in shock. Brilliant light shone from his fingertips, a mixture of gold and amber hues like the sun.

It was sun magic. Somehow, he had absorbed Apollo's power.

REBUILD
PANDORA

PANDORA COULDN'T KEEP HER EYES OFF THE Gorgon sisters. Even as soldiers and servants flitted about, repairing the throne room as best they could, she found her gaze drifting over to where the three sisters stood, conversing stoically with King Midas. They were almost identical—all three of them had pale skin, green eyes, and inky black hair, although one of them had the left side of her head completely shaved.

Pandora recognized the one who had healed Sol—Marina. She was the tallest of the three, her form slender and regal. She had a commanding air about her that made her stand out among the other sisters.

While Mona helped repair some of the earth tunnels that had collapsed during the attack, Pandora remained by Sol's side in case he awoke. He had been moved to a small cot on the opposite side of the throne room. The witches had offered a private chamber for him, but Pandora had refused. She needed to be here with the others, not only to ask for the Gorgon sisters' help, but also to accept her sentence. She refused to run and hide, even if it was alongside Sol.

Besides, she knew Sol would want to be here, too. He wouldn't want to miss anything. The minute he awakened, he could join the conversation.

With the help of magic and the dozens of servants and guardsmen repairing the underground palace, it didn't take long before the throne room was restored to its former glory. The golden statue of the hydra had been hauled away, and Pandora heard one of the servants mention a "vault" where other golden statues were stored. She vaguely wondered how many people Midas had turned to gold, and how many instances had been intentional.

Once the room had been cleared of debris and servants, Midas sank onto his throne. His hands were gloved once more as he rubbed his temples. Two of the Gorgon sisters stood next to him, whispering fervently to one another. The third sister—Marina—was locked in a romantic embrace with Romanos, heedless of any onlookers as their mouths claimed each other again and again. Pandora found herself entranced by the sight. So much passion and yearning. She wondered how long they had been apart. And gods, the way their bodies wrapped around one another with no restraint, holding nothing back...

"Trivia."

Pandora jumped, whirling to find Mona beside her. With flaming cheeks, Pandora cleared her throat and tucked a stray hair behind her ear. Then she frowned. "You... you called me Trivia."

"Is that all right? I'm sorry. I thought you preferred it. Or was that a lie?"

Pandora flinched at the casual way Mona assumed she had been lying. But could she really blame her, after everything she had done? "No, that was the truth. I do prefer it. Thank you."

Mona offered a tired smile, then gestured to Midas's throne. Evander had joined the Gorgon sisters and was making polite conversation. Across the room, Romanos and Marina finally broke apart and made their way to the throne as well.

"I think they're ready for us," Mona said in a hushed, reverent tone.

Pandora's heart lodged itself in her throat. Gods, she wasn't ready for this. But she squared her shoulders and cast one remorseful look at Sol, who still remained unconscious—before she followed her sister to the throne where Midas sat. She wrung her hands together, painfully aware of how every set of eyes fell on her, their gazes weighted with something heavy and final.

"We understand you were sent to us to be punished for your crimes," Marina said in a somber tone.

Pandora nodded, her mouth turning dry. Marina opened her mouth to continue, but Pandora blurted, "Wait. Please."

Marina's eyes narrowed at the interruption, but she waved a hand for Pandora to continue.

"I—I think Sol should be present for this." Pandora gestured to the figure lying on the opposite side of the room. "He—I—My actions brought about the death of his mother. I deceived him, more so than any other. He needs this closure."

Marina's keen eyes roved over Pandora, as if scanning her for any sign of deceit. After a moment, she offered a curt nod. "Very well. We will wait for the sun god to rise. In the meantime, we must discuss what is happening to the realms."

"It's the magic of Pandora," said Pandora. "Not me, but the goddess who came before me. The one who dabbled in the power of the Titans and created these dark forces. Her box was opened, and now, the dark magic is devouring everything it can get its hands on."

Marina nodded. "Yes, we were aware the box had been opened. We need to address two major issues: stopping the darkness from spreading, and repairing the realms that have been attacked."

Attacked. Pandora frowned at this. Marina spoke as if the magic from the box had only wounded the realms, not destroyed them.

Mona seemed to share her confusion. "The Underworld and Elysium were completely destroyed," she said slowly. "How—"

"An entire realm cannot be destroyed," Midas said. "There are fail-safes in place preventing them from being wiped from existence. The balance of our world hangs on it."

Mona glanced at Evander, whose brows were furrowed. "B-But we *saw* it. The darkness devoured everything in its path. The Underworld was completely eaten away."

"The basic enchantments surrounding the realm would have been destroyed, yes," Midas said. "But the fabric that binds the realm together remains intact. I have seen it myself in the reflection bowl."

Pandora's heart lurched, and Mona uttered a soft gasp, her hands flying to her mouth. "You—You've seen the Underworld?" Mona breathed. "Were there survivors? Is my sister there?"

"Yes," Romanos said. "Prue and Cyrus both survived. But Apollo is there as well. From what we can discern, he seeks the throne."

Heat coiled in Pandora's chest, a mixture of anger and indignation. What the hell was Apollo doing? He had no right to the crown. Did he believe Elysium was a lost cause? Was he so desperate for power that he would invade another kingdom to seize control?

"He can't," Pandora said, shaking her head. "Prue and Cyrus are too strong for him. And the citizens of the Underworld will follow their king and queen. Apollo has no chance."

Her words were full of conviction, but Pandora wasn't sure how much she believed them. Apollo was no fool; if he intended to take the throne, he likely had a scheme in place. He was not one to dive into a foolhardy plan on a whim unless he was certain he would prevail.

"The Underworld is not our greatest concern," Marina said, cutting a sharp glance at Pandora. "With two contenders for the throne, the realm is in good hands. Whoever emerges as the victor will want to have a thriving kingdom to rule over, so they will almost certainly put forth the effort to rebuild the realm. No, our priority is protecting *this* realm from an attack, and rebuilding Elysium so the souls have a place to rest."

"*Good hands*?" Pandora repeated, outraged. "Leaving my home at the mercy of Apollo is not what I would call *good hands.* Do you know the things he's done?"

She didn't realize how harsh her tone was until it echoed around them. Marina's eyes darkened, her chin lifting. Pandora could have sworn the Gorgon rose a few inches in height to tower over her.

"Do not question me," Marina hissed, her eyes changing to the color of flames, her pupils narrowing into slits. "Believe me when I say that Apollo *will* answer for his crimes as well." She cast a quick glance at Midas, whose jaw was rigid, his gloved hand forming a tight fist on the arm of his throne. "But there are more pressing matters to attend to. Right now, we need to send someone to Elysium to rebuild it before the restless souls bleed into the mortal realm."

"How do we do that?" Pandora asked. "My earth magic isn't strong enough." She glanced at Mona, who was frowning, her eyes distant. Pandora wondered what she was thinking.

"It is not just earth magic that's required," Midas said. "When Apollo designed the outer boundaries, he infused them with a fail-safe connected to both his and Gaia's magic. Only with a combination of their magic can it be activated, and from there, the wards can be rebuilt."

Pandora frowned. "We are daughters of Apollo and Gaia." She waved a hand between herself and Mona. "Surely, we can do it."

Before Midas could answer, Mona said, "No."

Pandora blinked at her sister. "Mona, what's wrong?"

Mona looked up, her gaze passing over each deity in turn. "I'm going to the Underworld to help my sister."

Marina huffed in exasperation. "That's not—"

"Try and stop me," Mona hissed, her eyes flashing. In this moment, she looked just as fierce as the Gorgon, her face hard and unyielding. Pandora had never seen her like this before.

"I'm going with her," Evander said, sliding his arm around Mona's waist. "My brother needs me as well."

"Neither of you is going anywhere until we figure out how to save Elysium," Marina barked.

"You have no authority over us," Mona snapped. "We are not your subjects, and you are not our queen."

"I am the vessel of Hestia, the fire goddess who gave her *life* for you!" Marina roared, and this time she *did* rise several feet in the air, her eyes burning amber and her hair floating around her as if it were underwater. Romanos suddenly grabbed Pandora's arm, whirling her around with her back to the Gorgon.

"What are you—" Pandora muttered, struggling against his grip, but he held firm.

"Do not look directly into her eyes," Romanos warned, and Pandora went still, the back of her neck prickling with awareness as a powerful energy flooded the room.

"Hestia dedicated her life to the protection of Elysium," Marina went on, her voice resonating and echoing as if several people were speaking. "Now, it is in our hands. You would do well to remember that Elysium is the home of your ancestors. You are not a mortal anymore, Pomona. You are a goddess. And your duty is to protect the home of your birthright."

A low hissing noise filled the air, and Pandora resisted the urge to look over her shoulder. Had Marina morphed into a snake?

"Marina," Rom called, his voice full of warning. "Settle your serpent. If you turn us all to stone, there's not much we can do for Elysium."

A chill skittered down Pandora's spine. "What is she?" she whispered.

"She has the soul of Medusa inside her," Rom said.

Pandora stiffened. *Medusa.* She only knew the name from stories, but the woman had died ages ago. Cursed with the hair of serpents, she had the power to turn others to stone with a single look.

She's like me, Pandora thought. *Marina is just like me.*

Except it seemed she had bonded with the soul, whereas Pandora was at war with hers. And she was losing.

Gradually, the powerful energies dispersed, leaving a chill in their wake. The hissing sounds vanished, and Romanos's grip on Pandora's arm loosened. Slowly, she turned back to the group to find Marina back to her normal height, her eyes returning to their usual green. She stared Mona down, and Mona glared in response.

"I will go," Pandora said quickly. "I will help rebuild Elysium. I have the blood of Apollo and Gaia in my veins." She wasn't sure what possessed her to say it, but she didn't want the Gorgon sisters attacking Mona.

Marina turned her steely gaze to Pandora before shaking her head. "You are not strong enough, and you do not possess sun magic."

"But I do," said a voice from across the room.

Pandora's heart seized in her chest as she turned to find Sol on his feet. He still seemed pale, and he was cradling one hand to his chest, but his gaze was firm as it locked with hers.

"I'll go with Trivia," Sol said, striding toward them. "We can activate the fail-safe together."

Pandora swallowed hard. How long had he been awake and listening? *He called me Trivia,* she thought. She wasn't sure if he had overheard what she'd said to Mona, or if he somehow knew that was the name she preferred.

She found she couldn't look away from him as his gaze held hers. Something intense stirred in those dark eyes, drawing her in, freezing her in place. It wasn't the same loathing she was accustomed to, but it was just as powerful, just as volatile. She feared if she kept looking, it would destroy her completely.

Why did you push me out of the way when the hydra attacked? she desperately wanted to ask him. *Why didn't you just let it destroy me?*

She couldn't deny it. Something had changed between them. They had both shown they would sacrifice everything to save each other.

But the darkness of her past couldn't be ignored. It wasn't something they could just brush past. Even if Sol did not hold hatred for her like he did before, it was possible nothing had changed between them. She was still a villain who had wronged him.

"It is an acceptable alternative," whispered one of the Gorgon sisters, jolting Pandora from her tangled thoughts.

"Perhaps," Marina said softly. "But we need—"

A deafening *boom* shook the ground and the walls, raining dust and dirt from above. For one horrible moment, Pandora thought another monster had come to attack. But a few servants darted forward, their eyes wide and full of excitement as they approached Midas and bowed deeply.

"What is it?" he demanded, glancing up at the ceiling with wary apprehension. "What has come?"

"My lord," said the first servant, a smile tugging at his lips. "It is Gaia. Gaia has come."

ADVANTAGE
PRUE

PRUE'S NIGHTMARES WERE PLAGUED BY Hyperion's dark eyes as he choked the life from her, his fingers tightening around her throat as darkness pressed in. She woke with a start, her neck throbbing in pain as if the Titan's hands had actually been wrapped around her. Light filtered into Cyrus's bedchamber, and Prue was twisted up in his bedsheets. She didn't remember falling asleep. Her face was sticky with tears.

And Cyrus had not returned.

Blinking sleepily, Prue sat up and surveyed the room, thinking perhaps he was dressing or bathing and she hadn't seen him yet. After climbing out of bed, she padded across the chamber, then peered into the bathing room. When she turned, she found a tray of fruits, cheeses, sliced bread, and raspberry tarts waiting for her in the sitting area. She popped a few grapes in her mouth, her stomach growling, then followed it with a heel of bread.

It wasn't until after she finished eating a generous helping of tarts that she realized a servant had been in here. Which meant someone had seen her in Cyrus's room and could very likely report to Apollo.

But as she glanced to the door for the tenth time, her stomach hollowed, and she feared the worst. If Apollo had killed Cyrus, then it wouldn't matter *who* saw Prue in this bedchamber.

She began pacing the room, wringing her hands together over and over as she deliberated what to do. Her instincts told her to charge after Apollo and demand to see her husband. But what if Hyperion was waiting for her? Would she survive another attack from him?

Besides, what if Cyrus's negotiations with Apollo were going well? What if she ruined everything by storming in on their discussion?

But she *knew* Cyrus... Even if he claimed to be civil, she knew his temper would get the better of him. He would threaten Apollo. Possibly even attack him.

And if Hyperion was there...

Prue stilled, her eyes flaring wide as the food in her stomach churned with anxiety. *Oh, Goddess...*

Would Cyrus survive an attack from Hyperion? If the Titan siphoned energy from him, would it kill him?

Caution be damned. Prue strode to the door, purpose and resolve flooding her veins. She'd waited long enough.

She yanked on the door handle, only to come face-to-face with Cyrus.

Prue yelped, and Cyrus clamped a hand over her mouth, his eyes wide with warning. Wordlessly, he walked her backward into the room before shutting and locking the door once more. Only when he turned to face her did she realize he was panting, and his face was a shade paler than usual.

"Cyrus?" she asked hesitantly.

His hands were braced on the door, his head bowed as he sucked in gulps of air. Hesitantly, Prue placed a hand on his shoulder. He didn't shake her off, so she tugged on him, pulling him to face her.

When he did, she almost staggered backward in alarm.

His eyes glowed *silver*.

Prue's blood chilled as she gaped at him, glancing over his form for any other sign of god power, like his tattoos or his horns or his silver hair.

But no. Only his eyes were different. And the longer she looked at them, the more the silver began to fade, slowly dimming to the blue of his human eyes.

"What—What happened?" she breathed.

"I attacked Apollo." His voice was strained.

"Dammit, Cyrus," Prue hissed, rubbing her forehead in exasperation. She was torn between amusement—because *of course* he hadn't been able to restrain himself around Apollo—and frustration that he would do something so stupid and reckless. "Did he hurt you?"

"No. In fact... when I put my hands on him, I—" Cyrus broke off, then cast her a wary look, as if afraid she wouldn't believe him.

Prue's expression softened. "What? You can tell me."

"I pulled on his power and struck him with sun magic."

It took a full minute for Prue to process his words. She merely blinked at him, uncomprehending, her foggy mind struggling to keep up. "I'm sorry, *what*?"

In a hushed whisper, Cyrus explained in detail his altercation with Apollo. When he was finished, Prue stared at him with a furrowed brow.

"Is it Hyperion's magic?" Cyrus asked. "Was it like this when he attacked you?"

Prue shook her head. "No, he turned my magic to ash and then ate it. And, from what you told me, it sounds like Apollo didn't use his powers *at all*, so there was no way you could have inhaled it like Hyperion did. How long did the sun magic last before it disappeared?"

"An hour. I went to the cave ruins to practice, to see what I could do. It wasn't very powerful, but it was vibrant. Like no magic I've ever felt before."

Prue rubbed her hands together, worry creeping into her chest. She wanted to believe this meant Cyrus's magic could come back. But she feared what Apollo would do. And she feared how his sun magic would affect Cyrus's human form.

"Prue, if I can harm him with my touch, this changes everything."

Prue looked at him, noticing the light in his eyes, the hope shining on his face.

"You can't," she said weakly. "Cyrus, you got lucky. If Hyperion is there next time, or, Goddess forbid, the other Titans, they will *kill* you."

"Not if I can draw from their magic and use it against them."

"And how long do you think your body can withstand that kind of strain? Cyrus, regardless of what strange siphoning ability you have, you are still a mortal. You can't endure as much as you could when you were a god."

Cyrus's jaw went rigid, and the hope in his eyes died. Cold settled into Prue's chest at the way his entire face seemed to dim. For a brief second, she returned to that horrible moment when he first awoke as a human and spat all those awful things at her.

Was he going to do it again? Was he going to claim death was preferable to being here with her?

She held perfectly still, her breath catching, her pulse

racing. *I'm going to lose him again,* she thought, fear sweeping over her like an icy wind.

Cyrus stepped closer to her and slid his hands around her waist, bringing her hips to his. Prue inhaled sharply, surprised at the contact. But the heat of his chest against hers was like a balm to her wounds, and she closed her eyes, reveling in his touch.

"We have an advantage here, love," Cyrus whispered, stroking loose curls away from her face and tucking them behind her ear with soft, delicate movements, as if she were made of glass. "We need to use it. Otherwise, this realm is doomed."

Prue shook her head, a lump rising in her throat. "We know nothing about this magic. What if it's a trick? A trap to get you to overexert yourself so the Titans can swoop in when you're weak and defenseless? What if—"

Cyrus's mouth crushed hers in a hard, fierce kiss, silencing her protests. She trembled, clinging to him, letting him claim her lips with his, letting his tongue sweep along hers. She felt herself melting into him, her fingers gripping his tunic, clenching the fabric to draw him closer.

Again and again, he kissed her, his tongue gliding along her lips and exploring the inside of her mouth. It felt as if he were kissing her for the first time, his movements hungry and desperate, curious and explorative.

When he finally pulled away, they were both gasping for breath. He brought his forehead to hers.

"I love you," he rasped.

Prue licked her lips, struggling to calm her racing heart. "I love you, too."

"We have no one else on our side," Cyrus said, withdrawing to look into her eyes. "It's only you and me against Apollo and Hyperion. And there may be more Titans coming. I don't know how to stop them. If this strange new magic is the way to turn the battle in our favor, we have to do it."

Prue knew he was right, but her insides quivered with terror at the prospect of losing him. She couldn't do this without him. Even if she managed to overpower Apollo, if she lost Cyrus in the process, she wouldn't be able to care for the realm. Not without her husband at her side.

Taking a slow, steadying breath, Prue raised a hand, revealing her palm to him. When Cyrus frowned, she said, "Take some of my power."

Cyrus withdrew a step, eyes wide. "What?"

"Just a bit of it. Let's see what you can do."

Cyrus was shaking his head. "No. I can't. Prue, it could hurt you."

"You need to train somehow. This is the best way. I can tell you how it affects me, and we can see if it works on other gods besides Apollo."

Cyrus stared at her, his eyes hard and unyielding.

Prue raised her eyebrows. "You said it yourself. We have to do it. You can't just rely on luck and good timing when we fight him."

With a sigh, Cyrus drew closer and slowly brought his palm to hers.

Nothing happened.

Prue rolled her eyes. "You have to channel that energy, Cyrus. If touching alone pulled power from me, I would've been reduced to an empty shell after what we did last night."

A half smirk played at Cyrus's lips before he focused intently on her palm. His brows knitted together, and a muscle feathered in his jaw. She recognized the fire brewing in his gaze: his fury. He was channeling the same rage he felt when he faced Apollo. Darkness swirled in his eyes, making them seem black for a moment instead of icy blue.

When he brought his hand to hers again, a cold chill seeped into her flesh, freezing her blood and making her gasp. Icy power flooded her, coursing through her veins. It felt so familiar...

Cyrus immediately jerked his hand away from her, flexing his fingers. Small tendrils of vines sprang from his hand, circling his palm. His face paled as he stared at the magic—*Prue's* magic—as it encircled him. The vines twisted and coiled, moving as if they were alive. They arched toward Cyrus like an animal that wanted to be stroked. After a moment, the vines receded, vanishing back into Cyrus's palm.

Prue cradled her own hand, staring at it. She thought she might find some kind of scorch mark or injury. But she saw nothing but smooth brown skin. Nothing to indicate Cyrus had wounded her by stealing a kernel of her power.

"Cyrus," she whispered before looking up at him. "That icy cold feeling—it felt like *your power.*"

He shook his head. "I don't understand."

"Remember when we were first bound together in Krenia?" Prue asked. "I summoned your black flames. And it felt... just like this. Cold and powerful and all-consuming."

Cyrus swallowed hard, his throat bobbing. "What does this mean? Is my magic back?"

Prue had no answer to this. If it *was* Cyrus's magic, it clearly wasn't the same. And if it wasn't... then what was it, and where had it come from?

A knock sounded at the door, and Cyrus grabbed Prue's wrist before hauling her to the bathing chamber. She opened her mouth to protest, to tell him it didn't matter, but that same fire still churned in his eyes, and she knew better than to argue with him.

He left to answer the door, and she stood there in the

bathing chamber, rubbing her arms to ward off the lingering chill of that strange power.

Subdued voices echoed from the main chamber. After a moment, the door closed, and Cyrus returned, clutching a small piece of parchment in his hands.

"What is it?" Prue asked, drawing closer to scrutinize the parchment.

"Apollo has issued a formal challenge," Cyrus said.

Prue's heart stuttered in her chest. "So soon? But the rest of the Titans aren't even here. Do you think it's because he's afraid of your new power?"

"Either that, or he's found a way to release the Titans on his own," Cyrus said, handing her the letter.

Prue's stomach clenched as she read over the words:

Apollo, God of the Sun and former King of Elysium, issues a formal challenge against Osiris, King of the Underworld. The battle will commence in three days' time in the Undead Wilds. Single combat, to the death. The winner will claim the throne of the Underworld. To refuse this challenge is to surrender the crown.

Prue stared at the words in horror. "Single combat?" she whispered. "But that means—"

"Only one of us can fight him," Cyrus said in a low voice. "And it has to be me."

SENTENCED
PANDORA

The moment those words were uttered, time seemed to freeze. Pandora was numb to her surroundings. All sounds became muffled. She merely stood there, eyes distant as the darkness raged inside her.

And she was powerless to stop it.

She felt weightless, impervious to the world around her. Her body was still like a statue; she couldn't even feel her limbs anymore. Her consciousness seemed to travel outside her body, soaring higher and higher.

Toward Gaia.

The soul inside her screamed and thrashed. Memories of a searing bright light and the pain of her body ripping apart flooded her mind. Her bones quaked from the intensity of it as the light burned brighter and brighter...

Distantly, Pandora registered that someone was speaking to her. Then Sol appeared before her, his beautiful face close to hers, his dark blue eyes full of concern. His warm fingers pressed into her shoulder, and she *felt* it. The heat of his body so close to hers.

Awareness crept in, momentarily drowning out the agony screaming inside her. Pandora found herself blinking, staring up at Sol as if she didn't recognize him.

But she did. She knew this sun god. He hated her. And yet, here he was, standing before her, trying to reach her.

Gradually, clarity returned, and she was able to make out sounds. They blared around her with alarming sharpness, making her flinch. Servants and guards bustled about, trying to make ready for the Goddess of the Realm.

But Sol's eyes remained fixed on hers. "Trivia," he murmured, stroking a finger down her cheek. "We can leave here. You do not have to face her."

Pandora shuddered from the tenderness of his touch, and fire coiled low in her belly as she envisioned him touching her elsewhere.

That was what she wanted: to lose herself in Sol's touch. To blot out the tortuous memories slicing through her. She knew if his hands were on her body, she would forget. She would forget her own name, her own past. All of it. If only he would keep touching her.

"Can't you do something?" Sol snapped at Mona. "You healed her before. Can you do it again?"

But Mona seemed as stunned as Pandora, her expression frozen in shock, eyes wide and face ashen. It seemed Pandora was not the only one apprehensive about seeing her mother.

"I have to face her," Pandora whispered. She wasn't sure if it was *her* voice or the voice of the soul who shared her body.

Sol's gaze snapped to hers, his brows knitting together. "No, you don't."

"I do." Pandora looked up at him, heat burning behind her eyes. "The darkness demands it."

"To hell with the darkness," Sol growled, gripping her arms firmly and lowering his head to look her directly in the eye. "*You* are in control, Trivia. Not her."

A tear spilled from her eye and raced down her cheek. "No, I'm not."

Sol's face slackened in surprise, but before he could respond, another boom shook the ground, this one far less violent than that of the hydra. A shimmer of gold light swirled in the center of the throne room, and a figure materialized. She had long black hair, vibrant blue eyes, and smooth brown skin. Her prominent chin made her look as regal as a queen. Her sharp cheekbones and shrewd eyes gave her a cutting persona that made Pandora believe the goddess could rip her to shreds.

And yet, at the sight of Gaia, Pandora's blood boiled, her chest swelling with white hot fury. The powers within her lunged, eager to devour the goddess, to tear her apart with her bare hands.

Why do you hate her so much? Pandora asked the soul within her, her hands trembling from the restraint it took to hold back the darkness within her. *She did nothing to you.*

She took everything from me, the spirit within her growled, enunciating each word with pure venom.

For a brief second, Pandora lost her hold on the powers inside her, shocked by the admission. Gaia had taken something from the original goddess? What was it?

Her hesitation cost her. In a flash, the vengeful soul wrestled control of Pandora's body, and she could no longer fight her off. She leapt, tackling Gaia to the ground, roaring in rage and anguish as she clawed at the goddess's face.

Gaia's arms flew up as she gripped Pandora's wrists, keeping her hands away from her face, her eyes wide and full of alarm. But other emotions flared in that expression. Grief. Sorrow. Pain.

"No," Pandora hissed in a voice that wasn't her own.

"You don't get to look at me with pity. *You did this to me.*"

She shoved harder, pinning the goddess to the ground. Her forehead cracked against Gaia's, slamming her skull backward into the hard earth. Gaia grunted, her hold loosening on her daughter's wrists. Pandora swiped her fingernails across Gaia's cheek, drawing blood.

Black shadows erupted from within Pandora, shooting outward, creating a dome around the two of them that sealed them off from the others. The shadows whispered and laughed as they danced around Gaia with hungry glee.

But Gaia made no move to stop her or the darkness. Only then did Pandora realize the goddess *could* have summoned her earth magic to strike her, to shove her away, to eradicate Pandora's shadows. But Gaia didn't use magic at all. She merely lay there, letting Pandora claw at her like a feral animal, letting the swirling black smoke swell and draw closer, eager to devour her.

Pandora registered two figures stepping through her shadows. They reeked of death magic—the only thing that could match the darkness of Pandora's box.

Death gods.

Hands gripped Pandora's shoulders, hauling her off Gaia. She spat and thrashed, the spirit inside her still desperate to cause pain, to tear off Gaia's head.

As Romanos and Evander dragged Pandora to the opposite end of the throne room, the shadows dispersed with an echoing scream of rage. Gaia slowly climbed to her feet, brushing her fingertips along the silver blood oozing down her face.

"You should let her go," Gaia said, her voice deep and powerful. "I deserve her fury."

Though her dark powers were gone, Pandora was still hissing and growling, flailing against the gods who held her. She was indeed like a caged animal.

"Do something!" Sol shouted, his eyes wide as he gestured to Pandora.

A kernel of warmth spread through her chest at the look of concern on his face, but it was drowned out by the screams inside her, the memories that engulfed her.

Kill Gaia. Kill her. Destroy her. Rip out her throat.

"Marina," Rom said in a strained voice as he struggled to contain Pandora, who continued to fight his grip on her. "Can't you help? You have Hestia's curse breaking abilities."

The Gorgon shook her head slowly, her eyes calculating as she surveyed Pandora. It was as if Pandora was a fascinating new species to observe, not a goddess in pain. "This curse is bound by the magic of the Titans. *Her* magic. It's stronger than mine. I can't do anything for her."

"Sol, you snapped her out of it before," Mona said,

her eyes brimming with tears as she looked beseechingly at the sun god. "Perhaps you can do it again. Please."

Sol's lips parted, his throat bobbing as he swallowed hard. He shot a glance at Gaia, then said, "Turn her away, so she can't see her."

Romanos and Evander both grunted as they shifted Pandora until she faced the earth wall of the throne room. Pandora screeched in fury, shoving hard against the death gods. But their grip was firm.

Then, Sol was there, his beautiful face before hers, his midnight blue eyes as bottomless as the sea. He pressed his hands to her face, fingers sliding under her chin and along her jaw as he cradled her like she was something precious.

His touch stilled her. She went limp, her arms held up only by the strength of Evander and Rom. Her eyes locked onto Sol's as if entranced by him. He was stunning, with his smooth blond hair and perfectly trimmed goatee, the smooth nose and square jaw and full lips that she had tasted not long ago.

And when he looked at her like that, like she was someone to be treasured, it unraveled the darkness inside her.

"Sol," she whispered.

He leaned closer until their noses brushed. Her eyes closed as she drank in the scent of him, the heat of his body so close to hers.

"You are here with me," he murmured, his voice low and soft and deliciously sultry. "Think only of me. My body and yours. The crash of the ocean waves. The salty sea air."

Pandora knew he was referring to their naked swim together, their bodies entwined, their laughter echoing. That had been the first time she'd let herself be free around him. And it had been exhilarating.

She took a deep, shuddering breath, then opened her eyes to meet his once more.

His eyes crinkled with his smile. "There she is."

Pandora brought her hands to his chest, fingertips running along the fabric of his tunic. His heartbeat stirred from underneath her hands, the rhythm a soothing pulse to the chaos raging inside her.

"Gaia is here," Sol whispered.

Pandora jolted, her body going rigid as her pulse began to race. That darkness flooded her senses again, threatening to take over.

"Stay with me," Sol murmured, running his fingers down her neck and settling his hands on her shoulders. "Trivia, stay with me. You are strong enough for this."

Pandora nodded, even though she didn't agree. She *wasn't* strong enough to fight the soul inside her. She had always been too weak. It was why she had devoted her life to vengeance; because she was powerless to resist it.

"I will be with you the whole time," Sol said. "You can overcome this. No matter what that darkness inside you demands."

Again, Pandora disagreed, but she clung to his words: *I will be with you.*

Perhaps, with Sol grounding her, she *could* do this.

Gradually, Pandora's mind cleared and her senses came back into focus. She registered the Gorgon sisters speaking with Gaia.

"Why have you come?" Marina asked. "What brings you to us?"

"My daughter," Gaia said. "I have come to face her, to accept whatever wrath she brings so her suffering may come to an end."

A choked laugh bubbled up Pandora's throat before she could stop herself. She kept her back to Gaia, afraid that same dark power would rise again, but she felt every pair of eyes shift to her.

"*Now* you've come?" Pandora called out, her voice ringing in the cavern. "I suppose you were too busy to visit over the past twenty years?" Beside her, Sol kept a firm grip on her arm, and she focused on the warmth of his skin on hers, using it to ground her and keep her present.

Gaia hesitated before responding with a defensive edge in her voice, "Apollo cursed me. I was confined to the mortal realm. There was no way for me to see you, unless you came here. But now, Prudence has freed me, and I sensed your presence here in my realm."

"Prue freed you?" Mona asked with a gasp. "Have you seen her? Is she well?"

"She is well, but she will be facing Apollo soon," Gaia said grimly. "I fear for her. For all three of you."

Pandora scoffed and shook her head, crossing her arms as she glowered at the earth wall in front of her. "I'm sorry, but I'm having a hard time believing anything you say. You've just lied *so many* times, it's getting hard to keep track."

"Trivia," Mona hissed in warning.

Pandora ignored her, clinging to the anger she felt toward her mother. There was a strange comfort in knowing it belonged to her and not the memories of her other life.

"Didn't she lie to you your entire life?" Pandora asked Mona. "She lied about who she was and who *you* were, then did nothing when you died and your soul was disconnected from your body."

"She couldn't do anything," Mona argued, but her voice sounded weak, as if she didn't quite believe it.

"Bullshit," Pandora growled, her arms quivering with rage. "She's the Goddess of the Earth. And a powerful witch. I don't believe she was completely powerless."

Mona started to speak, but Gaia cut her off. "She's

right. I had the power to use my magic for the benefit of others, but not myself. I could have done more."

The words should have satisfied Pandora, but they only made her angrier. "Is that supposed to be an apology?"

"I would love nothing more than to offer my heartfelt apologies, if you'll let me," Gaia said softly. "It's all I've yearned to do for twenty years now. But I sense you have more to say to me first."

"You abandoned me," Pandora cried, tears burning in her eyes. "You let him take me to that wretched realm, surrounded by demons and death magic, to be raised by a god who didn't give two shits about me. You could have cast spells, sent messages to the beyond, tried *something* to reach me, but you never did! Not once did you send a messenger or a vision or a tendril of your power to comfort me. Not once did you bother to explain yourself or try to know me. Only now, when *she* is ready to destroy you, when this soul inside me is close to taking over—*now* is when you decide to finally face me and apologize? No. I don't want to hear it. You're twenty years too late, and I refuse to listen to your half-assed apologies and explanations."

Silence rang in the throne room after her words, and Pandora hated herself for the tears that flowed freely down her cheeks.

Several minutes passed, but no one said a word. Gaia

did not try to continue apologizing. Pandora had no words left in her. And the rest of the crowd could only stare, wide-eyed at the two of them as if wondering who would speak next.

To Pandora's surprise, it was Marina who spoke first. Her voice was soft as she said, "I think we have decided on your punishment, Trivia."

Forgetting to face the wall, Pandora whirled to the Gorgons, bewildered by this subject change. But the three sisters were nodding, as if communicating through thoughts.

"Yes," said the sister with the partially shaved head. "A fitting sentence, I think."

"What?" Pandora said in disbelief. "I—I don't understand."

"To pay for your crimes, we sentence you to live in Elysium, to work with this sun god to rebuild it." Marina gestured to Sol, who straightened, eyebrows lifted in surprise. "You will also go with Gaia, who will train you to harness your earth magic so you can become powerful enough to activate the fail-safe within the wards. Once you do that, you are to rebuild the wards and the realm of Elysium so the souls can return to their resting place."

Pandora felt the blood drain from her face. She shook her head, her hands trembling. "I—No. I can't. I can't do that!"

"We have witnessed the power of the soul inside

you," said the third sister, her green eyes vibrant as she looked at Pandora. "It is strong enough, if it can be harnessed. Gaia can help you with this. To work alongside the goddess who evokes such uncontrollable rage from you would be a fitting punishment for the crimes you have committed."

"Please," Pandora said hoarsely, glancing between the Gorgon sisters. "*Please* don't do this."

"Our word is final," said Marina, her face like stone. "You three will leave for Elysium immediately."

DREAD

MONA

MONA COULDN'T DRAW HER GAZE FROM GAIA AS the throne room erupted into a flurry of preparations. She and Evander were preparing to return to the Rhea Desert with the fire witches to use their portal to travel to the Underworld. And Midas was showing Gaia, Sol, and Pandora the way to his own smaller portal, which only had access to Elysium.

Something tugged in her chest as she felt the moments slipping away from her. She had not seen her mother since the day she'd been resurrected in Faidon. Mona had merely walked past her mother, refusing to untie her restraints. Gaia had tried to prevent Prue from raising Mona from the dead. And her lies had made her untrustworthy.

So, Mona had left her there.

That wedge between them had only deepened with each passing day. Mona was torn between regret over the lack of reconciliation between them, and anger at the lies she'd been fed.

She wanted Gaia to know how much she'd hurt her.

But she also wanted her to know how much she loved her. And that, no matter what despicable acts she committed, she would always be Mona's mother.

In truth, it was Gaia whom she thought of when she had accepted Pandora as her sister. She was able to look past those things because they were blood. Like with Pandora, Mona wasn't immediately ready to forgive and forget. But she was willing to love in spite of the choices she'd made.

Now, she was losing her chance to make amends. Midas had bid Sol farewell. Romanos and the Gorgon sisters were climbing back through the tunnel that would lead them to where the fire witches waited for them.

And Sol, Pandora, and Gaia were headed in a different direction, through a back tunnel Mona hadn't noticed before. Mona's heart wrenched and twisted painfully as she watched them. Gaia was the last to leave, and she turned to glance at Mona, as if hearing her raging thoughts, her desperate plea to wait.

"Mama," Mona whispered, tears brimming in her eyes. She wanted to say, *Don't go,* but she knew there was no other way. Gaia needed to help rebuild Elysium before it was gone for good.

And Mona had to go to Prue. If Apollo was trying to seize the throne of the Underworld, her sister would need her help.

Gaia pressed a hand to her heart and bowed her head toward Mona. When she straightened, a single tear streaked down her face. She offered a watery smile that made Mona's throat tighten with emotion.

I love you.

We will speak soon.

I wish we didn't have to part ways.

Those were the words Mona read in her mother's gaze. She barely had time to nod—to show she under-stood—before Gaia vanished through the tunnel.

A shuddering sob broke through Mona, and she wept openly. Evander gathered her to his chest, holding her tightly as she expelled all her frustrations and grief. For so long, she had bottled it up, knowing there were more important matters.

But after watching her mother walk away, she couldn't hold back any longer.

She only allowed herself a moment to cry before she withdrew from Evander and impatiently wiped the moisture from her face. "I'm fine," she said thickly. "We need to go."

Evander dipped his head to look her in the eye. "I am so sorry, Mona."

Mona sniffed and nodded again. "It's all right. Really." When Evander continued to look at her with concern in his eyes, she stood on her tiptoes to press a gentle kiss to his lips. "I'm glad you're with me," she whispered.

He smiled softly, catching a tear with his thumb and brushing it away. "Me too."

Saffron, the earth witch from before, returned them to the Voiceless Jungle where Farah, Wren, and the other fire witches were patiently waiting. It felt like weeks since Mona had seen them, but in truth, not even a day had passed.

To her surprise, the witches were in their snake forms when Mona, Evander, Romanos, and the Gorgon sisters emerged from the curtain of ivy. Mona stopped short at the sight of so many huge serpents, her eyes growing wide.

The Gorgon sisters strode past her, all three of them sighing with contentment at the sight of the snakes. A golden glow encased their bodies, and they, too, shifted into identical white serpents that coiled on the forest floor, twining along the leaves before joining the others.

Mona watched with fascination. Some snakes were coiled within themselves, as if resting. Others were slithering to and fro, as if in search of food.

"What do you think it's like?" she asked Evander, her

eyes on the three white snakes as they darted into a shrub. A few moments later, a shrew burst free, and the snakes gave chase after it. "To be able to shift forms freely like that?"

Evander was silent for a long moment. "I wish I knew. I often wonder if things would have been different if Typhon had manifested himself as some sort of animal, instead of simply sharing my body." When Mona turned to look at him, his silvery eyes were full of sorrow. "I suppose I'll never know."

Mona took his hand, lacing her fingers with his. "He is still a part of you. That much was proven during the hydra attack."

Evander nodded, but his expression remained morose. "Yes. But it isn't the same. And it never will be again."

Mona drew closer to him, and he wrapped his arm around her, tucking her against his chest.

After the witches returned to their human forms, they set off through the jungle. Marina and her sisters led the way, as they knew the area the best. Mona lingered behind the others, lost in her thoughts. She wasn't eager to speak to anyone, and Evander seemed to sense this about her. He kept his hand clasped in hers as they walked in companionable silence. Thankfully, Marina and Romanos were able to fill Farah and the other witches in on what had transpired with King

Midas. Farah seemed alarmed but not at all surprised that a hydra had made its way into Midas's domain.

"It was only a matter of time," said the coven leader as they made their way through the ruins of the village of Sodara. "Between the two realms the darkness has already ravaged, there is only one left that still has anything of value to these creatures."

"Not to mention Midas's powers," Wren pointed out. "He's been hiding under the cover of a coven of earth witches, but now he's been discovered. More will be coming for him."

"Midas can handle himself," Farah said with a wave of her hand. "He has had far more training than the rest of us."

The rest of us. Mona frowned, and, before she could think better of it, she asked, "What do you mean by that?"

Several witches turned their heads to look at her.

"Midas is thousands of years old," Farah said, arching an eyebrow in Mona's direction. "He has had ample time to—"

"Not that," Mona interrupted. "What do you mean by *the rest of us*? You speak as if he is one of you. A witch."

Farah gave a single, slow blink. "Because he is."

Mona's brows lowered. "I don't understand."

"It is rare, but once every thousand years or so, a

powerful male witch emerges," Wren supplied. "In our case, it was Midas."

Our case. "Are you—Are you saying Midas is a *fire witch*?" Mona asked breathlessly, her head spinning with this revelation.

"He was, until Apollo cursed him," said Farah.

"That was after Apollo gifted Midas the power of the sun," Wren pointed out.

Mona shook her head, struggling to keep up. "So Apollo gave him his sun magic... but also cursed him?"

"Complicated, I know," said Wren with a smirk.

"That's nothing like the stories I was taught," Mona muttered, feeling frustrated and a bit betrayed that all the texts she'd studied about the deities from before had been wrong about this.

"And why do you think that is?" Marina asked with a chuckle. "Those of us blessed with immortality have the ability to rewrite those stories as we wish. Midas did this intentionally. He did not want everyone to know what he was capable of, nor did he want to attract too much attention to his witch magic. Male witches are often quite powerful, but not all covens see that as a blessing."

"Not to mention Midas knew the inner workings of spells like no other," said Farah. "According to Hestia, he could manipulate enchantments in ways Apollo never could. Apollo was jealous, and he felt threatened by this."

Mona fell silent at that, still frowning as she processed all this.

"I thought Midas was an alchemist," Evander said in his soft, steady tone.

"He was, after Apollo granted him sun magic," Farah said. "Then, the two worked alongside one another for hundreds of years. After Midas discovered the power to turn sun magic into liquid gold, Apollo wanted it for himself. He seized Midas's research, cursed him, and banished him to the Realm of Gaia."

Mona winced. Such a harsh sentence for someone who had done nothing wrong. "I wouldn't be surprised if *Apollo* had rewritten those stories as well."

"He has definitely rewritten a great deal," Marina said darkly, sharing a knowing look with her sisters.

Mona looked at Evander and found the concern in his eyes matched her own. They were both thinking of Prue and Cyrus and how they were facing such a deceitful and devious god at this very moment.

Mona prayed to the Goddess that she wouldn't be too late.

It took them less than a day's journey to make it back to the Rhea Desert. The trek across the dunes felt like an eternity with the desert wind whipping Mona's hair into her face and flinging dust particles in her eyes. Farah had lent her a scarf to cover her face, and she tightened it around herself. Despite the covering, the sand still managed to embed itself into every inch of her body.

Evander kept his hand locked on hers. Mona wasn't sure if he'd released his grip on her at all during their journey. She was grateful for his strength; it grounded her, keeping her from spiraling into panic at the thought of how long it was taking her to get to Prue.

Once before, Mona had made a treacherous journey across the sea and jumped into a whirlpool to save her sister in the Underworld. Looking back, Mona was shocked at her bravery. Had she really been that bold? It didn't seem like her at all.

In a sense, Mona felt that version of herself was stronger and braver. Right now, she was terrified, and she had Evander, a coven of witches, and three Gorgon sisters on her side.

So why did this journey feel so *final*? Why did she feel that, instead of coming to her sister's rescue, she would only arrive in time to witness her doom? The dread that filled her was unbearable and inescapable. It coiled inside her like a serpent made of ice, chilling her blood and dragging her down. Knots formed in her chest, cinching tighter with each step she took.

When they reached the hidden caves of the fire witch

coven, Farah removed her scarf and swiped sand from her face before turning to Mona. "With the powers of Gaia flowing through your veins, it should be enough to fuel the portal so you can travel through it."

"If it's not, we can help," Marina said, gesturing to her sisters, who both nodded.

"Thank you." Mona tried to smile, but all she managed was a weak grimace. "What will you do after this?"

"We are sending word across the realm to other fire witch covens," Marina said. "It's time to rally our forces. We cannot fight this darkness if we are separated like this."

Mona nodded, her throat tight. "I hope you prevail. And as soon as I know my sister is safe, I'll come back to fight alongside you."

Farah smiled and squeezed her shoulder. "You will always be welcome here, earth witch."

The crowd of witches slowly filed down the narrow passage that led underground. When they reached the massive cavern, several witches immediately shifted to their serpent forms, hissing and gliding along the rocky floor. Mona wondered if the shift was some form of release for them, a way for them to relax and be free. It certainly looked that way.

"I'll show you to the portal," said Wren, jerking her head toward one of the tunnels.

Mona remembered the way, but she was grateful for an escort all the same. The darkened tunnel seemed to swallow them whole as they wound through it, their footsteps echoing and bouncing off the walls.

It didn't take long for them to reach the metal archway. For a moment, Mona studied the etchings and designs, wondering what the symbols meant. Perhaps, if she made it back, she would ask Farah.

"May the Goddess protect you both," Wren said solemnly.

"Thank you," Mona said again, her voice strained. She shared a glance with Evander, and he nodded.

Mona remembered how to power the portal. She had done it in Elysium. Back then, her magic had felt so vast, so endless, that she felt like she could do anything.

Now, she felt weak and helpless, unable to save or help those she loved. What good was all this power amidst so much destruction? It felt futile to even try and stop it.

Even so, Mona stretched her hand forward, her fingertips brushing along the cold stone of the archway. Closing her eyes, she summoned her earth magic.

It took several tries. The weight of her frustrations and worries bore down heavily upon her, making it harder to conjure the magic that flowed through her. After a moment, life sprang forth in her chest, burgeoning through her body. The ground cracked as vines and thorns slithered forward. She pushed more, drawing as much energy as she could and funneling it into the archway.

The portal began to glow an ethereal pale blue that illuminated the dark cave, bathing her and Evander in light. The space underneath the arch shimmered and rippled like water.

"Are you ready?" Evander asked.

Mona nodded, even though she wasn't. But she couldn't afford to hesitate.

Prue was in danger. That was all that mattered.

With one last parting glance at Wren, Mona stepped through the portal, pulling Evander along with her.

SPACE

PANDORA

Pandora was trembling by the time she, Sol, and Gaia reached Elysium. She was covered in sweat, her bones weary and her mind clouded from the restraint it took to keep her darkness in check.

Every moment she stood alongside Gaia was filled with unbearable pain. Leashing the snarling monster inside her took all her effort. When they stepped through the portal and arrived on the barren beach, she sank to her knees, utterly spent from the taxing ordeal.

Gaia knelt by her side and touched her shoulder, as if to help her. The instant her mother's fingers brushed her skin, a hiss of pain erupted from Pandora, and she jerked away, her flesh on fire. Her mother's touch had burned her.

"Don't," she gritted out, wheezing through sharp breaths. "Please."

She hadn't meant to sound so harsh or enraged, but the words came out as a snarl. She had no energy left for controlling her voice. It was truly a miracle she could speak at all; every ounce of her body felt like it was being ripped apart.

Just like when Apollo had used his sun magic to tear into her.

No, not her. The goddess before her.

This isn't me, Pandora told herself. *It's her. Not me. We are not the same. I am different from her.*

But their souls were so entwined that Pandora didn't know what to believe anymore. She had no control. No sense of reality. The past and present melded together until her thoughts were incoherent, and she no longer knew the difference between what she wanted and what the vengeful soul inside her wanted.

Warm hands gripped her arms, and she instinctively flinched away. But it wasn't Gaia. She knew from the touch alone that it was Sol. Somehow, his large, smooth hands were so familiar to her that she knew without looking up that it was him.

"I can carry you, if you need me to," he murmured.

Pandora shut her eyes against the roaring in her ears. Distantly, she heard the lapping of ocean waves, which meant that some part of the Elysium enchantment had held, despite the destruction caused by Pandora's box.

The last time she'd been here by this very portal, Sol had stared at her with hatred in his eyes, pushing her to near death to allow as many people to pass through the portal as possible.

Remembering that powerful loathing and fury from him made her insides tremble for an entirely new reason.

"Why are you helping me?" Pandora whispered, still unable to look up at him. Light shone above her, and it was so similar to Apollo's magic that it made her stomach roil. She worried if she looked too closely at it, she would vomit all over Sol.

"Because the Gorgon sisters ordered me to," Sol said, his tone full of amusement.

Pandora shook her head, her skull throbbing. Gods, she couldn't take this much longer. "No. I mean, why are you being kind to me? You could kick me to the ground and refuse to speak to me, if you wanted. It would be no less than I deserved."

Sol was silent for a long moment. Pandora groaned from the weight of her memories and the screaming inside her. Her ears started ringing, and she thought for sure she would lose consciousness at any moment.

At long last, Sol said quietly, "I didn't realize... until I saw..." He broke off and cleared his throat. "When the darkness seized hold of you in that throne room, I saw just how much power she had over you. And I didn't know... Trivia, I had no idea how bad it was."

She choked on a dry laugh. "You thought I was lying?"

"Well, yes."

She winced. She deserved that.

"But everything I saw today showed me you are a prisoner to her memories and her darkness. You did not choose this. And you're fighting like hell against it."

Pandora slumped forward, but Sol caught her, cradling her to his chest. "I—I don't feel like I'm fighting," she whispered, her body now quivering as a strange chill claimed her. Her skin pebbled, and a cold sweat formed on her brow. "I f-feel weak. I f-feel like I'm losing."

Sol peeled her sticky, sweaty hair from her forehead and tucked it behind her ear. "Keep fighting, darling. You're stronger than you think."

She felt something soft brush against her forehead. For one delusional moment, she thought he might have kissed her there. But before she could decide if it was real or if she'd imagined it, she fell into darkness, succumbing to the pain at last.

.   .   .

Pandora awoke to the sound of crashing waves, this time much clearer than before. They washed over her as if she swam in the ocean itself, letting the soothing salty water flow around her. In her mind and heart, there was nothing but silence. Nothing but the sound of those pulsing waves.

In and out.

In and out.

She exhaled deeply, waiting for the memories and screams to assault her once more. But they did not. Warmth closed in around her, and she sighed with contentment, turning over to press into that comforting heat.

The heat moved.

Pandora's eyes flew open.

She was lying in a bed surrounded by translucent white drapes. Across from her, a set of open balcony doors revealed the oceanside.

A male grunt from next to her made her sit up so quickly that her head started spinning. Her heart leapt in her throat as she turned to find Sol blinking sleepily up at her, one half of his mouth curved into a satisfied smirk.

"Morning, beautiful." His voice was low and deliciously raspy, and it did despicable things to Pandora's pulse.

She practically fell out of bed, panic flaring as she

glanced over her body. Thank the gods she wasn't naked. But she *was* wearing a thin white shift.

Which meant either Sol or Gaia had changed her clothes. She didn't know which option was more mortifying.

She pressed a hand to her chest, struggling to control her breathing. "I—We—Oh my gods, Sol, did we..." She couldn't finish, and she covered her face with her hands, unable to look at him. Her face was on fire.

What had they done?

And why the hell couldn't she remember it?

Tell me my first time with this beautiful man wasn't when I was in the throes of insanity because of a former goddess.

And then, an altogether horrifying idea crept into her thoughts: had that former goddess possessed her body to be with her lover once more? She and Sol *had* been romantically entangled before the goddess's demise. And Pandora's darkness seemed more docile when Sol touched her.

Oh gods, no, please *no...* If another being or entity was using her body like that—

Sol offered a low chuckle. "Nothing happened, Trivia. I swear it. After you fell unconscious, you had these strange fits where your body would seize uncontrollably unless I held you. Gaia asked if I was comfortable lying next to you to ensure you got proper rest, and I said yes."

At the mention of her mother's name, an echo of those screams rang in Pandora's mind once more. She shut her eyes, struggling to clear her head. "Where—Where is she?"

"At the edge of the wards, trying to see how much damage has been done," Sol said, but Pandora heard the meaning behind his words.

She's keeping her distance so you don't lose your shit again.

Pandora ran a hand down her face. "The wards were destroyed, weren't they?"

"No. They were merely deactivated when—" Sol broke off, his eyes flaring with pain.

When Hestia died. Pandora quickly continued, "So, they can still be reactivated?"

"Apollo's side of the wards can. But his power alone was never enough to protect the realm. Gaia will need to infuse her own powers, or rather *your* powers, into the wards in order to strengthen them. It takes the magic of two deities to fully strengthen the protection of Elysium."

"I shouldn't be here," Pandora muttered, crossing her arms over her chest. "You and Gaia can do this without me."

"We could, yes." Sol scratched his chin. "But I don't

think that's the point. The point is to prove you can over-come that darkness inside you and access those goddess powers. This is an opportunity for you to become some-thing more than your curse, Trivia."

Pandora swallowed hard, trying not to feel intimi-dated by this. Already, she had failed. Only five minutes in Elysium, and she had let the darkness win.

Victory seemed impossible.

She changed the subject, frowning at the small bedchamber. A simple armoire rested against one wall, and on the opposite was a set of bookshelves. "What is this place?"

"One of the few homes that survived the attack," Sol said. "Gaia and I spruced it up a bit to make it fit for us."

"Us?" Pandora repeated, her heart skittering again.

"Well, it's clear you can't resist being around me." He gave her a lopsided grin. "You *need* me."

She scoffed, but the reaction was automatic only because he was being an arrogant prick like usual. But the truth was, he was right. If that darkness overtook her again, it was clear only Sol could bring her back.

The thought soured her stomach as she remembered the horror of imagining that former goddess controlling her body. Was she even herself anymore?

"Gaia found a small home across the street that she'll be staying in," Sol went on. "You will have your space from her."

With a sigh, Pandora sank onto the edge of the bed. "Space from her will not help my earth magic."

Sol sat up and scooted forward so they were side-by-side, shoulder-to-shoulder. "No, but we have to take small steps forward, not great leaps. This will take time, Trivia."

"I fear we don't *have* time," she whispered. "The magic from the box will sense Gaia's power. It could return and finish what it started."

"If it does, we will have enough time to go through the portal again," Sol said. "Between myself and Gaia, we are strong enough to fuel it. This isn't like before, with an entire city of people to evacuate. It's just the three of us."

Pandora flinched at the reminder of what she'd done. She'd caused so much destruction, so much loss of life. So many souls and people were now without homes because of her.

That's why you're here, she reminded herself. *To fix things.*

Her guilt would only fester and worsen if she allowed herself to sit here and do nothing.

She stood, letting her hands fall on her thighs. "I should find Gaia. We need to get started."

She was striding for the door when a warm hand grasped her wrist, stopping her. When she turned, Sol was looking at her, eyebrows raised. Only then did she register that he was shirtless, and that damned glorious sculpted chest was only inches away from her, taunting her.

Her mouth suddenly went dry.

"Trivia. You're in a shift."

Her eyes fluttered shut, embarrassment warming her cheeks. "Right. Any idea where I can change?"

"There are clothes in the armoire. I'll give you some privacy."

Pandora opened and closed her mouth, torn between begging him to stay and shoving him more quickly out the door. Before she could decide, Sol was striding out the door, and it closed behind him with a soft snap, leaving her alone with her thoughts and memories.

CHALLENGE
PRUE

PRUE HAD NEVER BEEN TO THE UNDEAD WILDS before. All she knew was that they were a dying wood with dark shadows and an even darker presence that couldn't be explained. The death gods often avoided the Wilds because they didn't want to tempt the darkness festering inside. Even Cyrus didn't know what dwelled in the seemingly haunted forest.

Now, with the magical construct of the Underworld in shambles, it wasn't a forest at all, but an expanse of misty darkness. Prue could sense nothing but Cyrus walking alongside her and the solid ground at her feet with each step she took. Everything else was obscured in shadow, a fog that concealed all and made her feel like she was walking on a cloud.

Of course Apollo would choose a place like this for the challenge. He likely hoped it would unsettle them.

Cyrus's hand was clamped tightly in hers, his form rigid and his steps unwavering. He exuded confidence and rage, his body lethal and powerful. Not a trace of nerves or anxiety or fear. He was nothing but the magnificent god Prue knew him to be. Even if he was mortal, even if his magic wasn't the same—he would always be that same otherworldly being to her.

For the past three days, they had trained together. Cyrus had siphoned her power a little at a time, then used it to summon flora at will. After Prue rested and recovered, he did it again. He had become more precise, able to determine how much power to drain in order to cast certain spells.

But she was afraid it wouldn't be enough.

She squeezed his fingers and took a steadying breath, trying to still the trembling within her chest. "I don't care what the terms of the challenge are," she whispered. "If he overpowers you, I'm interfering."

Cyrus cut her a sharp glance. "You can't. It will forfeit the terms."

"I don't care. If he's about to kill you, you're going to lose the challenge anyway." When he opened his mouth to argue, Prue said, "Wouldn't you do the same, if it were me?"

His mouth clamped shut, his brows lowering.

Prue almost laughed. "That's what I thought. Besides, I doubt Hyperion will stand by and do nothing if you overpower Apollo."

Cyrus heaved a shaky sigh, the only sign of his unease. "Prue, if you get too close, I—I'm not sure if I can protect you. I know nothing about this power. If I absorb too much magic, and it becomes volatile, you could get hurt."

"I can shield myself," Prue assured him. "My mother taught me how. Don't worry about me, Cyrus. No matter what, I'm not leaving you."

Cyrus halted, then turned to look at her, his expression stricken and his eyes filling with a panicked desperation. In a swift movement, he seized her face and kissed her deeply. His mouth glided over hers, his tongue sweeping along her lips and tasting her with expert precision. She gripped his tunic, fingers fisting the fabric as she drew him closer, intensifying the kiss with several strokes of her tongue. Her body molded to fit his, their hips aligning. His hands came along her waist, then slid lower until he cupped her ass. She gasped, withdrawing to give him a look that was part amusement, part confusion.

"What was that for?" she asked breathlessly.

"That was for all the moments I wasted not kissing you," he whispered, his hand catching one of her curls and coiling it around his finger. "You have always stood by me, Prue. Not once have you faltered, even during my most despicable moments. I do not deserve you."

Prue brought her hand to his cheek, trailing her fingertips along his jawline until he shuddered, his eyelids fluttering closed from the tender contact. "Don't worry," she breathed. "You can repay me by remaining by my side during my darkest moments. I'm sure there will be more of those to come."

He frowned. "Not if I have anything to say about it." He kissed her again, this time soft and gentle until her stomach dipped with heat and her body melted against him. She sighed into his mouth as he caught her lip between his and tugged gently. "I vow to spend every night worshiping your body, proving how sorry I am and how precious you are to me."

Half her mouth quirked upward, even as her toes curled from the sultry promise of his words. "Well, that sounds like an acceptable offer. But I will have to think on it."

He chuckled, the sound low in his throat, then withdrew, clasping her hand in his again as they walked forward once more.

When Prue sensed the powerful presence of Apollo, she stopped, and Cyrus followed suit. They stood there, side-by-side, waiting for their enemy to reveal himself.

Gradually, the mist parted to reveal Apollo in fighting leathers and metal spaulders that covered his shoulders. He had a wicked smile in place, his eyes glinting. Like Cyrus, he presented/ nothing but confidence.

"Come to watch the show, daughter?" Apollo called out, spreading his arms. "It should be an entertaining fight, if a bit short."

Prue only glared at him, refusing to be baited. "Where is your Titan leech?"

"Nearby, in case he is needed," Apollo said vaguely. "But don't worry. He won't interfere with the terms of our challenge, so long as *you* don't." He leveled a significant look at Prue.

She raised her chin. "I am here to support my husband. Nothing more."

"How noble of you," Apollo said with a mocking scoff. "But I'm afraid I must insist you remain twenty paces away. For your own protection, of course." He grinned.

Prue only gripped Cyrus's hand more tightly. He turned to face her, his expression eerily calm. "It's all right." Slowly, he extricated his hand and moved away from her, drawing closer to Apollo. A chill immediately swept over her as Cyrus's warmth disappeared. She rubbed her arms, swallowing around the lump of emotion in her throat.

Whispers echoed behind her, and she stiffened, glancing over her shoulder. Was this place truly haunted? After a moment, Prue sensed another presence drawing nearer. Her body tensed, expecting Hyperion to lunge for her. Her heart slammed painfully in her chest as she squinted, trying to peer through the mist.

Her breath caught in her throat as she made out not one, but *several* figures approaching. She stood straighter, alarm coursing through her. A scream built in her throat just before a familiar voice called out, "It's only us!"

Prue closed her eyes, trying to still her racing heart as Lagos came into view, followed by more than two dozen other demons. Some were members of the castle staff, while others she recognized from Erebos, the village of demons. A smile played at the edges of her mouth as she took in this crowd that had come to cheer on their king.

"What's this, now?" Apollo demanded, his voice laced with irritation. "You cannot ambush me with an army, nephew."

Cyrus had turned to stare at the crowd, his face pale and his eyes flaring wide with surprise.

"We are here in support of King Cyrus, the only *true* king of the Underworld," Lagos said, his voice ringing with authority.

Prue felt her eyes well up with tears of pride as she smiled gratefully at her friend. Lagos must have told all these demons what Cyrus had been doing—his deception toward Apollo, and the devotion to his kingdom that brought him here, facing the sun god who was far more powerful than he was.

"I did not ask any of you to come," Cyrus said, his voice full of uncertainty and shame. Prue knew what he was thinking: that he did not deserve this show of loyalty. That he was not a king who was worthy of them.

"We are aware of everything you have sacrificed for this kingdom," Lagos said, bowing deeply to Cyrus. "And this is how we show our appreciation."

"That's all well and good," Apollo said impatiently, "but you cannot—"

"The terms of your challenge do not prohibit an audience from watching," Prue called out. "If you did not want witnesses, you should have specified."

"That's not—I don't—" Apollo broke off, then sighed. "Fine. But I have brought my own witness as well. Hyperion, you can show yourself."

Like a phantom, the Titan materialized several paces behind Apollo, his dark and hungry gaze fixed on Prue. Her skin prickled with awareness, and she had the distinct impression that the taste of her magic had only made him ravenous for more.

He would devour her if he had the chance.

Her eyebrows lowered, and she bared her teeth at him. *Try and take it,* she thought. *See what happens.*

Something about the sight of her people rallying behind her husband had blotted out all her fear and concern. In this moment, she felt invincible. She hoped Cyrus felt the same.

"Oh, and the others as well," Apollo said idly. "They can show themselves, too."

Prue stiffened as several other figures appeared alongside Hyperion. Only then did she notice the sharp and pungent odor of their dark, unholy magic. It had been masked by the presence of the Underworld demons, but now it was stark and potent. She knew that scent...

It smelled like Kronos.

Prue's blood ran cold as the awful realization set in. Her chest constricted as she counted the dark forms that flanked Hyperion.

Eleven. And deep down, she knew that if Kronos were still alive, there would have been twelve figures standing there.

The Titans had arrived.

RESTRAINT
PANDORA

PANDORA WANTED TO FIND GAIA RIGHT AWAY, BUT Sol urged her to wait.

"Small steps," he reminded her. "If you pass out again, we'll have to start all over."

She'd wanted to protest, but he was right. She couldn't push herself too hard, or this would never work.

They started with leaving the house and stepping out into the open air. As soon as Pandora got a whiff of Gaia's potent magic—which swarmed and swelled around her like a fog—she felt ill and darted back inside.

A few hours later, she tried again, going as far as Gaia's front door before she had to retreat to the safety of her room once more.

It took a full day before Pandora could face Gaia without fleeing. The goddess was patient, waiting for

Pandora to come to her in her own time. This was both gratifying and infuriating. Pandora felt like a raging toddler, with Gaia placating her and waiting for her tantrums to subside. This was her *mother.* And she wasn't even trying to reach Pandora. Wasn't trying to apologize or explain or even look at her. And it stung more than she cared to admit. She wasn't sure what she was expecting—either a cold and callous being who held no remorse, or a mother so wracked with grief and torment that she would be on her knees, sobbing for Pandora's forgiveness day and night.

This woman was neither. She was aloof and distant, but the emotion in her eyes was so strong it tied Pandora's stomach into knots. And the way she had greeted her in the Voiceless Jungle... Well, Pandora had almost believed her grief had been real.

Or was it only an act? Was she only here to restore her former home without the interference of Apollo? Was Pandora merely another pawn in someone else's game?

She was tired of being used. She had been used her entire life for a vengeance that was not hers. The darkness inside her had promised it would be her ally, her supporter, a source of strength. But once it got what it wanted, it cast her aside, and now it was trying to take over.

Pandora clenched and unclenched her fingers into

fists as she stood on the threshold of Gaia's living room. She had made it into the house. Sol had gone ahead of her to warn Gaia of her approach. They had made it as far as the kitchen last time, with Pandora facing Gaia for a full minute before bolting.

Now, Pandora hesitated for a different reason. While she was concerned about the raging presence inside her, she was *more* afraid of finally facing her mother for the first time.

She is not a villain or a monster, Pandora told herself. *But she is not a warm and caring person. She will not show you love or compassion. She is not a mother to you.*

It was a difficult line to walk, between the frantic urge to tear out Gaia's throat and the desire for a mother she'd never had. Pandora had to keep the darkness at bay, to keep herself from attacking Gaia again. But she couldn't allow herself to believe Gaia was the warm and caring person she wished her to be.

Shoving down her unease, Pandora took a deep breath and followed the small hallway that led past the kitchen and toward the sitting room.

Gaia was perched on the sofa, back straight and hands folded in her lap. Sol stood next to her, arms crossed. He turned to look up at Pandora's entrance, his brows furrowed and his eyes full of concern. He strode toward her, immediately clasping her hand in both of his, pressing his warmth into her. He knew how his touch affected her, and already, the soothing balm of his heat melted into Pandora, and she sighed, exhaling in relief. Within her, the darkness ebbed, dulling into something faint and manageable.

"Daughter," Gaia said, inclining her head. Her shrewd eyes flitted from Sol to Pandora and back again, but she said nothing about the way they clung to one another.

"Gaia," Pandora said curtly. She refused to call this goddess anything but her name. She did not deserve to be called *Mother.* This woman was ultimately a stranger to her. Nothing more. "Should we move to the outer wards?"

"No," Gaia said. "Not yet. We will begin right here."

Pandora blinked. "Here?"

"Yes. Please sit." Gaia gestured to the armchair on the opposite side of the room.

Pandora hesitated for only a moment before obeying, easing onto the very edge of the cushion in case she needed to bolt from the room. Sol stood next to her, his hand on her shoulder.

Gaia leaned forward, scrutinizing Pandora in a way that made her want to squirm. She forced herself to keep still, to meet Gaia's stare with her own.

"Can you summon your earth magic for me?" Gaia asked. "I need to understand its essence if I am to work with it."

Pandora nodded, then closed her eyes. Her brow furrowed as she tried to sift through all the hatred and rage boiling inside her. Even with her eyes closed, she could still sense Gaia's presence, her earthy smell and powerful aura. The darkness within her festered and thrashed, screaming to be released.

Pandora grunted, struggling to see past it. But the former goddess's power was too strong. It was everywhere, consuming her thoughts, her body, her very being.

"Her hatred for me is overpowering you," Gaia observed.

Pandora exhaled in a huff of exasperation and opened her eyes. "Why? Why does she hate you so much?"

For some reason, Gaia's gaze flicked to Sol and back to Pandora before she replied, "She sought the throne of Elysium."

Pandora's head reared back, and she felt Sol stiffen beside her, his hold on her shoulder tightening just a fraction.

"When I married Apollo," Gaia went on, "I took the opportunity away from her. So, she sought out the Titans, hoping their power would help her seize the crown by force."

"Apollo wasn't king yet," Sol said, his voice low. "You two married well before Jupiter's demise."

Gaia looked at him again, sorrow and regret stirring in her gaze. She said nothing, but Pandora's stomach dropped as realization set in.

"It wasn't just the throne she wanted," Pandora whispered. She suddenly felt ill as the churning in her gut intensified. "It was... *Apollo*."

Oh gods, she was going to be sick. She was going to retch and vomit right here on Gaia's carpet.

The soul inside of her loved *Apollo*. Her father.

Something hissed inside her, all venom and anger, and Pandora realized the soul did not love Apollo. Not anymore. Not after what he had done.

But once, long ago, she had.

Pandora looked up at Sol, blinking through the fog of her mind, to find his expression hard as stone as he glared at Gaia.

"You're lying," he said.

"I am not," Gaia said firmly. "It is true. When she realized she had no chance with Apollo, she sought out another sun god to help her get closer to him, to bring him down if she could not have him for herself."

Sol stepped toward Gaia, withdrawing his hand from Pandora. The darkness immediately swelled, crowding her vision, threatening to drag her under.

Distantly, she heard Sol growl, "Stop it. This is a *lie*. I knew her. And she wouldn't—" He broke off with a sharp inhale. Pandora knew he'd been about to say *She wouldn't do that,* but this wasn't true. The goddess had been ruthless and power hungry. She *would* have done whatever was necessary to seize power. It was what had led to her downfall in the end.

"I am sorry," Gaia said softly.

Sol was panting now as if he'd run a mile. For a long moment, he said nothing, but his breaths became more ragged and desperate. He turned and stormed from the room, his heavy footsteps echoing.

"Sol!" Pandora cried, rising to follow after him.

"Let him be," Gaia said. "He must process this without the reminder of the woman he once loved."

Pandora shot a hateful look at Gaia. "Why did you do that? Was that truly necessary?"

"It was necessary for *you* to understand the full extent of her rage," Gaia said smoothly. "Sol would have found out eventually."

Pandora shook her head, her hands quivering with fury. She was torn between chasing after Sol and strangling Gaia. The earth goddess *was* cold and callous. She didn't care that she'd hurt Sol, who had done nothing but strengthen and support Pandora since the hydra attack. His loyalty was something she did not deserve. But he was here, doing his duty to his kingdom. And now Gaia was crushing him with the revelation that his lover had only used him to get to Apollo. That the passionate love that had shattered him for centuries was built on nothing but lies.

"Do you feel it?" Gaia asked. Her voice was so quiet Pandora almost didn't hear her over her own violent thoughts.

"Feel what?" Pandora snapped.

"Your own rage. It's stronger than hers now, isn't it?"

Pandora gritted her teeth. "That's what this is? Some kind of test for me?"

"That is the whole reason we're here," Gaia said, her expression stoic and unapologetic. "To harness your earth magic so we can rebuild Elysium."

"You can do this without me," Pandora bit out. "You and Sol can activate the fail-safe."

"Pandora, you don't seem to be understanding me." Gaia leaned forward, her eyes sharpening.

"Don't call me that."

Gaia blinked. "What should I call you?"

"Trivia. I am not her. I am not the same as her."

"Very well, then. Trivia, you must understand. This is more than just your punishment. It is more than just a training exercise to help you with your magic. The soul inside you is dangerous and has already ripped apart two realms. It is connected to the very darkness that seeks to bring down our existence. If I can teach you to quiet the voice inside you and trust your own magic, to grow your powers and make you strong enough to complete this task, then it will silence the presence inside you. You will become stronger than her. She will no longer be a threat to you or to our realm."

Our realm. As if Pandora and Gaia could ever belong to the same place.

No, Pandora had grown up in the Underworld. *That* was her home.

But if what Gaia said was true, then Pandora could finally be free. The soul would still be living inside her, but it would be silenced. Pandora would be in control of her body and her mind.

She would be able to shut off these thoughts and emotions. She would be able to live her own life.

The idea was so foreign and yet so appealing... It loosened the tightness in her chest and made her feel weightless. The possibilities were almost overwhelming. What would she even *do* with her life? Her entire purpose had been revenge. What would she do without it?

"Fine," she said in a clipped voice. "Where do we start?"

"We should wait for Sol to return," Gaia said.

Pandora shook her head. "No, I need to do this without him."

Gaia tilted her head, looking at her with interest. "Why?"

"Because... because he is too connected to *her*. It's why his touch affects me so much."

Gaia smiled, her eyes sparking with amusement. "Is that what you think?"

"Obviously," Pandora said through gritted teeth. She wanted to smack that smug expression off the goddess's face.

"If his touch is only a connection to Pandora, then why does it seem to soothe you?"

"Because it soothes *her*."

"So, that voice inside you, it grows louder when he is near? Her emotions intensify when he touches you?"

Pandora faltered at that. Because, in truth, Sol's touch helped to quiet those voices and emotions. It helped bring her clarity.

"If Sol was connected to that soul inside you," Gaia went on, "then his presence would make things worse. Pandora's emotions would fight harder to escape and to reach him. They would drown you out completely." Gaia clasped her hands together on her lap, her eyes intent as she focused on Pandora. "Trivia, I believe it is *your* love for Sol that grounds you. He is your anchor, tethering you to this world and this life, not the one that came before."

"I don't love him," Pandora said automatically, even as her chest constricted from the lie. *Was* it a lie? Well, it had to be. There was so much betrayal tangled up in her association with Sol. How could two people possibly come to love each other after all that? He was her rival, the man she'd hated as a child. His behavior was insufferable.

And yet... He had stood by her. They had saved each other in more ways than one. He had willingly come to Elysium with her. He had shared a bed with her, knowing it was the only way to calm her.

A knot of emotion formed in Pandora's throat, and she couldn't breathe. The reality of her feelings for Sol swelled until it nearly suffocated her.

"That's it." Gaia scooted forward, then stretched out her hand. "Focus on those feelings, and take my hand."

Pandora shook her head, unable to think clearly. Her confusion and disorientation were like a storm in her mind.

"Take my hand, Trivia." Gaia flexed her fingers.

Pandora sucked in a sharp breath, then snatched Gaia's hand.

Immediately, an explosion of darkness burst forth, shrouding everything in inky black shadows. Pandora cried out, back arching, and tried to withdraw her hand, but Gaia clung to her fingers, tightening her grip.

"Hold on to those emotions!" Gaia cried out over the screaming shadows that filled the room. "You are in love with Sol. Don't hide from it any longer. You love him, and you hate me. You hate me for hurting him."

Pandora threw her head back and roared into the darkness, tears streaming down her face. A mixture of rage and grief, sorrow and doubt, regret and longing coursed through her so violently she thought she might faint.

"That's it, daughter," Gaia urged.

White hot anger flared in Pandora's chest, and she screeched, "Don't call me that!"

"You are my daughter," Gaia went on. "Regardless of how much you hate me. I birthed you. I loved you. I still love you. No matter what happens or who tries to take you from me, I will always love you."

"No!" Pandora screamed as sobs tore through her, ripping from her chest. "Please, stop!"

"I wanted to search for you," Gaia continued. Around her, the shadows began to flicker. "But I was so afraid that if I found a way to reach you, Apollo would find out. He would take Prudence and Pomona from me, and I would be alone."

The shadows continued swirling, but they were fainter now. Light bled through the darkness, illuminating the shape of Gaia before her.

"It was selfish," Gaia said, her voice breaking. "I will never forgive myself for not trying harder. I should have done more for you, daughter. And I am so terribly sorry."

"I don't *want* your apologies!" Pandora cried. "They

mean nothing to me! And they can't take away the suffering you caused."

"I know," Gaia said. "That is a burden I will carry for the rest of my existence."

"No, it's *my* burden, too! You think I care that you feel *guilty*? That you got to live your life on that island with my sisters, free to do as you pleased, while I rotted away in the Underworld? You think I care that it tore you up inside? It doesn't make *anything* better to know you feel badly about it. You aren't apologizing for me—you're doing it for *you* to assuage your guilt. So shut the hell up and leave me alone!"

She screamed the last words until her throat was raw, until tears filled her eyes, blurring her vision. When she blinked rapidly to clear them away, she gasped, dropping Gaia's hand in shock.

The shadows had completely dispersed. And in their wake, a bed of vines and leaves lay at her feet, covering the carpet completely.

Gaia wiped tears from her eyes, her face suddenly more haggard than before. Her voice was strained, but her eyes gleamed with pride as she said, "Well done, daughter. Well done."

SIPHON

CYRUS

AT THE SIGHT OF HIS PEOPLE RALLYING TO support him, Cyrus's chest was in knots, his thoughts cloudy with shame and guilt. He did not deserve this. He wasn't worthy of their loyalty. And they shouldn't have come to this place to watch his defeat.

But now, at the sight of those eleven Titans alongside Apollo, Cyrus's stomach roiled, and panic flared within him.

"I should thank your lovely wife," Apollo taunted, his expression full of glee. "Were it not for her, I never would have found the Book of Eyes. The power within it proved strong enough to allow the remaining Titans access to the Underworld."

No, Cyrus thought, numb with disbelief. This couldn't be true. Surely, this was only a nightmare, and he would wake at any moment to find Prue next to him in bed and the Titans still safely locked in Tartarus.

But no. The Titans were *here*. He was too late. Even if he could defeat Apollo in the challenge, how could he possibly send all eleven Titans back to Tartarus?

Dread and despair filled him, dragging his heart down to his stomach. He couldn't do this. It was futile. Why should he even bother? Apollo had won either way.

"Cyrus!" Prue called, jolting him from his thoughts.

With weary eyes, he looked at his wife, who still stood several paces away. She looked at him, and her lavender eyes flared wide. Fear shone there, but also a resolute determination that he envied. He had always admired that about her. She was relentless. And she never faltered.

She nodded at him, then pressed her hand to her chest. He remembered her words from that night: *No matter who you are, or what you are... I am yours, Cyrus. Always.*

Cyrus's eyes burned with emotion as he stared at her, inclining his head to show he understood. His gaze shifted behind her, to the crowd that had come to support their king.

They had come for *him*. Prue was here for him.

He wasn't alone. And he wasn't just fighting for his own life; he was fighting for theirs, too. For his kingdom. For the future of his people.

For the woman he loved more than his own soul.

Slowly, Cyrus turned to face Apollo once more, resolve coursing through him. Apollo's smug expression only fueled Cyrus's motivation to win, to wipe that slimy grin off the sun god's face.

Apollo spread his hands, eyebrows raised. "Shall we choose our weapons?" He snapped his fingers at one of the Titans behind him, but before they could bring forth an arsenal, Cyrus spoke.

"No weapons."

Apollo froze, eyes narrowed as he looked at Cyrus with suspicion.

"No weapons," Cyrus repeated, his voice loud and firm. He wanted to choke the life out of Apollo with his bare hands.

Apollo smirked, then chuckled. "Very well, then. Suit yourself. I can easily kill you with my magic alone."

Cyrus said nothing. Let Apollo believe he had the advantage. Perhaps he'd forgotten what Cyrus had done to him before. Or maybe he hadn't noticed that Cyrus had channeled his own magic in front of him.

"Are you ready?" Apollo asked.

Cyrus nodded.

From behind the sun god, Hyperion bellowed, "Let the challenge commence!"

Cyrus immediately broke into a sprint, lunging for Apollo before he could summon his sun magic. He needed to close the distance between them as quickly as possible. His siphoning powers wouldn't work unless he could touch Apollo.

His opponent reacted quickly. In seconds, Apollo was wielding a brilliant gold orb between his fingers. He flung it toward Cyrus, who dived out of the way, rolling in the dirt to avoid getting struck. He was on his feet once more, gasping for breath, his shoulder burning from the impact.

But he couldn't let his mortal body slow him down. The fate of his kingdom depended on this.

More light soared toward him. Cyrus ducked, then dived again. This time, the magic seared into his right arm, and he roared in fury. The smell of scorched flesh reached his nose, and he lost all feeling in his upper arm.

He didn't dare look at the wound. He knew it was bad. If he looked, it would distract him from his task.

Take him down. Then assess your injuries.

Breathing sharply through his teeth, Cyrus moved again. There were only a few steps between them now, but Apollo was circling him, keeping that distance. He knew. He knew what Cyrus was trying to do.

Apollo's mouth curled into a satisfied smile, and Cyrus knew he was doomed. All Apollo needed to do was keep striking Cyrus from afar until he was too winded to continue. And Cyrus would never get close enough to touch him.

Despair threatened to take over once again, but Cyrus refused to give up. He scanned his surroundings, searching for something he could use to his advantage.

"Regretting not choosing a weapon, nephew?" Apollo taunted.

Cyrus ignored him. A long, jagged stick rested on the ground nearby. He snatched it up, then slashed it in the air directly in front of Apollo. As expected, Apollo reared back to avoid getting hit. Cyrus swung the stick again and again, forcing Apollo backward. The eleven Titans formed a wall behind him; Apollo wouldn't get far, not without colliding with someone.

Apollo glanced uncertainly over his shoulder, realizing he was running out of space. The Titans shifted, inching backward to give Apollo more room, but Cyrus could tell the sun god was uncomfortable being this close to them. Sunlight burned between Apollo's palms, and he unleashed his power.

Cyrus dropped, falling flat on his stomach, keeping low to the ground as the power blasted right above him, singeing the top of his hair. Sweat poured down his face as he rose to his feet. He swung his stick wide, arcing to the left. Apollo fell for the bait, shifting to the right. Cyrus let the stick fall, leaping for Apollo and managing to tackle him to the ground.

Before the sun god could retaliate, Cyrus's hands

were on his throat, pressing hard. He bared his teeth and growled, "Your reign ends now, oh great one."

All the anger and power he felt from before flooded through him. He pictured Prue, her face tear-stained and her neck bruised after Hyperion's attack. In his mind, he saw Apollo's apathetic expression, completely unaffected by the fact that his daughter had been assaulted.

Heat burned between Cyrus's hands, the power growing until his fingers began to quiver with intensity. The air thrummed, and Apollo's eyes bulged as he struggled to breathe.

A heavy force collided with Cyrus, knocking him backward. He groaned, his arms scraping against the ground as he struggled to rise.

Hyperion's dark eyes were fixed on him, one arm lifted as dark shadows spilled from his fingers.

Cyrus glared at the Titan. In an ordinary challenge, this was grounds for disqualification. But with the Titans unleashed, anything was possible. Cyrus didn't want to risk igniting a civil war. If the Titans decided to attack, his people would be the first to die.

From the ground, Apollo climbed to his feet, massaging his neck. He nodded at Hyperion, who dropped his arms and withdrew to the line of Titans.

Cyrus's breath seized within him. *Dammit.* As long as the Titans were backing Apollo, Cyrus would never win.

Power simmered in his veins, eager to be unleashed. But Cyrus had to save it for the right moment. He likely only had one shot. Apollo wouldn't be foolish enough to let Cyrus touch him again. And now that Hyperion had seen firsthand what Cyrus could do, he wouldn't let it happen, either.

Strike him straight through the heart, Cyrus told himself. A single strike of a god's power at full blast would be enough to kill him. But it had to hit him directly in the heart.

Cyrus brought his hands together, and a pulsing vibration quaked through his fingers.

Apollo staggered back a step, his face paling, as he realized what Cyrus was about to do. His gaze flicked behind Cyrus as if searching for a way out. He brought his own hands together, no doubt to summon power to deflect Cyrus's blow.

Cyrus unleashed the full strength of his sun magic, just as Apollo did the same... but his hands weren't pointed at Cyrus.

Time seemed to freeze as someone shouted from behind him. Cyrus's heart constricted in his chest as he heard Prue scream.

"No!" Cyrus roared, turning to see Prue fall to the ground. Lagos caught her by the shoulders before she collapsed. Her eyes were still open, but a searing black mark stained her shoulder.

Her *shoulder.* Not her chest. She wasn't dead.

"Finish her!" Apollo bellowed.

Cyrus faced the sun god once more, finding him on the ground, clutching his bleeding arm.

Cyrus had missed.

But he didn't have time to dwell on this. Hyperion strode forward, his venomous gaze fixed on Prue. He wielded his hands together, conjuring shadows, then blasted them straight at Prue.

Cyrus didn't think. All he knew was he couldn't let this vile beast destroy his wife. He dived, catching the Titan's magic straight through his chest, absorbing the impact before he crashed to the ground. Screams echoed around him, and the smell of burning flesh stung his nostrils. Pain—blistering and unbearable—rocketed through him. He faintly heard Prue shouting his name before he succumbed to darkness.

COLLIDE
PANDORA

"More," Gaia commanded.

Pandora didn't bother stifling her irritation at the commanding tone ringing in her mother's voice. "More *please.*"

"I am not your subordinate. I do not owe you any manners or politeness."

This had become the routine between them over the past two days. They stood on the shore near the edge of the wards, the ocean waves lapping around them.

Gaia was urging her to create a wall of vines that could completely block the wind. From the wind tousling Pandora's red hair all over her face, it was clear she was failing.

Pandora flicked her wrists, clinging to the anger flaring within her, using it to fuel her power. Vines and brambles climbed from the ground, twining around her feet. But the foliage moved slowly, as if something were blocking its movements.

"More," Gaia said again.

"I'm *trying*," Pandora snapped. "It won't come."

"It won't come because you haven't accessed your true powers. Pull on it more, Pandora."

"It's Trivia," she bit out. "My name is Trivia."

"Prove it. Prove you aren't the goddess trapped inside you, but your own woman with your own magic. Show me."

Pandora stifled a cry of frustration and flung her hands toward Gaia, envisioning her ivy coiling around the earth goddess's throat until she choked.

Gaia's blue eyes glinted, as if she knew exactly what Pandora was thinking. "You can't do it without him, can you?" Gaia asked.

"What?" Pandora was too exhausted to decipher her words.

"You need Sol."

A lump rose in Pandora's throat, but she forced it down and shook her head. "He doesn't need to be dragged into this."

"You should send for him."

"He's been through enough," Pandora said sharply. "And I will not *send for him,* as if he is some lackey to be ordered around."

Gaia's eyes narrowed as she scrutinized her. Pandora refused to meet her gaze, worried her mother would see more than she wanted her to.

In truth, Pandora was being a coward. Ever since Gaia had revealed that the passion between Sol and his former lover had been nothing more than a means to take down Apollo, Pandora feared what she would find when she finally confronted Sol once more. Would he despise her all over again? Would he resent her for what the goddess had done to him?

She didn't want to look into those midnight blue eyes and see loathing again. Her heart wouldn't be able to handle it.

If Gaia noticed this turmoil on her daughter's face, she didn't remark on it. Instead, she said, "Let's try something else. Focus on the goddess. Pandora."

Pandora stiffened, nostrils flaring. "I thought the whole point was to leave her out of this. I don't want her growing stronger."

"You won't. I want you to focus on how much you despise her. Think about what she has done to you. To those you love. What has she taken from you?"

Pandora's lips pressed together. "This won't work."

"Humor me."

With a sigh, Pandora let her hands fall against her thighs. "And what if it gives her control, and she forces me to attack you?"

"I can defend myself."

Pandora recalled how she'd lunged at Gaia in the Voiceless Jungle. The earth goddess had not fought back. Pandora had the distinct impression that Gaia refused to fight her. If it came down to it, would the darkness kill Gaia because she would not defend herself against it?

Pandora hated how the thought of killing her mother caused her so much pain. She held no affection for this woman. She loathed her, actually.

But she also didn't want to be the cause of her death. She had caused enough suffering in her life. To add even one more casualty to that list would be too much. The weight of that grief, that shame, was unbearable, and she couldn't possibly carry any more.

"Try it," Gaia urged. She spread her hands, flexing her fingers toward Pandora as if preparing to summon her magic if she needed to.

"Fine." Pandora's eyes closed, and, reluctantly, she thought of the soul inside her. It had been quieted ever since Gaia had evoked Pandora's own emotions. But as she prodded it, opening herself up to those thoughts and that darkness, the energy in her shifted and swirled.

"No," Gaia said firmly. "Do not let her out. Think about *your* feelings toward her. You are still in control."

Pandora's fingers clenched into tight fists. She shut down the darkness, burying it deep, as she instead focused on her own thoughts.

She has taken everything from me.

She broke Sol's heart.

Pandora's fists began to tremble. A quivering intensity shook through her, boiling her blood and rattling her bones.

She cursed me to a life of misery.

She haunts me every day and night.

Pandora's breaths came sharp and fast, and rage coursed through her, heating her body as it churned violently.

She lied to me.

Betrayed me.

Used me.

She cares for nothing and no one.

Something exploded within her as if a volcano had erupted. With a roar, Pandora unleashed the strength of her power, letting loose her hatred and fury. The air shimmered with magic, the power tickling her nostrils.

When her eyes opened, they met a wall of ivy blocking the sea completely from view. The leaves shifted in the wind, but they were layered so thickly that not even a tiny breeze ruffled her hair.

A breathless laugh escaped her, and she couldn't stop the disbelieving smile from spreading across her face.

"You are holding yourself back," Gaia said.

Pandora turned to find Gaia watching her carefully, as if afraid of what she might do next.

Her smile fading, Pandora asked, "What do you mean?"

"You are so afraid of letting her free that you hold yourself back. I think you are having trouble discerning her thoughts from your own."

"Of course I am," Pandora snarled. "She lives inside my body. She takes over my thoughts. I question every-thing because of her."

"But with each summoning of your earth power, you solidify your own intentions. You separate yourself from her. I believe you *know* your own emotions, Trivia. You just have to trust them."

Pandora swallowed hard. "I can't," she whispered.

Gaia stepped closer. "You *can*. You can do this, daughter."

Pandora's eyes closed. She was too tired to demand that Gaia not call her that. She was too tired to argue. And above all, she was far too tired for this fight. She wasn't strong enough to resist the goddess inside her. When her powers unlocked, she knew deep down that that was when the darkness would strike. It would try to take over in the very moment she felt confident enough to conjure the magic on her own.

Right now, it was merely biding its time, waiting for its opportunity.

"I... will try," Pandora said at last. "But I have to rest."

Gaia nodded once. "Of course. We will resume in the morning." She turned to leave, then paused, glancing back, her eyes surveying the wall of ivy that separated them from the waters. "Do check on Sol, will you? If he is in pain, he could use a friend right now. And I don't believe I qualify." A small smile lit her face.

Pandora was about to say that she didn't qualify either, but Gaia had already turned to leave, her feet gliding in the sand as she made her way back to the village.

Like the coward she was, Pandora stood on the threshold of the house she and Sol shared, unable to take that final step and open the door. She didn't want to see him. She didn't want to witness the pain on his face, the misery of losing the one love he'd ever known.

She didn't want to know that he was mourning the loss of that despicable goddess.

And, more than anything, she didn't want to see him yearn for another woman. A woman who was not her.

She wasn't strong enough for it. Not tonight.

She turned, not sure where she was intending to go —perhaps she was crazy enough to ask Gaia if she could sleep in her house for the night—when the door opened.

Her heart lurched in her throat as she whirled to face Sol. His hair was mussed, as if he'd been running his hands through it repeatedly. His dark eyes were wide and a bit crazed. He wore a loose tunic that was open at the front, revealing a smattering of chest hair.

"Trivia," he said softly.

Pandora's throat closed, and she couldn't speak. She couldn't even breathe.

"Why are you just standing there? Come inside." Sol stepped back to let her through.

As if of their own accord, her feet moved, and she stepped over the threshold. Sol closed the door and turned to face her, rubbing the back of his neck.

"You're back," he said awkwardly.

"I am." Her voice was strained, and she kept her gaze fixed on the ceramic floors.

"Did—Did she hurt you?"

Confused, Pandora looked up at Sol. His eyes were full of fear. "What?"

"Did Gaia hurt you?"

Pandora frowned. "No, of course not. Why would you think that?"

Sol shot her an incredulous look. "She was manipulating you. She was using me to hurt you. It's why I stayed away."

Realization dawned on her. Sol figured out that Gaia was provoking her emotions, trying to draw them out. "I —Well—No, she didn't hurt me. Not physically. In fact, it actually worked. It helped me sift my emotions from...”

“From hers,” Sol finished.

The last thing Pandora wanted to do was remind Sol of the former goddess. She took a shaky breath and said, “Are *you* all right?”

He cocked his head at her. “Why wouldn't I be?”

“The things Gaia said...” Pandora trailed off and shook her head. “She shouldn't have done that to you. You don't deserve to suffer any more for this.”

“Well, I *was* upset at first,” Sol admitted. “But I wasn't as upset with Pandora and her lies as I was with myself. I was angry I let myself cling to the idea of her. I let her torment me for years, even long after she'd died, only to find out that what we had wasn't... well, it wasn't real.” He shook his head. “I needed some time to think, but once I processed everything, I realized Gaia had been manipulating *you*. So, I thought it would be best if I stayed away.”

Pandora could only stare at him, her pulse racing from his admission. “So you—you're all right?”

To her surprise, Sol offered her a crooked smile, his eyes glinting with amusement. “Were you worried about me, Trivia?”

“Of course I was! Gaia revealed that Pandora was using you to get to Apollo. You stormed off, enraged. I—

I thought—" She broke off, unsure of how to finish that sentence.

I thought you were still in love with her.

I thought this changed everything for you.

I thought you hated me again.

Sol crossed his arms, which drew Pandora's gaze to the hint of that muscular chest under his tunic. Her throat turned dry, and she found herself forgetting her thoughts entirely.

"You thought... what?" Sol prompted, eyebrows raised. The gleam in his eyes told Pandora he was thoroughly enjoying this.

Pandora was torn between fleeing the house and punching the smirk off his face. She wanted to yell at him for tormenting her like this, but... didn't she deserve it? Hadn't she done the same to him?

She was tired of hiding. She was tired of pretending. And above all, she was tired of fighting what she felt for him.

This would all be over soon. And she had a horrible feeling that the darkness inside her wouldn't let her live through this. She only had right now, and she was determined to make it count.

With a deep breath, she said in a steady voice, "I was afraid for the longest time that you wanted me to be *her.* That you were disappointed that I wasn't. I need you, Sol.

You are my rock during all this, even though I don't deserve it. I don't deserve *any* of this. I—I never meant to fall in love with you. But I did. And now, I couldn't stop it even if I wanted to. I am hopelessly lost in my love for you, and I would do absolutely anything for you. Even if it means giving you the space to grieve a woman I could never be."

The air was still after her confession, and Sol watched her with an unreadable expression. The humor in his face was gone, but the intense look in his eyes made her want to squirm. She forced herself to hold his gaze as he took slow and measured steps toward her. Her heartbeat thundered loudly in her chest until it was roaring in her ears by the time he stood before her.

"You would do anything for me?" he asked, his voice low and soft.

"Yes," Pandora breathed, every ounce of her body coiled tightly by the warmth of his body so close to hers. Close enough to touch. Close enough to taste. She stared up at him, lips parted, knowing that if she stood on her tiptoes, her mouth would brush his.

He raised a hand, catching her hair and twining it around his finger. His knuckle grazed her cheek, and her breath caught in her throat. Then his mouth was at her ear, his whisper brushing her flesh and making her shiver with longing.

"I want to remove every layer of clothing on your body so I can worship you properly," he murmured. "I want you on that bed, your legs spread for me so I can taste you like I did on that balcony. I want your mouth on my cock so we can finish what we started in the library. I want *all* of you, Trivia."

Her skin pebbled, and her stomach turned molten from his words. Slowly, she drew back to gaze up at him, to see if he was teasing her. He couldn't possibly be serious...

But that dark and sensuous look in his eyes... She'd only seen him like that once before: in the library, when she'd been sucking on him, unraveling him, making him come undone for her.

"Will you do that for me, Trivia?" he asked.

Gods above, she couldn't speak. She completely forgot how to breathe. All she could do was stare at him, mesmerized by his midnight blue eyes and the look of yearning on his face.

"Why?" Her voice was barely more than a whisper. "Why don't you hate me?"

He huffed a laugh at that. "I tried, darling. Believe me, I tried. But the moment that hydra came for you, as much as I wanted to deny it, I knew I couldn't lose you. And I'm tired of fighting it. Aren't you?"

Gods, she was. She really, truly was. She was torn between falling to her knees and sobbing at his feet for his forgiveness, and pulling him to her so she could kiss him fully.

Sol watched her expectantly, those blue eyes inviting and full of a dark seduction she was powerless to resist. Pandora couldn't find any words, so instead she tugged on the corset strings of her bodice, pulling them loose. Sol's eyes tracked the movement, and his pupils flared. When it was free, Pandora lifted the corset over her head and let it fall to the floor. Her loose tunic now billowed around her.

Sol swallowed, his throat bobbing. But she wasn't finished. Her hands fumbled with the waistband of her trousers, tugging and wriggling until they slid from her hips and fell to her ankles. Her gaze held Sol's as she carefully stepped out of them.

She had never completely bared herself to a man. With the lovers she had taken, it had been nothing more than a carnal need to fulfill. She had always lifted her skirts for whatever demon of the Underworld could satisfy her.

Her hands shook as she pulled the tunic over her arms and let it fall with the rest of her clothing. Then she stood there, letting Sol appraise her naked form, waiting for him to turn away in disgust. She was no divine beauty, and she knew he'd taken plenty of of lovers. But unlike her, his had been the most stunning goddesses of Elysium. How could she compare?

Sol drew closer, his eyes wide and his lips parted. His hands settled on her shoulders, and his skin was warm and smooth against hers. She closed her eyes as his fingers trailed down her arms, his touches ever so gentle. Her breathing turned unsteady as his palm skimmed over her navel, then traveled up to her breasts. He cupped one, and her stomach dipped, her head rolling back.

"I wish I could paint you," Sol whispered, his thumb pressing against her nipple. A low moan poured from her lips. "You are magnificent, Trivia. Every part of you."

She exhaled a strained chuckle. "Liar. You've seen plenty of naked women, I'm sure."

"Oh, I have."

She kicked his shin, and he laughed.

"Trivia, there's no comparison. It's not just your bronze skin and fiery hair and golden eyes... But your spirit and passion and temper. Gods, it drives me mad."

Pandora snorted. "Is that good, or bad?"

He ducked his head and brought his mouth to her shoulder. "Both." He dragged his tongue along her skin, and she gasped when his teeth clamped down on her. Her hands fisted his shirt, her hips rolling against his. "You have a fire like no other, Trivia. A fire I want to feed and fuel until it burns me. I want your flames to consume me entirely."

"Then what are you waiting for?" Pandora challenged. "I'm naked and ready for you, Sol. Or will you make me stand here like this for you all night?"

"Mmm," he purred against her skin, his lips moving to her neck. "Well, you aren't exactly suffering right now, are you?" His tongue glided along the column of her throat, and she jerked as pleasure rolled through her. "Besides, I enjoy having my way with you like this."

Pandora shoved his shoulders until he stumbled away from her, his eyes flaring wide with surprise. She grabbed him by the shirt, then spun him around to pin him against the wall. With a growl, she ripped the shirt in two, then managed to tug it off his body.

He laughed again, his smile widening. "There's that fire."

She pressed her hands into his chest, relishing the feel of his hair and muscles. Her fingers trailed down his abdomen, over every ridge and curve.

"You toy with me," she whispered, her fingers sliding underneath his trousers, "and I'll toy with you."

She gripped him firmly in her hand, and he jolted against her touch. His hands grasped her waist tight enough to bruise. "Shit, Trivia."

"You said you wanted my mouth around your cock." She knelt before him, then tugged his trousers all the way to the floor. She stared up at him. His eyes were closed, his head leaning against the wall. His arousal twitched, and she smiled.

Without warning, she brought her lips to his length, then ran her tongue along the tip.

Sol groaned, the sound low and hoarse. His hips bucked, and she took him deeper into her mouth.

"Oh, that mouth of yours," Sol ground out, thrusting harder. "Gods, Trivia, that wicked mouth..."

Pandora couldn't stop herself from smiling as she flicked her tongue against him once more, then dragged her teeth along the sensitive skin.

"Trivia, if you—" He broke off with another groan. "If you keep doing that, I'm—I'm—"

She sucked and nipped at him, tasting him thoroughly.

All too suddenly, he withdrew from her mouth. She gasped, reeling backward in surprise. Before she fell rather ungracefully on her bare ass, Sol scooped her up, cradling her to his chest. She yelped in surprise, her arms coming around his neck. His eyes were wild and intense, but he managed a cocky half-smile.

"I told you I wanted your legs spread, my beautiful goddess. I don't want to come until I'm between those glorious thighs of yours."

She found herself laughing as he carried her to the bedroom. With ease, he deposited her onto the bed. She stared up at him with a smile, then spread her legs as he'd demanded.

A low sound rumbled from his throat as he climbed onto the bed, his body poised above hers. His golden hair hung from his head, tickling her shoulder and cheek. He kissed her, his mouth claiming hers with bruising intensity. She arched upward, leaning into his touch, craving him more and more. His tongue slid between her lips before colliding with hers. She moaned into his mouth, her arms coming around his neck to bring him closer.

His lips moved to her collarbone, dragging kisses along her neck until he stopped just above her breasts. He took her nipple in his mouth, then rolled his tongue over it again and again.

Pandora cried out, her head thrown back as lightning crackled in her veins. Gods above, she lost her mind when he licked her like that.

"Your—Your—" She broke off with a gasp when he caught her nipple between his teeth. Her mind emptied, and she lost all sense of where she was.

"My what?" he murmured against her breast.

Pandora blinked, dazed, struggling to recall what she'd been about to say. "Your tongue... is just as wicked."

He chuckled, the sound vibrating through her. Much to her dismay, he withdrew from her breasts to look down at her, his eyes sparkling with mirth. "Ah, but how am I to resist such a perfect bosom?" His eyes held hers as he cupped a breast again, then squeezed the nipple between his two fingers.

Pandora's hips rolled as a strangled sound poured from her mouth. "Gods, Sol..."

His other hand slid down her thigh before brushing between her legs. Her blood heated when he found the moisture gathered there. He dragged a finger along her center, then lifted that finger to his lips.

"Mmm." He licked his finger, his eyes still on her. "So delicious."

"Sol," Pandora rasped. It was all she could manage; only his name.

"When I said you drive me mad," he said, leaning in so his nose brushed hers, "I meant that from dawn until dusk, you consume my thoughts, my heart, my mind. You evoke my rage, my frustration, my desire. You draw out everything from me, even the pieces I want to keep buried forever." He kissed her again, his lips moving urgently and hungrily over hers. "I love you, Trivia." Another kiss. "And I want you to keep consuming me forever."

Pandora's hands threaded through his hair, tugging at the golden strands to pull him closer to her. Her mouth opened wider for him, letting his tongue ravish her completely. Gods, the smooth feel of that tongue as it explored every part of her mouth... It nearly shattered her completely.

"Take me, Sol," she gasped. "Please."

His hands were on her thighs again, and he hitched her legs upward before settling himself between them. "Well, as long as you said *please*..."

She didn't have time to laugh or growl at him. In one swift movement, he slid inside her, and awareness exploded through her body. Her eyes closed, her head rolling back as pleasure built inside her, coiling tightly. Her legs wrapped around him, her heels digging into his back. He thrust deeper with a loud groan, his hands still on her thighs as he spread them wider. He filled her so completely, so fully and perfectly, that she could die right there.

They seemed suspended in time as he held himself still, letting them both feel this collision of their souls and bodies, this acceptance of the feelings they'd been fighting for so long. His dark eyes held hers, flaring wide with a wildness she wanted to explore. She wriggled her hips, demanding more. But he slid out of her instead, and she pulled on his hair, growling a string of expletives.

He laughed. "Patience, love." Then, he drove into her again, and a ragged moan burst from her. He withdrew, then pushed into her again. Each time, he shoved inside her with more intensity, and his pace quickened. Harder and harder he slammed into her until her whole body jerked with each thrust, the bed frame shaking and creaking. His grunts matched the rhythm of his thrusts, and they turned feral and manic as he uttered sounds she had never heard him make before.

He shifted her hips, angling her legs higher in the air

so he could drive into her even deeper. Her vision blurred as pleasure rocketed through her with violent fervor. Every nerve of hers was on fire as he pounded through her again and again. Her moans turned into shrieks and screams, her throat raw as each cry was wrenched from her by force. She no longer knew her name, and she no longer cared about anything but his frantic movements. She could feel him moving inside her, and gods, the friction of him thrusting into her over and over was enough to push her over the edge.

"Sol—*Sol*—" Her fingernails raked down his back as he buried his face in her neck.

Her hips rocked, matching his movements as she urged him onward, wanting more. She was so close to the edge. Fire coiled tightly inside her, ready to spring free. She wanted to tumble off the cliff with him.

Stars danced in her vision, and tears pricked her eyes. She gasped out his name again as release spiraled through her, colliding with the pent up desire burning inside her. It erupted like a volcano, cascading through her body and making her tremble. Soon after, Sol followed, roaring as he came, his body spasming with his own climax.

Pandora clutched him tighter, burying her face in his chest. She could feel his heartbeat racing along with her own. She clung to that, letting it ground her. He had fallen off the edge with her, and now they had both shattered.

For a long moment, they didn't move. Their arms and legs were tangled, and Sol was still buried inside her. She wanted to cling to this moment forever, to preserve it and never let it go. She was still gasping for breath when he drew back to look at her, his eyes full of exhausted satisfaction.

"Damn, Trivia," he panted, swiping the sweaty hair away from her face. "That fire of yours will be the death of me."

She arched against him so she could kiss him, and he groaned when the movement shifted his cock inside her. "I hope not," she murmured against his lips. "Because I want many more nights like this with you."

He laced his fingers with hers, then brought them to his mouth, brushing kisses against each of her knuckles. "So do I."

REBORN

PRUE

THE SPLIT SECOND BEFORE THE TITAN STRUCK her, Prue realized how foolish it had been for her to come here.

She was Cyrus's weakness. And it didn't occur to her until this moment that Apollo would exploit that to win the challenge.

She ducked at the last second, but the lightning from the Titan's unholy power managed to slice into her shoulder, making her bones rattle. Shooting pain spiraled up her arm, and her skin was on fire. With an anguished cry, she cradled her arm, looking frantically for Cyrus. If he had turned to her... If his back was to Apollo...

"My queen!" Lagos shouted, darting in front of her. His big form momentarily blocked her view of Cyrus.

"It's a trap!" Prue shrieked. "Cyrus, *look out!*"

A blinding white light flashed, and another bolt of lightning cracked in the air. Prue dropped to the ground, arms covering her head. Lagos instinctively shielded her with his arms as they both waited for the blow.

But it never came.

Shouts and screams echoed around Prue, and Apollo was bellowing something she couldn't make out.

Panting, Prue rose to her feet, her heart hammering madly in her chest.

Please, no. Oh Goddess, please no...

"Prue," Lagos said, but she pushed past him, desperation pounding within her. Her pulse quickened when she noticed the figure lying on the ground.

"No," she whispered. Horror pooled in her gut, and her stomach sank with dread. "*No.*"

Then she was running, ignoring Lagos's protests behind her, gritting her teeth against the blinding pain in her arm. She sprinted until she reached Cyrus's side. A charred black spot marred his tunic, and steam rose from the wound.

"Cyrus!" she cried in a broken voice. Her shaking hands hovered over his form as she tried to determine what she could do for him. Should she put pressure on the wound?

No, she needed to see if he was still breathing first...

Tears poured down her face, and she choked on a

sob, but she couldn't stop. With trembling fingers, she pressed her hands to his chest, then his neck, waiting, trying to keep still as she listened for a heartbeat.

Silence. Stillness. Then...

Thump, thump.

"Thank the Goddess," Prue whispered, closing her eyes in relief. The pulse was faint, but it was there. She just needed to heal him before his injuries claimed his life.

"*Kill her*!" Apollo roared.

"Prue!" someone shouted.

Prue looked up in time to see Hyperion storming toward her, venom in his gaze as his hands stretched toward her. She didn't have time to run, and even if she did, she refused to leave Cyrus's side.

She was about to die. They both were.

Shrieks of alarm filled the air as something swooped down from above, clipping Hyperion on the shoulder. Hyperion grunted, knocked over from the force of whatever had flown at him. Prue crouched low, her arms clutching Cyrus to her as she surveyed the sky—or rather, the gray expanse that had once been the sky.

Her breath caught in her throat, and she squinted in confusion at the flying figure.

It was a man with glowing translucent wings that beat behind him like ghosts. When he arced, turning back toward her, Prue's eyes flared wide.

It was Evander.

Before she could process this, the ground split, and cracks formed all around her and Cyrus. From the fissures sprang forth vines and roots, curling forward, each one bearing sharpened barbs.

"Mona," Prue whispered in disbelief. She wanted to climb to her feet, to run to her sister, but she couldn't leave Cyrus. Instead, she clung to him, bringing his head into her lap as she witnessed the chaos erupt around her.

The Titans scattered as Evander dived for them once more, his hands outstretched. Prue caught a glimpse of pearly white claws extending from his fingers. He slashed, and one Titan wasn't quick enough. Evander's claws raked through his shoulder, and black blood bloomed. The Titan screamed in rage, falling to the ground and clutching the wound. Apollo crouched low, cowering with his arms above his head as he tried to avoid Evander's strikes.

"Prue!" shouted an achingly familiar voice.

Prue looked over and found Mona racing toward her. Her long, black hair whipped behind her, and she wore a corseted tunic and leather pants. She dropped beside Prue, and the sisters embraced. Prue's tears fell anew at the sight of her sister. Goddess, it had been so long since they'd seen each other.

"What are you doing here?" Prue asked in a strained voice. "It isn't safe!"

"That's exactly why I'm here," Mona said with a smile. "I couldn't leave you to deal with this on your own."

Prue's lower lip wobbled, and she started to cry once more. There was so much strength and confidence in Mona's face that it almost made her unrecognizable. She had a fierceness about her that had never been there before. Gone was the meek, bookish sister she'd grown up with in Krenia. This woman was every bit the goddess Prue knew her to be.

"Mona," Prue choked, lifting Cyrus's head on her lap. He still wasn't moving. "Can you heal him? Please."

Mona frowned as she looked over Cyrus. "What happened to him?"

"One of the Titans struck him."

"No, I mean..." Mona faltered, and Prue realized she was noticing Cyrus's all-black hair and unmarked skin.

"He's mortal," Prue whispered.

Mona stared at her, eyes wide with alarm. "*What*?"

"There isn't time to explain! Can you heal him?"

"I—I will do what I can."

Apollo was shouting something at the Titans. Prue looked up and found him gesturing wildly to the crowd of demons standing with Lagos.

"No," Prue whispered in horror. "*Lagos!*" she cried, waving her arms frantically. "Get them out! *Go!*"

Lagos glanced from her to Apollo, finally understanding. He shouted urgently at the crowd, and within moments, they were fleeing the Undead Wilds.

But the Titans were faster. They surged forward, easily overtaking the crowd. One of them slammed into the earth, cutting off their escape.

Prue pressed her hands into the ground, summoning her magic. Vines and leaves coated the earth, slithering toward the Titans. One by one, her vines yanked on their ankles, tethering them to the ground. Each one yelped, clawing at the restraints, but Prue's magic had bought her people time. They darted around the Titans, continuing their hurried movements.

"Shit," Prue hissed as one of the Titans inhaled deeply. Her foliage turned to ash, and he sucked it up, then roared in triumph. White light burned in the sky, and he struck. A demon fell with a loud cry before the Titan extended a clawed hand and ripped out his throat.

"*No!*" Prue screamed, jumping to her feet. She summoned more magic, then froze as the Titan met her gaze. A hungry smile spread along his face.

He wanted her to conjure her magic. He wanted to devour it, too.

It would only make him stronger. She couldn't.

But her people were falling. The Titans were inhaling her magic, breaking free of her hold on them as they preyed on the innocent people of the Underworld.

"Prue!" Mona cried.

Prue turned to her sister, but before she could face her, more lightning burst in the sky, momentarily blinding her. She shielded her eyes as the glow burned against her, searing her face and warming her blood. A roar of fury exploded around her, making the ground tremble.

And on his feet before her was Cyrus. His eyes were all-white, and they crackled like the lightning dancing from his fingers. His chest was rising and falling with heavy breaths, and his teeth were bared.

"C-Cyrus?" Prue breathed, pressing a hand to her chest in an attempt to calm her racing heart.

Cyrus roared again, then brought his hands together. A ball of lightning formed between his palms, and he unleashed it toward the crowd of Titans attacking his people.

The light collided with them, and white light sizzled through them, scorching their bodies. The Titans went flying in different directions until they collapsed into charred heaps on the forest floor.

"No!" Apollo roared, but when Cyrus flexed his arms toward him, the sun god paled and backed away from him, his face stricken with terror.

Prue gaped at her husband, unable to comprehend what was happening. Her heart pulsed a frantic rhythm in her chest, and she thought she might faint from a mixture of shock and relief.

He was alive. And yet... what *was* he?

He was not a human, but this wasn't death magic, either.

"Cyrus," Prue said again, her voice louder now.

Cyrus's eyes shuddered, and gradually, the white light faded to the usual icy blue. Slowly, his gaze lowered to meet hers. Her heart lurched painfully as their eyes locked. She held her breath, waiting for recognition or hatred or... *some* kind of awareness to dawn on his face. Would he despise her again? Would he forget her entirely?

"Prue," he said, his voice raspy. In a swift movement, he closed the distance between them, grasping her arms and helping her to her feet. Prue threw her arms around him and wept into his chest. The scorch mark still stained his shirt, and the sight of it only made her cry harder.

"I thought I l-lost you," she sobbed, clinging to his shirt.

"Shit!" Cyrus cried suddenly, shoving her behind him. He brought his hands together once more, and lightning split the air before barreling into a Titan, who had been only a few steps away from reaching Prue. The Titan's entire body seized as Cyrus's strange magic electrocuted him. Then, he fell over, motionless.

Prue stared, wide-eyed at the fallen Titan. He did not rise.

"Cyrus, what is this magic?" she asked. "How?"

"I—I think I siphoned their powers." Cyrus lifted a hand, staring at it in disbelief. "When they struck me, I absorbed the magic."

Prue's blood ran cold. "You—You have *Titan* magic within you?"

Cyrus met her gaze. "Yes. I do. But I'm not sure how long it will last. We need to use it while we can."

A shadow slammed into the ground before them, pearly wings outstretched. Panting, Evander strode toward them, not even fazed by Cyrus's appearance or his new magic. He merely inclined his head. "Brother."

Cyrus offered a grim smile. "It's good to see you, Evander."

"I can't hold them off forever." Evander gestured to Cyrus's raised hand. "But it looks like your magic can do more damage than mine."

"Did the civilians get out?" Prue asked.

Evander nodded. "One Titan tried to cut them off, but I took care of him. Unfortunately, my blows are not fatal, so it's only temporary."

"That's all right," Prue said. "With the crowd gone, we don't have to hold back any longer."

She stepped around Cyrus, now standing side-by-side with him. Mona appeared on her other side, her eyes bright with determination.

In front of them stood Apollo, still shouting orders to

the Titans. But there were fewer of them than before; now, only seven remained, and many of them looked reluctant to follow Apollo's orders.

"Apollo!" Cyrus bellowed, his voice ringing around them.

The sun god turned to face him, then blanched at the sight of the four deities prepared to fight him.

"Your Titan attacked me," Cyrus said, his voice loud and commanding. "You have breached the terms of our challenge."

"No," Apollo sputtered, shaking his head.

"You have forfeited your right to the throne," Cyrus continued. "The kingdom is mine."

"*No!*" Apollo screeched. He frantically flung his hands toward the Titans. "*Stop him!*"

The Titans drew forward, but their steps were slow and measured. Instead of surrounding Cyrus, they formed a small circle around Apollo.

"We are finished, Apollo," said Hyperion in his low and deep voice. "We have done our part. Our bargain has been fulfilled."

"You haven't done *shit*," Apollo spat. "I'm not King of the Underworld!"

"That was not our agreement. We vowed to help you during the challenge. And we did. But we will not follow your orders any longer."

"We are finished," said the Titan next to Hyperion—a

beast of a man with deep purple skin, lengthy claws, and two large ram horns protruding from his temples.

"You're *not* finished." Apollo's cheeks were turning red, and his eyes were wild with rage and panic. "You obey *my* command, and I order you to—"

The purple Titan didn't let him finish. With a swift motion, he stabbed his claws right through Apollo's chest.

Prue shrieked and clapped a hand over her mouth. The Titan pushed harder until his claws completely impaled Apollo's chest. Silver blood bubbled from the sun god's mouth, dribbling down his chin. With a hoarse, wet cough, he crumpled, then slid backward. The Titan withdrew his claws as Apollo's form collapsed in a heap on the ground.

Shit, Prue thought as the purple Titan turned his black eyes toward her. "Do not get in our way, little goddess."

"We cannot let you roam freely," Cyrus said, his voice still resonant despite the sight of Apollo's dying form. "You must return to Tartarus."

A few of the Titans laughed. Some of them growled, baring their teeth in fury.

"Try and stop us," Hyperion challenged, spreading his arms as he smirked at Cyrus. "It will be fun to watch you fail so spectacularly."

"Cyrus," Prue whispered, gripping his arm tightly

before he advanced on the Titans. He may be wielding the Titans' power, but as far as they knew, he was still mortal. All it would take was one swipe of that purple Titan's claws, and Cyrus would be dead.

Cyrus fixed his blue eyes on her, and they were full of pain and regret. "You need to get out. Take your sister."

"No!" Mona said.

"Like hell," Prue hissed. "If anyone should leave, it's *you*, Cyrus."

"I can't just let them go," Cyrus whispered, his voice pleading. "They will destroy the realm. They'll slaughter our people."

A knot formed in Prue's throat as she looked at the sorrow in her husband's eyes. She thought of the arrogant, power-hungry god she'd first met and how little he had cared for those around him, even his own subjects. This man before her was so very different. He was willing to give his life for his people—for *her*. He was willing to battle an impossible foe, even if it meant his own death.

Heat stung her eyes as she continued to stare at him. But Prue refused to cry any more. She had done enough of that already.

"Then I will fight with you," she said softly, lacing her fingers through his. "For our people."

Admiration shone in his eyes, and he nodded once.

He glanced over her shoulder to meet Evander's gaze. "Evander—"

"We're staying," Evander said, arms crossed in defiance. Beside him, Mona lifted her chin, eyes flashing.

Prue took a shaky breath as she turned to look at the Titans. They were already advancing toward them, their steps casual and slow, as if this fight would be nothing more than an inconvenience to them.

But Cyrus wielded that same power. And Mona and Prue had embraced their goddess powers. Evander still had his demonic qualities, though they were a strange echo of what they had once been.

The four of them were a force to be reckoned with.

The thought sent fire shooting through Prue's veins, and she clung to that strength, using it to fuel her courage. With a shout, she raised her fist, then slammed it into the earth. The ground shook, and the cracks in the ground widened to massive crevices. The holes spread, causing rocks and roots to crumble as a wide crater formed between them and the Titans. It continued spreading, and the Titans began backing up in alarm. But Prue pressed onward until the hole swallowed up two of the Titans. Their screams echoed as they fell and then, with a loud *thud,* they went silent.

Cyrus looked at her with a mixture of surprise and pride.

Prue gave him a wicked smile. "Let the games begin."

BETRAYED

PANDORA

As much as Pandora wanted to linger in bed all day with Sol, she knew they had an important duty to fulfill.

But that didn't mean she had to rush out of the house that morning.

He woke her by kissing her shoulder, allowing his tongue to roam the expanse of her naked skin. After that, she was straddling him, hands pressed to his chest and her head thrown back as he thrust into her again and again, drawing out ragged moans from her.

Once they'd finished, she managed to get half dressed before Sol came up behind her. His arms snaked around her waist, and his fingers inched up her abdomen to massage her breasts.

The tunic she'd been trying to button had fallen in

tatters to the floor as Sol pushed her up against the wall. Her legs wrapped around him, and he took her all over again, burying himself between her legs and crying out her name as he came a second time. Pandora had to admit his stamina was impressive; nothing at all like the feeble demons she'd tousled with in the Underworld.

Perhaps that was the benefit of tangling with a sun god.

"If you don't stop, we'll keep Gaia waiting all day," Pandora panted as Sol withdrew from her. She retrieved a new tunic from the wardrobe.

"Well, if you would stop looking so damn enticing, it wouldn't be so difficult to resist," he quipped, shooting her a lazy smile over his shoulder.

She couldn't help but grin back at him. It was hard to refuse, especially with how uncertain their future was. The darkness from her box could arrive at any moment, as could the Titans. Plus there was Apollo to deal with. There were too many threats, and Pandora had crossed too many lines to consider herself free.

With the voices and the rage inside her, she would *never* be free. And she refused to drag Sol down with her.

So, she would treasure these moments. Because they very well could be her last.

When they were both finally dressed and ready to leave, Sol drew her in for one last tantalizing kiss— ensuring his tongue ravished her mouth completely—

before they left the house. Her skin and blood were still humming from their lovemaking, and despite the ache between her legs, all she wanted to do was drag Sol back to bed. Perhaps the day would be uneventful, and they could continue their exploits well into the night...

But, of course, she wasn't so lucky.

As they approached the outer wards where Gaia waited for them, Pandora immediately knew something was wrong. The air felt thinner, and the winds were stronger. There was also a heady darkness swirling in the air that was all too familiar to Pandora.

"Shit," she whispered, then broke into a run to reach Gaia's side. Sol said nothing but followed suit.

When Gaia turned, her face was stricken with fear. "We are out of time."

"The Titans?" Sol asked, looking around.

"No. The magic of Pandora's box. It has found us." Gaia turned to Pandora. "It doesn't matter if you are ready or not. We need to try to reactivate the wards. *Now.*"

Pandora nodded, ignoring the spinning anxiety within her stomach. She should have been quicker to rise this morning. If the realm was destroyed all because she and Sol hadn't been able to keep their hands off each other, she would never forgive herself.

"I need you to summon her," Gaia said in a low voice.

Pandora's heart lurched, and her eyes narrowed. "What?" That wasn't part of their plan.

"Summon the goddess within you. Let her magic infuse this area." Gaia spread her arms to indicate the grassy ground at their feet.

"Why?" Pandora snapped. "That's a terrible idea."

"We need to lure the darkness *here*. Distract it from what we'll be doing at the fulcrum."

Pandora swallowed hard. They had not practiced this. The plan was for her and Sol to use their combined magic to activate the wards. But the darkness was here now; they hadn't expected it to arrive so soon. "I've never summoned her at will before. And if she overtakes me..."

"I'll be here." Sol took her hand in his. "I'll stay by your side the whole time."

Pandora looked at him and found nothing but earnest determination on his face. The solid confidence in his eyes filled her with newfound bravery, and she found herself nodding. "All right."

"It will be the opposite of our training," Gaia said. "Close your eyes, and think of *her* emotions. *Her* memories. Not yours. Learning the difference will help you when we reach the fulcrum, so this exercise will be good for you."

Sure it will, Pandora thought doubtfully, but she obediently closed her eyes. The fury inside her had ebbed, thanks to her training and Sol's generous touches last night. Ignoring her instincts to leave the sleeping goddess be, Pandora mentally prodded her, summoning those old memories that had haunted her for most of her life.

The screams.

The burning bright light.

Her soul and body, ripped apart by Apollo's magic.

Pandora slid her hand free from Sol's grasp, and the absence of his warmth only coaxed the darkness forward. A roar built in her chest as the presence inside her stirred to life.

Pandora inwardly cringed at the swelling emotions that intruded on her thoughts.

Pain.

Agony.

Kill them all. Kill them now!

Pandora forced her eyes open and shifted her gaze to Gaia, knowing it would anger the darkness the most.

As expected, a shrill scream echoed in her mind, and Pandora lunged. At the last second, she reeled in those emotions, shutting her eyes again and taking Sol's hand, squeezing his fingers tightly to block out the voices. With her other hand, she flexed her fingers, extending her arm toward the wards. Darkened shadows erupted from her fingertips, saturating the air and stinging her nostrils with the sharp smell of death magic.

"Gods, I never thought I would have to smell that again," Sol muttered.

Pandora blinked. The sound of his voice jolted her from the haze of her memories, and she dropped her hand as the shadows dissipated. "What? Death magic?"

"Not just death magic. Titan magic."

Pandora's stomach soured, and she released his hand again, stung by the reminder that she possessed something inside her that was so foul to him.

Sol took both her hands this time, tugging her toward him so she was forced to meet his gaze. He ducked his head to look into her eyes. "I love you, Trivia. Not this soul inside you. But *you*. Never forget that." He brushed his knuckle under her chin and brought his mouth to hers in a teasing, gentle kiss.

Pandora found herself trembling from his touch, and when he withdrew, she took a shuddering breath.

"I think that did it," Gaia said. "Come. We must get to the fulcrum as quickly as possible."

The air was roaring with turbulent wind by the time Pandora, Gaia, and Sol reached the courtyard that marked the peak of Elysium's magic. In the center was a pedestal surrounded by pillars and braziers. A small copse of trees lined the courtyard, and at the edge of the fulcrum was a cliff facing the ocean.

Pandora's hair billowed around her, and she stared up at the darkening sky with a sense of foreboding. The last time her magic had come to her, she had felt relief, fully believing her revenge was about to be complete. She had shattered her relationship with Sol and revealed her true nature to Apollo.

Oh, how naïve she had been.

"Trivia," Gaia murmured, her blue eyes sharp as they fixed on her.

Pandora blinked away the memories and focused on her mother.

"You can do this," Gaia whispered. "I know you can. You have always had the power within you. And you are stronger than you think."

Pandora's throat welled up with unexpected emotion at the intense look on Gaia's face. The earth goddess truly believed in her. Even though they were essentially strangers and Pandora had sought her death for most of her life, Gaia still trusted her and believed she could do this.

Pandora's eyes burned, and she knew if she spoke that she would start crying. So instead, she merely nodded.

"I will stay down here and warn you if the magic gets too close," Gaia said, inclining her head toward the raised platform of the fulcrum. "But it must be you two on the fulcrum."

Pandora looked at Sol. "Are you ready?"

He offered a grim smile. "Let's rebuild the world, love."

Hand-in-hand, they hurried across the courtyard and toward the dais. Energy hummed in the air with each step Pandora took, and by the time she reached the center, she felt like she was wading through water. Her grip on Sol's hand tightened as they helped each other push through the swelling power around them. It burned against her skin, and Pandora could only assume the magic of Elysium could sense the approaching threat and was strengthening its defenses.

Please, she begged the magic. *Please let us in. We can stop this. Just let us in!*

As if the magic responded to her plea, the air cleared, and Pandora and Sol finally reached the top of the dais.

"Go," Sol panted, squeezing her hand. "Do what you must. I'm here for you."

Pandora nodded, then closed her eyes. The turmoil of her thoughts was difficult to sift through as they raged inside her, awakened by the presence of the box's magic.

My emotions, she thought. *I must access my emotions. Where are they?*

She thought of the intense pleasure and passion she'd experienced with Sol the night before. He was *hers*. Not the other goddess's. But hers alone.

She thought of the pride on Gaia's face, and the softness of that look they had shared. Pandora no longer felt hatred for her mother. A wary sort of acceptance had drifted between the two of them, and more than anything, Pandora wanted to explore that, to see if it could strengthen into something akin to love. She had never before known the love of a parent, and it wasn't until this very moment that she realized just how much she wanted it. How much she would sacrifice for it.

"Sol!" Pandora cried over the rushing wind. "If we don't make it through this—"

"Trivia, don't!" Sol moaned, his voice anguished.

"If we don't make it through this," she shouted over him, "please know that I love you with every facet of my being. And if we survive, I will spend every day of my existence atoning for what I've done to you. I swear it."

"Well, I will accept your atonement in the form of long, sweaty nights with you naked in my bed."

She chuckled, her chest tightening as she tried not to let the laughter pull her out of the magic she was trying to conjure. Sol's echoing laugh resonated in her mind, and she clung to that, to the way it made her heart soar and her skin tingle. The warmth of him, the feel of his hand in hers...

Pandora gasped as earth magic rocketed through her with violent fervor. Were it not for Sol's grip on her, she would have fallen from the force of it. Even though her eyes were closed, she could *sense* the flora spilling over the dais at her feet. Grass sprang upward, tickling her legs. Branches crowded her, forming a cocoon around her and Sol.

"My turn?" Sol asked.

She could only nod, trying to hold on to the burgeoning magic flooding from her. It felt like a dam had burst, and she couldn't contain the power. Alarm flared inside her, and she feared the darkness would take hold of her because she was losing control. It was too much. Too fast.

But then Sol's light bled through her eyelids, glowing and brilliant. Her hand warmed in his as he summoned his power. The dome of branches encased the light, as if the two of them stood alone in the center of a lantern.

The air vibrated through her bones. Sol clasped her other hand, and their magic united. It all came together in a brutal clash of earth and sun, light and flora, green and gold. The collision shook the ground, making Pandora's blood sing. It was so similar to the way their bodies collided last night when they finally came together after so much hatred and animosity. And now, their magic was doing the same.

Power roared in Pandora's ears. A smile spread across her face. It was working. The fail-safe was activating. Soon, the wards would return, strengthening Elysium's defenses once more.

In the distance, Gaia was shouting something.

Pandora's eyes flew open, and she met Sol's confused look with one of her own.

Then, she felt it. Darkness surged, drawing closer. Through the gaps in her branches, the darkening sky now looked charcoal black.

The magic of her box was here.

How? she thought in a panic. She and Sol had done everything they were supposed to. The wards were supposed to be reinforced, not torn down to make way for the very darkness they were trying to stop.

But all around her, she felt the magic flickering. Whatever power flowed between her earth magic and Sol's sun magic was fading, like the dying embers of a fire.

Abruptly, Pandora released Sol's hands, trying to tear through her dome of branches in search of Gaia. Something had gone wrong. She must have made a mistake, because the magic was *here,* and they were too late...

"*It's a trap!*" Gaia screamed.

Pandora froze, her blood chilling. What had gone wrong? Had the darkness of her box somehow tricked her?

She grabbed Sol's arm, intent on fleeing the dais and taking shelter... where? Where could they run? The darkness had them cornered now.

A burst of gold light filled the center of the dais— sun magic. Pandora shot a bewildered look at Sol.

"It—It's not me!" he cried, shaking his head.

Pandora tugged him backward, away from the light as it grew in size. A shape appeared, spreading until it formed the figure of a tall male.

When the light faded, Pandora staggered backward in shock.

The man who stood before them was Midas. His head was tilted back, a look of relief on his face. He grinned broadly, his gloved hands spread wide.

"Ah, thank you," he said, chuckling. "I've been waiting for this moment for *centuries*. And now, thanks to you, I am finally free."

TAKEN
EVANDER

EVER SINCE HE HAD STEPPED THROUGH THE portal and entered the Underworld, Evander could sense echoes of Typhon all around him. It wasn't nearly as potent as when the creature occupied his body, but it was there. Typhon wasn't gone. And that knowledge brought him more comfort than he had expected.

And when he had seen Cyrus lying there unresponsive, while the Titans surrounded him, Typhon's wings and claws had appeared of their own accord. It was as if the demon inside Evander was still there—and it was enraged that his brother was in danger.

Now, he was standing alongside Cyrus and Prue and... and Mona. Gods, all he wanted to do was grab Mona and fly her far away from here. But he had learned firsthand that Mona did not follow anyone else's rules, particularly when it came to her sister.

Mona wasn't going anywhere. And neither was he. Even if this meant the four of them were taking their last stand and these Titans would wipe them from existence, he would not be moved.

Prue pushed more of her earth magic into the ground, and a few more Titans fell into the crater. But it was temporary. Everything they did was temporary.

Only Cyrus had the power to kill them.

"I'm with you, brother," Evander told him. "Just tell us what to do."

Cyrus nodded, his eyes on Prue as she mentally dragged more Titans into her abyss. "Bring them down. Wound them." Cyrus met his gaze at last. "I'll take care of the rest."

Evander nodded, then spread his wings. He shot a warning look at Mona. *Don't die,* he thought to her.

She nodded, understanding his plea and answering it with a request of her own: *Stay alive, Evander.*

He would do his damndest. With a beat of his wings, he shot upward, flying high above the trees. His claws outstretched as he darted back down. He lanced through one Titan, then another. The third was ready for him and launched his massive fist into Evander's shoulder. He grunted, veering to the left to avoid crashing into the

Titan. But hot blood gushed from an injury in his arm, slowing him down.

The Titan growled, drawing closer. Evander's wings flapped repeatedly, drawing him away from the beast, but the Titan was faster. So much faster than Evander anticipated. One moment, he was several feet away, and the next, he was there, his meaty fist clamped on Evander's uninjured arm, dragging him downward.

Evander roared as agony ripped through him. But suddenly, his pearly wings receded, as if they had indeed been nothing more than a ghost.

The Titan gawked and released him, stunned by the disappearance of the wings. Taking advantage of his stupor, Evander struck, driving his fist into the Titan's gut. He struck again and again, pushing the Titan backward. He finally aimed a kick, sending the Titan flying, black blood trickling down his chin.

A crack of lightning split the air, illuminating the ground in front of Evander. Light exploded around the Titan, and then, his body was nothing more than a charred husk.

Evander turned to glance appreciatively at Cyrus, who nodded in return. Another Titan lunged, and Evander intercepted this one, summoning his ghostly wings once more. But they felt weaker than before. He had a feeling they wouldn't last much longer. Typhon's presence had receded, now only a whisper from within.

In the distance, Mona was summoning vines, wrapping them around each Titan's foot. But the Titans were inhaling her magic like it was a feast, drawing power from it. It only seemed to make them stronger as they drew closer to her.

"Mona, stop!" Evander shouted, soaring toward her.

But he wasn't quick enough.

A Titan grabbed her by the throat and lifted her off her feet. Mona scrambled, her legs flailing and her fingers clawing at his fist, trying to free herself.

Evander pumped his wings harder, furiously trying to make his way over to her.

Then Prue was there, a long branch in her hands. She stabbed the Titan in the back with it, shoving it all the way through the man's tough flesh. Inky blood oozed from the wound, and he immediately released Mona.

Prue grabbed her sister's hand, pulling her to her feet and ushering her away from the Titan. Cyrus's lightning crackled once more, and then the Titan was dead.

"Retreat!" roared the purple-skinned Titan, waving his hand to the others.

Relief swelled within Evander. *Thank the gods.*

"Grab her!" cried another Titan.

Evander's eyes widened, and his heart dropped like a stone. The Titans wanted *Prue.*

His gaze flicked to the two sisters. Their hands were

clutched together as they tried to escape the Titans, but they were surrounded.

"Cyrus!" Evander bellowed.

Cyrus followed his gaze, then slammed his hands together. Lightning stuck again and again, leaving scorch marks in the earth. One Titan cried out, falling to his knees.

"Now!" said the purple Titan. He spread his hands, fingers twisting in the air, as if he were weaving threads.

A rippling black hole formed in the earth at his feet, and a fierce wind billowed around them, making the trees sway.

Shit. The Titan had opened a damn *portal.*

"No!" Evander cried, his wings pumping harder. But the magic of Typhon was spent, and, too suddenly, the wings vanished, sending him careening. He landed hard in the dirt, rolling to soften the blow. But his arms ached, and something had torn in his leg. Still, he crawled forward, desperate to reach Mona and Prue. They were shouting something incoherent to one another, clinging to each other.

Cyrus was sprinting forward, unable to use his lightning because the Titans were too close to Prue. He couldn't risk hitting her.

Prue summoned more branches, wielding them as weapons. But the four Titans now surrounding her inhaled deeply, and the branches turned to ash.

Prue fell to her knees, her face growing paler by the minute. Evander knew the siphoning of her magic was taking its toll on her. Mona's arms came around her, trying to drag her to safety.

"Mona, go!" Evander screamed. "Get out of there!"

Mona shot him a look of frustration mingled with sorrow, then shook her head slowly. Tears streamed down her face.

Another streak of lightning, but this one struck too far to make an impact. One of the Titans shot a gleeful look at Cyrus over his shoulder.

The Titan knew they'd won. And from the widening of Cyrus's eyes and the pallor of his skin, he knew it, too.

"Prue!" Cyrus roared. His eyes were all white now as lightning danced around his fingertips. Power emanated through him, and yet... he was still powerless. He could do nothing but watch as the Titans put their hands on Prue, tugging her arms behind her back.

"Don't!" Cyrus begged, his face crumpling. "Please, spare her! This is not her fight!"

The purple Titan bared his teeth at Cyrus. "Oh, but it is, little death god. And when you are ready to negotiate for her freedom, you know how to reach us."

Cyrus's cry was swallowed up in the roaring wind as the last remaining Titans shoved Prue and Mona through the portal. Evander's fingers raked through the dirt as he frantically clawed his way forward, desperate to save them, to stop the portal from closing...

With a deafening *boom*, the black hole vanished, and the wind died. Nothing but silence and stillness followed. Evander was gasping for breath, his face covered in tears he didn't realize he'd shed.

And Prue and Mona were gone.

OFFERING

PANDORA

PANDORA'S MIND COULDN'T COMPREHEND WHAT she was seeing. King Midas was... here? Even though he was supposed to have been cursed to never return to Elysium.

"Uncle, what is this?" Sol asked slowly, his brow furrowing. "How are you here?"

"I do apologize for the deception," Midas said, bringing his hands together with a sigh. "But it was the only way to ensure you would do your part to free me."

Pandora shook her head, finally finding her voice. "Explain yourself. What did you do?"

"I told you that in order to activate the fail-safe within the wards, you had to combine sun magic and earth magic," Midas said, his eyes glinting with triumph.

"But in truth, the combination of the two actually... summons *me*."

Alarm raced through Pandora. *No.* He couldn't be serious. "You're lying," she said at once. "Gaia would have known."

"Gaia knows *nothing* about the wards," Midas snarled. "I was the one who put them there. I was the one who included the fail-safe in order to bring me back when the time was right. With sun and earth magic, my powers can be restored. And with the death of sun and earth, my curse will be lifted."

Pandora's blood ran cold at the word *death*. She stepped forward, placing herself between Midas and Sol.

Midas laughed. "Don't fret, my dear. I don't mean any harm to you or my nephew. It's Gaia and Apollo I want. Your powers should have summoned them both. Gaia was already here, of course, but Apollo..." Midas frowned, then glanced behind them as if in search of the sun god. "Well, either he found a way around my fail-safe, or he's already dead." He laughed again. "I suppose I'll have to kill Gaia and see what happens."

He made for the steps leading to the courtyard, but Pandora stood in his path, glaring at him.

"You will not touch my mother."

Midas's eyebrows lifted. "That's a bold claim coming from the woman who almost tore out Gaia's throat merely days ago. Where is that bloodlust now, darling? I could use your help with this."

Pandora shoved his shoulders so he staggered backward, but he was still chuckling. The sound of his laughter infuriated her, and she advanced, prepared to kick him down...

But then he removed his gloves, and his fingers shimmered with gold light.

"Trivia." Sol grabbed her arms, tugging her away from Midas. "Don't."

Midas smiled and wiggled his fingers at her as he descended the steps to the courtyard.

Frantic, Pandora shoved away from Sol and followed after Midas. Instantly, her magic receded, and the dark storm of the box's power roared in the sky above them. Funnel clouds formed as the power converged, and laughter and screams from within the darkness echoed around the fulcrum.

Gaia stood at the edge of the courtyard, her chin lifted as Midas advanced toward her. "Very clever deception," she acknowledged. "But it is no good. My death will not free you."

"Don't try to weasel your way out of this one, Gaia," Midas said. "You've lived in freedom for long enough. It's my turn now."

He lunged for her, but Gaia summoned a wall of tree

bark to block him. Growling, Midas lunged again, but Gaia stopped him with a thick row of bushes.

Pandora was running for her mother without thinking. Sol shouted after her, but she ignored him. After everything, after years of suffering, she couldn't just stand there and watch this man kill her mother.

She had to do something.

Gold light speared from Midas's fingertips, slicing through branches and leaves as he made his way toward Gaia. All it would take was a single touch, and Gaia would be gone forever.

Thunder boomed in the distance, and Pandora froze, staring up at the darkening sky. Her heart lurched as the swirling shadows drew closer.

It would devour them all. It didn't matter if she could stop Midas; the darkness would seek Gaia's life first.

How could Pandora save her mother? Despair crashed through her, and she fell to her knees.

Titan magic, whispered a voice within her.

Blinking through tears, Pandora glanced up, recalling how she had begged Farah, the fire witch coven leader, to consider turning to Titan magic to stop the darkness. *That magic isn't to be trifled with,* Farah had said.

But that magic was already here. It lived inside Pandora. If she could access it, perhaps she could use it to close up the box once more.

"Time to come out, Pandora," she whispered, nudging that goddess's presence once more. It didn't take much to coax her out; the swirling shadows called to her.

Screams echoed in her ears, and she rose to her feet, making her way toward the dueling deities. Her eyes were fixed on Gaia, which she knew would infuriate the goddess.

Come for her, she taunted. *She is right here. Come and claim her.*

The goddess within her roared with fury, thrashing against Pandora's restraints.

And Pandora let go. She dropped her defenses and let the soul's anger and trauma and vengeance burst forth. Just like when she stood on the fulcrum, the dam burst, gushing forth. But this time, it was the darkness of Pandora. Inky black shadows spilled forth, pooling along the floor.

Gaia and Midas halted their fighting to stare at her, sensing the powerful presence of the Titan magic.

"No," Gaia breathed.

"Sol, get her out of here!" Pandora shouted, but her voice was not her own. It was layered with another voice. Another soul.

"I'm not leaving you!" Sol cried.

"*Sol!*" Pandora screamed, desperate to make him understand this was the only way. "I couldn't save your mother for you. But you can save mine. Please, I am *begging* you!" Tears spilled from her eyes, but she kept her gazed fixed on that dark, swirling vortex that was coming for her.

Midas yelped and scrambled away, but Pandora gripped him firmly by the arm, careful not to touch his skin. She held him there, and when he reached for her, trying to use his powers to turn her to gold, she kicked him in the groin, and he crumpled. With her boot, she held him there, refusing to let him go.

"Now, Sol!" she shrieked.

To her relief, Sol obliged, taking Gaia's arm and wrenching her away from the storm.

"No!" Gaia moaned, reaching for her daughter. "I will not lose you again, Trivia! *No!*"

A sob tore through Pandora as she aimed her black magic for the shadows in the sky. "Come for me!" she called. "Come for this power!"

The shadows released a cry of delight as they drew closer, swallowing up Pandora and Midas. When the tornado had enveloped them, Pandora unleashed it all with a roar of pain.

"With the power of the Titans, I seal up this darkness. Let it be contained and controlled, sealed up by my essence. Let it forevermore be bottled up within the box from whence it came."

A harsh, grating screech reverberated from within

her as the goddess realized what she was doing. Once more, Pandora saw that blinding light as Apollo destroyed her. The force of that power ripped her apart for a second time, and this time it truly *was* her. Not another person's memories, but *hers.*

Pandora's.

Trivia's.

They were now one and the same.

Pandora fell to her knees. Beside her, Midas sobbed like a child as the darkness consumed them both. Walls closed in on them, trapping them alongside the darkness. As the box sealed them up, Pandora caught a glimpse of Sol struggling to pull Gaia away from the scene. But the two watched, horror-stricken, as the black shadows ripped Pandora's soul from her body, using her aura to contain it all.

I love you, she thought to them just before she was yanked from eternity, doomed to drown in the box's depths forevermore.

VOW

CYRUS

CYRUS KNELT ON THE FOREST FLOOR, PRESSING his hands into the dirt where the Titans' portal had vanished. His fingers sifted the earth, his hardened gaze fixed on those small grains, trying to determine if there was any trace of Titan magic remaining. Anything he could use to track them so he could get his wife back.

Evander appeared by his side. Cyrus could feel his brother's panic mounting; Evander's fingers kept clenching into fists, and he was trembling.

"Cyrus," Evander said, his voice strained. He seemed moments away from combusting entirely. "We have to do something. Mona—I can't—"

"Wait," Cyrus said, his voice surprisingly calm given the turmoil raging in his chest.

My wife is gone.

The Titans have her.

She is gone.

The rage and desperation swirled within him like a storm, twisting faster and faster until he felt ready to burst.

But he forced himself to remain still. He closed his eyes, searching within himself for that god sense he had trusted for so long.

It was so very different now; not at all like he remembered. He wasn't sure if it was his mortal body or the Titan powers flowing through him.

He had expected the Titan magic within him to fade, like Apollo's had, but it was still there. Perhaps it was because that particular brand of magic was stronger than any other.

The air pulsated, and the earth began to tremble. Cyrus pressed his fingers deeper into the earth until the dirt covered his hands entirely. Sparks ignited along his arms, and lightning crackled in the air. He sensed Evander jumping backward to avoid getting struck.

A deep, pulsing thrum resonated from within the earth, warming Cyrus's fingers and coaxing the flames of his power to life. The magic of the realm encircled him, claiming him as the rightful ruler of the Underworld once more. It should have accepted him immediately after Apollo had forfeited the challenge. But the power of the Titans had been overwhelming, no doubt making it difficult for the magic of the Underworld to reach Cyrus.

But it was here now.

In the silent stillness following the Titans' departure, Cyrus was ready to be anointed by the realm's magic once again.

But unlike before, when Cyrus had taken the crown from Aidoneus, there was something *else* in the air. Something he had never sensed before.

Whispers echoed in the Wilds, shifting through the trees like a breeze. The murmurs grew louder and more fervent. Branches swayed and leaves fell. The whispers of the dead made the hair on Cyrus's arms stand on end. He suppressed a shiver, keeping his eyes closed as he embraced that strange power roiling through him.

"Cyrus," Evander said again, his voice soft with warning.

King, the voices seemed to say. *Our king has awakened. Our king is here.*

Cyrus's eyes flew open, and from the way his brother stiffened, he knew his eyes were all white. But Cyrus felt nothing but pure, raw power coursing through him. What had once been intoxicating to him now existed only to serve one purpose: to find Prue.

"Kneel," Cyrus said, his voice powerful and commanding.

Evander immediately took a knee before him, bowing his head to the King of the Underworld.

"I wasn't talking to you, brother," said Cyrus.

The whispers multiplied until they sounded more like a raging tornado than a cacophony of voices. From within the depths of the Undead Wilds, the restless and wayward spirits finally revealed themselves. Hundreds of translucent white figures appeared, ready to serve their king. For eons, they had been stranded, disconnected from their souls. When Cyrus had first claimed the throne, he hadn't been worthy of the power of this realm. And these spirits had known it. They had avoided him, refusing to bow.

But now, with the reigning power given to him a second time, the Wilds had come to life. The spirits who had haunted the realm for so long were finally emerging.

And, one by one, the pearly spirits knelt to the ground, bowing their heads to Cyrus just as Evander had.

This time was different. Cyrus had changed. He was willing to make sacrifices for his people. He was ready now, when before he had only been hungry for power.

"I am sorry it has taken me so long to be worthy of the crown," Cyrus said, addressing the spirits. "But I swear a solemn vow to you that if you help me rescue Prue and Mona, I will see to it that you are finally freed. That your souls will find rest at last."

The spirits said nothing. They continued bowing before Cyrus, their forms motionless. While the whispers had ceased, an eerie wind shook the trees, whipping against Cyrus's face and tousling his hair.

Then, the whispers returned. With one collective voice, the spirits replied, "We accept."

NOTE TO THE READER

Thank you so much for reading! I greatly appreciate you taking the time.

If you would be so kind, please leave a review to let others know what you thought of the book!

ACKNOWLEDGMENTS

My heart is full as I consider how many incredible individuals helped me bring this story to life.

My Tuesday Tribe, for your support and many brainstorming sessions when I had writer's block.

My fabulous beta readers: Jenni, Tori, Melissa, and Kari. Without your critical input, this book would not have made it! Your suggestions were monumental in shaping the story.

My stellar ARC team for your enthusiastic reading and reviews! Thank you for your willingness to dive in and leave reviews so promptly! You all are amazing.

Kay Moody, for your incredible proofreading skills.

art_jake, for the stunning art you created for the reversible dust jacket.

To all my Kickstarter backers: a monumental thank you for your support and your pledges. Without you, the gorgeous special editions for this book never would have been possible. Thank you so much for your contributions.

And, above all, thank you Alex, Colin, Ellie, and Isabel. Your smiles and laughter bring joy to my life. All of this is for you.

ABOUT THE AUTHOR

R.L. Perez is an author, wife, mother, reader, writer, and teacher. She lives in Florida with her husband and three children. On a regular basis, she can usually be found napping, reading, feverishly writing, revising, or watching an abundance of Netflix. More than anything, she loves spending time with her family. Her greatest joys are her two kids, nature, literature, and chocolate.

Subscribe to her newsletter for new releases, promotions, giveaways, and book recommendations! Get a FREE eBook when you sign up at subscribe.rlperez.com.